Disney's TALESPIN

THE OLD MAN AND THE SEA DUCK

Adapted by
Lee Nordling

MALLARD PRESS

Illustrated by
Vaccaro Associates, Inc.

Twin Books

"I love flying!" said Baloo, taking a sip of soda pop. He snapped the steering yoke to the right and banked the *Sea Duck* between two walls of rock in a towering mountain range. The peaks of the mountains disappeared high above the clouds.

4

Kit sat in the copilot's seat scanning a chart while Wildcat looked on. "I think I've found a pass we can fly through," said Kit excitedly. "Turn left . . . now!"

"Right-o!" laughed Baloo, banking his plane into the pass.

"Miracle Pass," said Kit. "I wonder why it's called that."
The *Sea Duck* clipped a ledge and started spinning toward the ground. "Because if you make it through, it's a miracle!" said Baloo.

The force of the diving plane sent Wildcat staggering around the cargo hold. He grabbed a strap to steady himself, but it came loose, releasing a load of coconuts. Wildcat ducked as the coconuts bounced forward into the cockpit.

Just as Baloo pulled the *Sea Duck* from its nose dive, one of the coconuts smacked him on the back of the head. Moaning, he sailed safely through the last of Miracle Pass, then slumped over the steering wheel.

"Baloo!" Kit cried. "Wildcat, come quick! Baloo's hurt!"

Wildcat tried to take control of the plane. Kit eased
Baloo out of the pilot's seat and splashed soda pop on
his face.

"Baloo! Can you hear me?" said Kit. "Are you okay?"

"No," said Baloo, opening his eyes. "I'm sticky."

"Well, at least you're awake," said Kit, relieved. "Do
you feel well enough to fly?"

"I think so," said Baloo, looking at all the lights and
switches on the control panel. "But what makes you
think I'm a pilot?"

"Uh-oh!" said Kit, looking at the bump on Baloo's head. "Wildcat, we've got a problem. Baloo doesn't remember how to fly!"

"Then let's teach him!" said Wildcat, as they soared toward a dark wall of clouds. "But I hope this isn't going to be a crash course!"

Wildcat opened the emergency box and pulled out a book called *How to Fly*. Kit helped Baloo back into the pilot's seat.

"'Step one'," read Wildcat, just as the *Sea Duck* flew into a giant storm cloud. "'Do not ever, ever, *ever* fly into a giant storm cloud' . . ."

The *Sea Duck* tossed and turned as lightning crackled across the rain-swept windshield. "The lesson's over!" cried Baloo, letting go of the steering yoke. "I quit!" Wildcat lunged forward to grab the yoke.

"You can't quit!" said Kit. "You're the only one who can save us!"

Then another splinter of lightning struck the right engine.

"What was that?" said Baloo, as the plane spun into a nose dive.

"Our signal to bail out!" said Wildcat, reaching for their parachutes.

As they pulled on their parachutes, another jolt of
lightning rocked the *Sea Duck* and sent Kit and Wildcat
flying out of the hatch. The hatch slammed shut and
jammed. Baloo was trapped inside the falling plane.

Kit and Wildcat opened their parachutes. Wide-eyed, they watched the plane spin closer and closer to the ground.

"Jump, Baloo! Jump!" cried Kit. But they never saw Baloo jump, and the *Sea Duck* soon disappeared.

17

Baloo scrambled into the pilot's seat and grabbed the yoke. "Somebody help me!" he screamed. "I'm caught in a storm!"

"What storm?" said a scratchy voice from the radio. Baloo looked out the window. The storm was gone.

"My runway lights are right below you, son," said the voice.

Baloo looked down at the dark narrow landing strip and shook his head. "But I can't fly," he whispered, "much less land."

"Horselips!" said the voice. "I'll talk you down. By the way, son, my name is Joe."

Shaking, Baloo followed Joe's step-by-step instructions. Soon the *Sea Duck* touched down, bobbing and bouncing its way along the runway.

Baloo staggered out of the plane. The runway lights made it difficult to see anything but the dim outline of a few buildings.

An old man with a cane limped onto the landing strip and said, "Congratulations, son. You would've lost your other engine in another thirty seconds and cracked up for sure."

That was the last thing Baloo heard before he fainted.

Meanwhile, Kit and Wildcat were very worried. They had hiked all the way back through Miracle Pass to a small town called Zambizi Flats. There, they borrowed a jeep and began their search for Baloo. But although they looked all night, it seemed that Baloo and the *Sea Duck* had disappeared into thin air.

The next morning, Baloo awoke on a cot in an old airplane hangar. He got up and glanced at the snapshots that were pinned to a bulletin board by the door. They were of Joe as a fighter pilot ace and flight instructor. There was a medal pinned below the photos that read, "Legion of Valor—Joe McGee."

Baloo whistled softly and went outside. Joe stood next to the *Sea Duck*, tightening a bolt. "Good morning, son," said Joe. "The radio's shot, but she's ready for takeoff!"

Before Baloo could say a word, Joe continued, "And
don't worry about having to get over the cliffs that ring
this valley. There's a tunnel at the end of the runway
that any good pilot can get through."

"But . . . but I can't fly," said Baloo. "I don't
remember how."

Joe smiled. "Son, you landed in the right place."
Baloo turned to see a sign that read "Joe's Flying
School" above the hangar door.

Later that day, Baloo sat in the open cockpit of a small, one-man plane, banking left, banking right, and diving down.

"Pull up! Pull up!" Joe yelled. "You're going to crash!"

Baloo panicked and yanked so hard on the yoke
that it came off in his hands. The plane went crazy
and bucked Baloo out of the cockpit and onto the
hangar floor. Joe shook his head, stepped over to the
floor-mounted airplane, and pressed the "off" button.

"Let's try it again," sighed Joe.

Bit by bit, Baloo mastered the floor-mounted plane.
Then he practiced in a plane that was hung from the
ceiling by wires, and only crashed ten or twenty times.
Finally, he was ready for the big time!

Baloo was nervous. The glider drifted gently off the edge of the tall cliff, then caught the wind and clung to it. Joe leaned forward from the back seat and told him he was doing fine.

"Look around you, Baloo," said Joe. "Up here you're free as a bird. The skies are yours!"

With Joe's help, Baloo flew the glider through a series of stunts. "Try to have some fun," said Joe, clapping Baloo on the back. "You've remembered how to fly, but you've forgotten what flying is all about!"

But some of Baloo's memory had come back. He remembered the terrifying flight through Miracle Pass.

After Baloo landed, Joe said, "Well, I think you're
ready to solo."

"S-s-solo?" said Baloo with a gulp. "Let's do it another
day. Okay, Joe? The weather looks a little rough right now."

Joe looked up at the sky and saw one puffy, white cloud.

The next morning, Baloo's trick knee was bothering him.

The morning after that, Baloo lay on his cot and sniffed an onion until his eyes watered. When Joe came in, he said, "Son, you look awful!"

Baloo sniffed. "Sorry, Joe, but I just don't feel up to going up."

"That's okay," said Joe, walking toward the door. "I've got some work to do outside. If you need anything, just holler."

32

After Joe left, Baloo breathed a sigh of relief. A few moments later, he heard a loud crash and ran outside. Joe lay on the ground by a ladder, clutching his leg. "I think it's busted," said Joe. "You've got to fly to Zambizi Flats and get Doc Cooper! It's twenty miles due north!"

Without thinking, Baloo rushed for the *Sea Duck*, leaped in, cranked the engine, and streaked down the runway. As Baloo flew through the tunnel and out of the valley, Joe raised his hand and cried, "That's the way, son!"

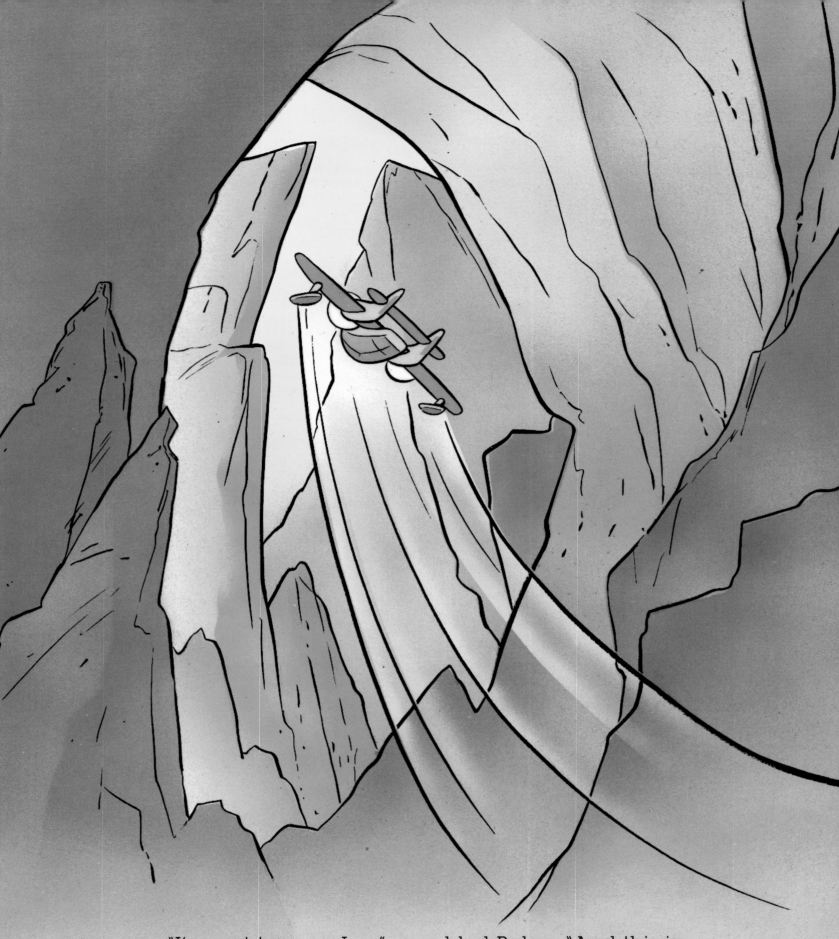

"I've got to save Joe," mumbled Baloo. "And this is the only fast way to get where I'm going!" He tightened his seat belt, turned the yoke, and banked the *Sea Duck* straight into Miracle Pass. He was in trouble from the beginning.

Baloo jerked the yoke back and forth as the *Sea Duck* clipped boulders and ledges and cliff sides. Each time he recovered, he was jarred by another near miss. Finally Baloo ran out of luck. The *Sea Duck* lost altitude too quickly, and went spinning out of control.

As Baloo tried to recover, he heard Joe say, "Try to have some fun. You've forgotten what flying is all about!"

As if a curtain had parted, Baloo glimpsed a moment in his past when he and Kit swooped high above the clouds. Baloo let out a whoop. "I remember!" he cried, pulling the *Sea Duck* out of its spin.

Later, on the outskirts of Zambizi Flats, Kit and
Wildcat were returning for their third tank of gas.
They had all but given up hope when Kit heard the
familiar sound of twin engines. He looked up to see
the *Sea Duck* pass overhead, then land. Kit cheered.

Kit and Wildcat drove up as Baloo was rushing out of the doctor's office with Doc Cooper. "Baloo, what happened to you?" said Kit.

"There's no time to explain!" said Baloo, pushing everyone into the plane. "Someone needs our help!"

Baloo taxied down the street, then roared into the sky.

Baloo flew the *Sea Duck* as well as he ever
had, barely blinking on his return trip through
Miracle Pass. He was the first one out of the
plane when it landed.

"Joe! We're here!" cried Baloo, rushing toward
the hangar.

But Joe wasn't there, and everything looked different . . . older. Baloo's voice echoed through the empty, dusty hangar.

"Joe! Mr. McGee! Where are you?" cried Baloo.

"Joe McGee? Is this some kind of joke?" said Doc Cooper. "Joe McGee passed on twenty years ago!"

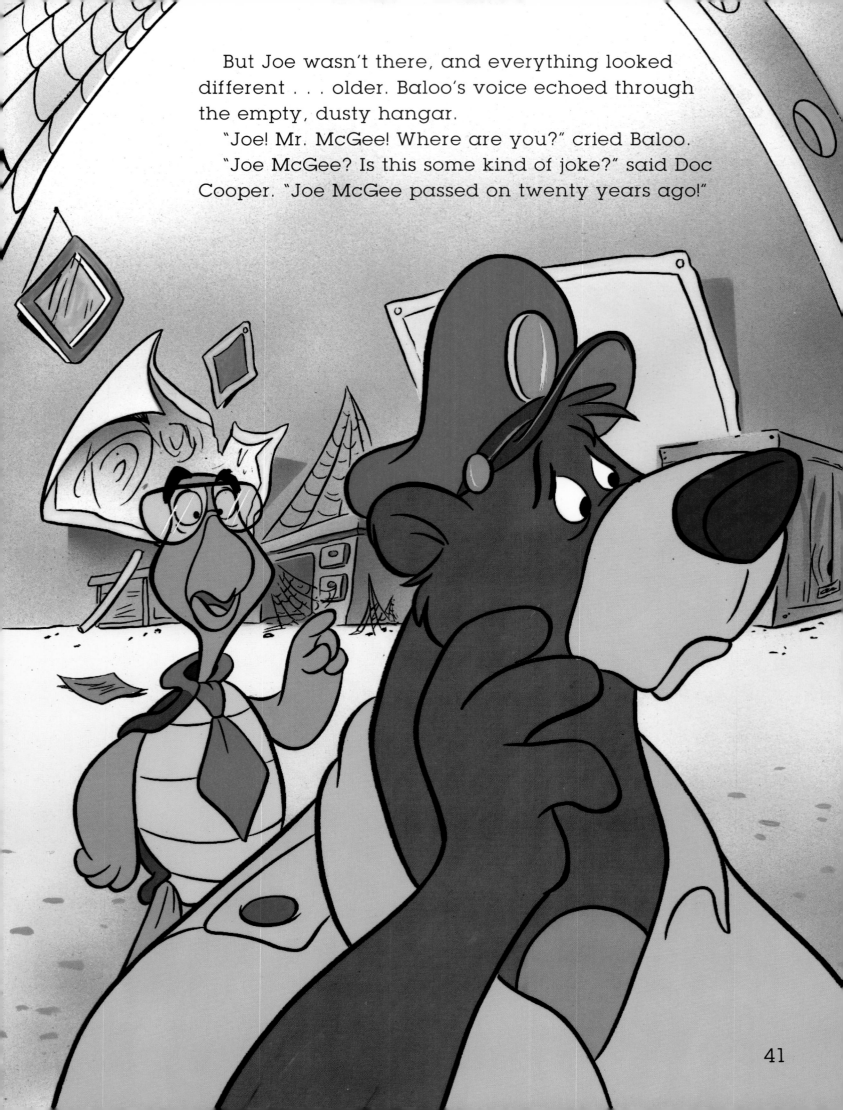

41

Baloo shook his head in disbelief and walked over to Joe's desk. "No, you don't understand," he said. "I left him here less than an hour ago. He taught me how to fly again . . . he . . . he . . ."

Doc Cooper put his hand on Baloo's shoulder. "He taught a lot of flyers," said the doctor. "Some say he was the best . . . but that was a long time ago."

Baloo's eyes brimmed with tears as he glanced through the snapshots on the bulletin board. Then he smiled, took one of the pictures down, and put it in his pocket.

Once they were all back inside the plane and ready for takeoff, Baloo took the photo out of his pocket and placed it on the instrument panel. "Thanks, Joe," he whispered.

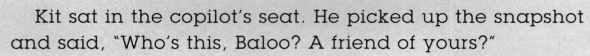

Kit sat in the copilot's seat. He picked up the snapshot and said, "Who's this, Baloo? A friend of yours?"

Baloo glanced at the old, worn photo of Joe and him together.

"Yeah, kid," said Baloo, smiling. "He's a very old friend."

45

As the *Sea Duck* rolled down the runway, heading for the tunnel, a voice echoed on the wind. It was a voice that only Baloo could hear.

"Look around you, Baloo," said Joe. "You're free as a bird! The skies are yours!"

Selenium in Biology and Human Health

Raymond F. Burk
Editor

Selenium in
Biology and Human Health

With 30 Illustrations

Springer-Verlag
New York Berlin Heidelberg London Paris
Tokyo Hong Kong Barcelona Budapest

Raymond F. Burk
Division of Gastroenterology
Department of Medicine
School of Medicine
Vanderbilt University
Nashville, TN 37232 USA

Library of Congress Cataloging-in-Publication Data
Selenium in biology and human health / Raymond F. Burk, editor.
    p.   cm.
    Includes bibliographical references and index.
    ISBN 0-387-94080-4 (acid-free paper: New York). — ISBN
3-540-94080-4 (acid-free paper: Berlin)
    1. Selenium—Physiological effect.   2. Selenium in human
nutrition.   I. Burk, Raymond F.
QP535.S5S435   1993
574.19'245—dc20   93-4691

Printed on acid-free paper.

Typeset by Best-set Typesetter Ltd., Hong Kong.
Printed and bound by Edwards Brothers, Inc., Ann Arbor, MI.
Printed in the United States of America.

9 8 7 6 5 4 3 2 1

ISBN 0-387-94080-4 Springer-Verlag New York Berlin Heidelberg
ISBN 3-540-94080-4 Springer-Verlag Berlin Heidelberg New York

to Eni, Teresa, and the memory of Stephen

Preface

This volume reflects the current strong interest of biological scientists in selenium. The idea for the book originated at the Fifth International Symposium on Selenium in Biology and Medicine, which was held in Nashville in 1992. That meeting provided evidence that selenium is attracting the attention of scientists working in a variety of fields. In molecular biology, the study of selenium is adding a new and unexpected chapter to the story of the genetic code and its translation. In biochemistry, selenoproteins are being recognized as the mediators of the biological effects of the element, and new selenoproteins are being recognized and studied. Finally, in medicine and public health, selenium has human health implications that range from effects on heart disease to a possible relationship with cancer.

Contributors to this book have reviewed developing areas of selenium research from the perspective of the investigator. These reviews will be useful to selenium researchers for their critical approach and to other scientists as an update on the development of the selenium field.

Nashville, Tennessee   Raymond F. Burk
March 1993

Contents

Contributors

Georg Alfthan
National Public Health Institute
Mannerheimintie 166
SF-00300 Helsinki
Finland

Antti Aro
National Public Health Institute
Mannerheimintie 166
SF-00300 Helsinki
Finland

John R. Arthur
Rowett Research Institute
Bucksburn, Aberdeen
Scotland AB2 9SB
United Kingdom

Nelly Avissar
Strong Children's Research Center
University of Rochester Medical Center
Rochester, NY 14642, USA

Geoffrey J. Beckett
University Department of Clinical Biochemistry
Royal Infirmary
Edinburgh
Scotland EH3 9YW
United Kingdom

August Böck
Lehrstuhl für Mikrobiologie
Universität München
Maria-Ward-Strasse 1a
D-8000 München 19
Germany

Raymond F. Burk
Division of Gastroenterology
Department of Medicine
Vanderbilt University School of Medicine
Nashville, TN 37232, USA

In Soon Choi
Laboratory of Experimental Carcinogenesis
National Cancer Institute
National Institutes of Health
Bethesda, MD 20892, USA

Harvey J. Cohen
Strong Children's Research Center
University of Rochester Medical Center
Rochester, NY 14642, USA

Alan M. Diamond
Department of Radiation and Cellular Oncology
University of Chicago
Chicago, IL 60637, USA

Howard E. Ganther
Department of Preventive Medicine
University of Texas Medical Branch at Galveston
Galveston, TX 77550, USA

Dolph L. Hatfield
Laboratory of Experimental Carcinogenesis
National Cancer Institute
National Institutes of Health
Bethesda, MD 20892, USA

Kristina E. Hill
Division of Gastroenterology
Department of Medicine
Vanderbilt University School of Medicine
Nashville, TN 37232, USA

Jussi K. Huttunen
National Public Health Institute
Mannerheimintie 166
SF-00300 Helsinki
Finland

Clement Ip
Department of Surgical Oncology
Roswell Park Cancer Institute
Buffalo, NY 14263, USA

Jae-Eon Jung
Laboratory of Experimental Carcinogenesis
National Cancer Institute
National Institutes of Health
Bethesda, MD 20892, USA

Kenneth C. Kleene
Department of Biology
University of Massachusetts at Boston
100 Morrissey Blvd.
Boston, MA 02125-3393, USA

Takeshi Ohama
Laboratory of Experimental Carcinogenesis
National Cancer Institute
National Institutes of Health
Bethesda, MD 20892, USA

Jianhua Piao
Institute of Nutrition and Food Hygiene
Chinese Academy of Preventive Medicine
Beijing 100050
China

Roger A. Sunde
Nutrition Sciences Group
Colleges of Human Environmental Sciences and
Agriculture, Food and Natural Resources
University of Missouri
Columbia, MO 65211, USA

Pertti Varo
Department of Applied Chemistry and Microbiology
University of Helsinki
Helsinki, Finland

Yiming Xia
Institute of Nutrition and Food Hygiene
Chinese Academy of Preventive Medicine
Beijing 100050
China

Introduction

Raymond F. Burk

Knowledge of selenium in biology and human health is accumulating at a rapid rate. The application of immunological and molecular biological tools to the study of selenium has led to the recognition of several new selenoproteins in the recent past, and there are indications that many more will be discovered in the future. Success has been achieved in understanding how selenium is incorporated into proteins, and reasonable estimates of nutritional requirements for the element have been made. The purpose of this book is to present reviews relevant to selenium in biology and human health from the perspective of authors who are producing much of the new knowledge.

Selenium research in biology began over 60 years ago with the quest for a toxic principle in plants grown in parts of South Dakota and Nebraska. Animals eating those plants exhibited a variety of injuries to the nervous system, the liver, and the integument. Studies carried out at the South Dakota Experiment Station (Franke, 1934) and elsewhere determined that the toxicity was caused by selenium, which had been taken up in proportion to its concentration in the soil and incorporated into amino acids by the plants. Other areas of high soil selenium were identified and the significance of selenium as a naturally occurring toxicant was established.

The agricultural research community directed a great deal of effort to the study of selenium toxicity. Analysis of forages was carried out in all areas of the United States and a "selenium map" was constructed (Rosenfeld and Beath, 1964). It demonstrated that there were many circumscribed areas in the Great Plains region, and a few elsewhere, which produced plants with very high selenium content. Three other types of areas were also described: High selenium but not toxic, moderate selenium, and very low selenium. The very low selenium areas were later found to be areas where grazing animals, pigs, and poultry suffer from selenium-deficiency diseases. The map was used to restrict the use, for feed, of plants from very high selenium areas.

During the period from 1954 to 1957, selenium was shown to be required by bacteria (Pinsent, 1954), mammals (Schwarz and Foltz, 1957), and birds (Patterson et al., 1957). The work in animals was accomplished because selenium has relationships with other nutrients. Dietary liver necrosis had been described in rats in 1935 as a spontaneous necrosis of the liver which begins in the centrilobular regions and becomes massive. It occurred in rats fed from weaning on a yeast-based diet. The diet was first shown to be deficient in vitamin E when inclusion of that vitamin prevented the development of dietary liver necrosis. Addition of sulfur amino acids also prevented necrosis. Tissue extracts which contained neither of these substances were also efficacious and this led to the concept that a "factor 3" existed. This factor was selenium and, in retrospect, the effect of sulfur amino acids was probably due largely to their contamination by selenium. Thus, inclusion of either selenium or vitamin E in the diet prevented the development of dietary liver necrosis. This linked the function of these nutrients and led to a search for selenium responsiveness in a number of animal diseases known to respond to vitamin E.

In the late 1950s and the 1960s many of these vitamin E–responsive animal diseases were shown also to respond to selenium. They included mulberry heart disease and nutritional liver necrosis in pigs; exudative diathesis in poultry; and white muscle disease in sheep. This latter condition is especially prevalent in low-selenium areas on the selenium map. This information led to the use of selenium in animal feeds in low-selenium areas. Supplementation improved livestock health but it has raised concerns that it could cause selenium accumulation in some ecosystems and lead to toxicity. This is an area of concern and controversy.

In the 1960s selenium was shown to have effects independent of vitamin E. Second-generation selenium-deficient rats fed diets with adequate concentrations of vitamin E developed cataracts and did not grow (Whanger and Weswig, 1975). Male rats raised on severely selenium-deficient diets from weaning grew more slowly than controls and developed aspermatogenesis. These studies made it clear that selenium was an essential nutrient independent of vitamin E.

In 1973 selenium was shown to be a constituent of glutathione peroxidase (Rotruck et al.) It was demonstrated that the activity of this enzyme fell drastically in selenium deficiency. This appeared to explain the relationship of selenium with vitamin E. It was postulated that these two nutrients provided a one–two defense against free-radical oxidant injury: Vitamin E would scavenge free radicals and selenium-dependent glutathione peroxidase would remove any hydroperoxides which resulted from free radicals that escaped the action of vitamin E. This attractive concept has proven to be simplistic.

Several selenium-dependent glutathione peroxidases have now been characterized. Sunde discusses cellular glutathione peroxidases in chapter 3 and Cohen and Avissar discuss plasma glutathione peroxidase in chapter 4. Even though their *in vitro* functions seem to dictate oxidant defense roles for the glutathione peroxidases, there is scant direct evidence for such functions. There is even evidence for selenium-dependent oxidant injury protection independent of glutathione peroxidase (Burk et al., 1980). Sunde points out in chapter 3 that cellular glutathione peroxidase exhibits some of the characteristics of a storage depot for selenium. Thus, study of the selenium-dependent glutathione peroxidases continues to be active, and it seems certain that a great deal remains to be learned about the functions of this family of enzymes.

In 1976 selenocysteine was identified as the form of selenium in a selenoprotein isolated from *Clostridium sticklandii* (Cone et al.). Subsequent work has demonstrated selenocysteine to be the form of selenium in other selenoproteins, including glutathione peroxidase. Selenomethionine is incorporated into proteins, but most evidence points to this being a random substitution for methionine residues with minimal effect on the function of the protein. Other forms of the element have been suspected in a few proteins containing the element but none have yet been identified. Thus the only *physiological* form of selenium known at the present time to occur in proteins is selenocysteine.

The DNA codon for selenocysteine is TGA. A fascinating series of studies reported over the last 7 years has elucidated the mechanism by which this codon, which usually causes termination of translation, designates incorporation of selenocysteine into the primary structure of bacterial selenoproteins. Böck summarizes these studies in chapter 1. The mechanism in eukaryotes is analogous but differs in some aspects. The eukaryotic tRNAs involved in this process are discussed by Hatfield et al. in chapter 2.

Two selenoproteins have been described in recent years in which the primary structure contains more than one selenocysteine. Selenoprotein P is an extracellular glycoprotein postulated to have an oxidant defense role. It is discussed in chapter 6 by Hill and Burk. The mitochondrial capsule selenoprotein of sperm is developmentally regulated. It is discussed by Kleene in chapter 7.

A number of biological effects of selenium have been identified (Burk, 1983). The toxicities of several substances are affected by selenium deficiency. Many drug-metabolizing enzyme activities are altered by it. Hepatic heme metabolism is defective in selenium-deficient rats and glutathione metabolism is altered in them. The effect of selenium deficiency on glutathione metabolism is discussed by Hill in chapter 8. The underlying biochemical causes of these effects remain uncertain for the most part and uncovering them remains a major challenge for the future.

Selenium deficiency was shown to be relevant to human health by the demonstration in China that it was a necessary condition for the development of Keshan disease (Keshan Disease Research Group, 1979). This disease is a cardiomyopathy, which is often fatal and was a major public-health problem in China until recently. Its decreased incidence in recent years and its potential significance to the understanding of oxidant injury of the heart are discussed by Xia et al. in chapter 10.

For many years there have been suggestions that selenium protects against cancer. This possibility has stimulated numerous epidemiological as well as animal studies. Ip and his collaborators have used their knowledge of selenium metabolism to design studies in chemoprevention which seek to minimize the toxicity of selenium while exploring its cancer-prevention value. He and Ganther discuss in chapter 9 some of their novel approaches to the use of selenium in cancer prevention in animal models.

Selenium has been known to be involved in thyroid hormone metabolism for over a decade. Recently the enzyme which converts thyroxine to triiodothyronine in liver, kidney, and thyroid has been demonstrated to be a selenoenzyme. Arthur and Beckett discuss the effects of selenium on thyroid function in chapter 5 and point out that observations in man suggest that selenium deficiency can contribute to the development of cretinism.

Because of low soil selenium in Finland, the blood selenium level of Finns was found to be lower than that of residents of many Western countries. In order to raise the selenium status of the population, Finland embarked in 1984 on a program of adding selenium to fertilizers. The latest results of this program are reported by Varo et al. in chapter 11. This chapter has great significance because it reports a careful study of the effects of the supplementation on selenium levels in food and in human blood. It provides useful information on the effects of supplementing populations with selenium.

The chapters in this book cover a broad range of topics from basic research to human studies. They illustrate the broad front along which studies of selenium are making an impact.

REFERENCES

Burk, RF. Biological activity of selenium. Ann Rev Nutr 3:53–70; 1983.

Burk, RF, Lawrence, RA, Lane, JM. Liver necrosis and lipid peroxidation in the rat as the result of paraquat and diquat administration. J Clin Invest 65:1024–1031; 1980.

Cone, JE, Del Rio, RM, Davis, JN, Stadtman, TC. Chemical characterization of the selenoprotein component of clostridial glycine reductase: identification of selenocysteine as the organoselenium moiety. Proc Natl Acad Sci USA 73:2659–2663; 1976.

Franke, KW. A new toxicant occurring naturally in certain samples of plant foodstuffs. I. Results obtained in preliminary feeding trials. J Nutr 8:597–608; 1934.

Keshan Disease Research Group. Observations on effect of sodium selenite in prevention of Keshan disease. Chin Med J 92:471–476; 1979.

Patterson, EL, Milstrey, R, Stokstad, ELR. Effect of selenium in preventing exudative diathesis in chicks. Proc Soc Exptl Biol Med 95:617–620; 1957.

Pinsent, J. The need for selenite and molybdate in the formation of formic dehydrogenase by members of the coli-aerogenes group of bacteria. Biochem J 57:10–16; 1954.

Rosenfeld, I, Beath, OA. Selenium. Geobotany, biochemistry, toxicity, and nutrition. New York, Academic Press; 1964.

Rotruck, JT, Pope, AL, Ganther, HE, Swanson, AB, Hafeman, DG, Hoekstra, WG. Selenium: biochemical role as a component of glutathione peroxidase. Science 179:585–590; 1973.

Schwarz, K, Foltz, CM. Selenium as an integral part of Factor 3 against dietary necrotic liver degeneration. J Am Chem Soc 79:3292–3293; 1957.

Whanger, PD, Weswig, PH. Effects of selenium, chromium and antioxidants on growth, eye cataracts, plasma cholesterol and blood glucose in selenium deficient, vitamin E supplemented rats. Nutr Rep Int 12:345–348; 1975.

Chapter 1

Incorporation of Selenium into Bacterial Selenoproteins

August Böck

In 1954, J. Pinsent discovered that *Escherichia coli* produces gas from formic acid only when the medium is supplemented with the trace elements molybdenum and selenium (1). Thus, *E. coli* was the first organism for which a biological role of selenium was demonstrated. It took almost 40 years to identify the enzyme responsible for formate oxidation under the aerobic conditions used by Pinsent: It is formate dehydrogenase O (FDH$_O$), which presumably is a respiratory chain-linked enzyme coupling formate oxidation to O$_2$ reduction (2). In addition to FDH$_O$, *E. coli* possesses two other formate dehydrogenases: FDH$_N$ couples formate oxidation to nitrate reduction (3). FDH$_H$ is a component of the formate hydrogenlyase complex and delivers the electrons withdrawn from formate to hydrogenase 3, thereby reducing protons to elemental hydrogen (4,5).

All three formate dehydrogenase isoenzymes possess a seleno-polypeptide as a constituent subunit. The selenopolypeptide subunits of FDH$_N$ and FDH$_O$ are 110 kDa (2,3) in size. They cross-react immunologically (6), but they are genetically distinct and their genes are expressed under different physiological conditions (2). FDH$_H$, on the other hand, possesses an 80-kDa selenopolypeptide subunit (5,7). Selenium-containing formate dehydrogenases are present also in several *Clostridium* (8) and *Methanococcus* (9) species. In those cases investigated, selenium is present in the selenopolypeptide as a covalently bound selenocysteine residue (9,10).

Other selenium-dependent enzymes from bacteria are hydrogenases and a glycine reductase. Glycine reductase is present in those obligate anaerobes that are able to carry out a Stickland reaction whereby electrons withdrawn from one amino acid are transferred to glycine as acceptor. The reduction of glycine to ammonia and acetate is coupled to substrate-level phosphorylation (11). One of the three subunits of the glycine reductase complex, protein P$_A$, carries a selenocysteine residue (12).

There are several reports on hydrogenases which contain selenium (13). The best-studied example is the NiFeSe hydrogenase from *Desulfovibrio baculatus* (now *Desulfomicrobium baculatum*). Selenium is one of the coordination sites via which the catalytically active nickel is liganded to the protein (14); however, the identity of the selenium-containing moiety with selenocysteine has not been proven yet by protein-chemical methods. Its existence has only been delineated from the fact that the gene sequence contains an in-frame TGA codon (15) which—in the case of the *E. coli fdhF* (coding for the selenopolypeptide of FDH)—is responsible for directing the cotranslational insertion of selenocysteine.

SELENOCYSTEINE IS COTRANSLATIONALLY INSERTED INTO THE POLYPEPTIDE

Early studies of bacterial selenoprotein formation yielded the important, but at the time unexplainable, result that bacteria grown in the absence of selenium in the medium do not contain immunologically detectable "apoprotein" of the selenium-dependent enzyme (cited in ref. 16). The implication of this result was only understood when it was found in 1986 that two genes coding for selenoproteins contain an in-frame TGA codon in the sequence (17,18), which suggested a cotranslational mode of incorporation of the nonstandard amino acid. As a consequence, in the absence of selenium, decoding of the selenoprotein mRNA pauses or terminates at the UGA codon determining selenocysteine incorporation. Under conditions of mRNA surplus (when the gene is located on a plasmid), a polypeptide fragment can be detected in the cells which corresponds (by size and immunological reaction) to the portion of the selenoprotein reaching from the N-terminus to the position of selenocysteine in the polypeptide chain (19).

A direct proof of the cotranslational incorporation of selenocysteine was then provided in experiments in which a reporter gene like *lacZ* was fused downstream to the portion of the *fdhF* gene containing the TGA codon. Read-through into the *lacZ* mRNA and formation of β-galactosidase occurred only when (1) selenium was present in the medium, and (2) when a functional pathway of selenocysteine biosynthesis and incorporation was present (20,21).

COMPONENTS REQUIRED FOR SELENOCYSTEINE BIOSYNTHESIS AND INSERTION

The classical approach of mutant isolation and characterization was followed for the identification of cellular components involved in seleno-

TABLE 1.1. Genes and their products required for selenoprotein formation.

Gene	Map position (min)	Molecular size (kDa)	Structure	Function
selA (fdhA)[1]	80	50.7	α_{10}; 10 PLP[2]	Selenocysteine synthase
selB (fdhA)[1]	80	68.8	α	Translation factor
selC (fdhC)[1]	82	95 nucleotides		tRNA^{Sec}
selD (fdhB)[1]	38	36.7	α	Selenium activation

[1] Previous gene designation (22).
[2] Pyridoxal-5-phosphate.

protein formation. W. Leinfelder isolated hyperacidifying mutants of *E. coli*. He showed that one class of them mapped at the *fdhA* locus and that this locus harbors two genes, now designated *selA* and *selB* (19). *fdh* lesions had previously been described as being pleio-tropically defective in both FDH$_H$ and FDH$_N$ activities (22). The previously described *fdhB* and *fdhC* mutants (now designated *selD* and *selC*, respectively) were then analyzed and also shown to carry defects in selenium metabolism (19). All four genes were cloned and sequenced and the respective gene products were purified. Table 1.1 summarises their properties.

selC Codes for a tRNA

The nucleotide sequence of *selC* suggested that its product is a tRNA species (23). This was confirmed by determining the primary structure at the RNA level (24). The *selC* encoded tRNA is charged with L-serine by seryl-tRNA ligase; in comparison to cognate serine-accepting tRNA species, however, the ligase displays about tenfold-reduced K_m and K_{cat} values for this tRNA, which probably reflects the low de-mand for selenoprotein synthesis (25). The analysis of bulk tRNA from cells grown in the presence of [^{75}Se] selenite revealed that this tRNA is aminoacylated with selenocysteine *in vivo* (21). Mutants with lesions in *selA* and *selD* were unable to form selenocysteyl-tRNA *in vivo* whereas those blocked in *selB* accumulated increased amounts of it in comparison to wild-type *selB* strains (21). The following conclusions could be drawn from these results: (1) Selenocysteine biosynthesis occurs from an L-seryl residue charged to tRNA; (2) the products of *selA* and *selD* have a function in the conversion of seryl-tRNA to selenocysteyl-tRNA; and (3) the *selB* gene product is involved in a step "beyond" selenocysteyl-tRNA formation, possibly in the decoding process at the ribosome (21). Based on the function of the *selC* gene product, this tRNA was designated tRNA^{Sec}. tRNA^{Sec}—in comparison to all other elongator tRNA species—bears a number of unusual structural properties: (1) It has an anticodon complementary to UGA; thus, tRNA^{Sec} could be considered a "natural UGA suppressor," but it will be shown later that this tRNA does not serve as a suppressor of "ordinary" UGA codons; (2) tRNA^{Sec} possesses an 8-base-pair-long aminoacyl-acceptor helix; (3) a number of bases located at normally invariant positions deviate from the consensus (23); and (4) it contains a modification pattern unique for *E. coli* tRNA species (24). Analysis of tRNA^{Sec} from *Proteus vulgaris* revealed that these unique structural features are conserved (26).

Biosynthesis of Selenocysteine

Exchange of the hydroxyl group of seryl-tRNA^{Sec} by a selenol moiety requires the activation of the hydroxyl. Data in the literature had indicated that this activation may consist of O-phosphorylation both in *E. coli* (27) and in eukaryotes (28). However, when the *selA* gene product had been purified it was discovered that the protein carried a chromophore identified as pyridoxal-5-phosphate (PLP) (29). PLP-dependent catalysis obviates O-phosphorylation of the seryl residue and suggests a 2,3 elimination of a water molecule, creating an aminoacrylyl-tRNA (i.e., dehydroalanyl-tRNA) intermediate to which HSe$^-$ can be added. This reaction mechanism could be proven experimentally (30); it closely resembles that followed by tryptophan synthase (31) or cystathionine-γ-synthase (32). It remains to be seen whether selenocysteine is synthesized in eukaryotes via the same pathway as in *E. coli*.

Evidence for the chemical form of reduced selenium acting as the substrate for SELA (now termed selenocysteine synthase) was provided only recently (33,34). This selenium donor molecule is the product of a selenide-dependent cleavage reaction of ATP catalyzed by SELD whereby the β-phosphate of ATP is released as inorganic phosphate and the γ-phosphate forms a product with HSe⁻, possibly a phosphoroselenoate (33,34). Indeed, a direct phosphorus−selenium bond could be demonstrated recently by nuclear magnetic resonance (NMR) analysis of the SELD reaction product (34). Selenocysteine synthase exhibits a high specificity for this substrate since other nucleophiles like selenide and sulfide are not used (30). The amino-acrylyl moiety, therefore, must be well shielded within the binding site at selenocysteine synthase and only accessible by the cognate substrate.

Selenocysteine synthase is a homooligomer of 10 subunits, each one carrying one PLP prosthetic group (29,30). One seryl-tRNA^{Sec} molecule is bound by two subunits, as judged both by biochemical and electron-microscopical analysis (30,35). Since the aminoacyl-tRNA is covalently bound to the PLP, high-resolution (2 nm) images of the enzyme-substrate complexes could be obtained. They revealed that five tRNA molecules are bound tangentially to the fully saturated disc-shaped enzyme (35). Under conditions of limited saturation, complexes with one, two, three, or four bound tRNAs were observed, indicating that binding is not subject to cooperativity (35).

Selenocysteine synthase reacts only with seryl-tRNA^{Sec} and not with any of the seryl-tRNA^{Ser} isoacceptor species (30,36). This indicates that the enzyme differentiates structural features of the tRNA. Indeed, a loose interaction was observed with uncharged tRNA^{Sec} (36).

SELB IS A SELENOCYSTEYL-tRNA^{Sec}-SPECIFIC TRANSLATION FACTOR

SELB displays sequence similarity to elongation factor Tu (EF-Tu) and initiation factor 2α (IF-2α) over its 240 N-terminal amino acids (37). The similarity involves not only the protein domains implicated in the binding of guanine nucleotides but also primary structure elements outside those regions (37). Like EF-Tu and IF-2 SELB binds GTP and GDP, the association constants being 1 μM and 10 μM, respectively. The higher affinity to GTP obviates the need for a GDP displacing factor like EF-Ts. SELB, in addition, binds selenocysteyl-tRNA^{Sec} stoichiometrically; no interaction was observed with seryl-tRNA^{Sec}, a fact that explains the extremely high selectivity for selenocysteine insertion even in the presence of an excess of seryl-tRNA^{Sec}. In contrast to EF-Tu, therefore, SELB differentiates the aminoacyl residue of the tRNA.

Förster et al. investigated whether EF-Tu is able to interact with selenocysteyl-tRNA^{Sec} (38). It was found that the affinity of EF-Tu for tRNA^{Sec} is at least 200-fold below that for seryl-tRNA^{Ser}, irrespective of whether tRNA^{Sec} was charged with serine or selenocysteine. The general conclusion, therefore, is that SELB is able to form a ternary complex with GTP and selenocysteyl-tRNA^{Sec} and that it has a function alternate to that of EF-Tu (37).

Analysis of the mRNA Context Required for Decoding UGA with Selenocysteine

The discovery that a nonsense codon is used to direct the insertion of a nonstandard amino acid into protein raises questions about this mechanism: (1) Why can't this nonsense codon function as a termination signal, and (2) which features of the mRNA are responsible for this particular nonsense codon and not any UGA termination codon being decoded with selenocysteine. Clearly, the mRNA context had to play a differentiating role.

The question was studied by introducing deletions on the 5' and on the 3' side of the TGA codon within the *fdhF* gene and by fusing the segment carrying the deletion in-frame to the *lacZ* gene (39). Read-through of the UGA in these constructs was measured by β-galactosidase activity and the values corresponded exactly to the capacity for selenocysteine insertion. The results obtained indicated that a stretch of about 40 nucleotides at the 3' side of the UGA codon were required for full read-through. Upstream sequences were not essential but the nucleotides neighboring the UGA immediately at the 5' side seemed to modulate the extent of read-through. Within the 40-nucleotide stretch a putative hairpin structure could be formed.

This secondary structure was subjected to an extensive mutational analysis, which revealed that it contains features that are absolutely required for selenocysteine incorporation determined by the UGA codon adjacent on its 5′ side (40). The most important element was the sequence of the loop region; almost any base change resulted in a grossly decreased read-through. Other important structural requirements were the length of the helical region of the hairpin and the base pair adjacent to the loop (40). Corroborating results were published by Berg et al. for the translation of the FDH$_N$ selenoprotein mRNA (41).

INTERACTION BETWEEN SELB AND THE mRNA

The existence of a specific nucleotide sequence about 18 bases downstream of the UGA codon forces the conclusion that this recognition element must interact with some component of the translation machinery, the most plausible candidates being some ribosomal compound or translation factor SELB. This interaction supposedly leads to (1) prevention of termination and (2) specific recognition of the UGA for selenocysteine incorporation.

A first indication for a specific interaction between SELB and the hairpin structure within the *fdhF* mRNA comes from genetic experiments. An *fdhF* gene segment carrying a hairpin with a mutation in the loop region was fused to *lacZ*. As a consequence of the mutation there was no read-through over the UGA and β-galactosidase activities were at background levels. *selB* mutants were then generated and screened for translation of the UGA. Several suppressor *selB* alleles were obtained that promoted read-through in the context of the mutated hairpin (A. Herzog and A. Böck, unpublished results).

By means of two different strategies a direct interaction between SELB and the *fdhF* mRNA secondary structure could be demonstrated. First, the accessibility of the mRNA segment for chemical modification and RNase attack was analyzed. Evidence was obtained for the *de facto* existence of this structure, and it was found that the hairpin loop region was protected in the presence of SELB (C. Baron and A. Böck, unpublished data). Second, by means of mobility shift experiments it could be demonstrated that SELB forms a quaternary complex with selenocysteyl-tRNA, GTP, and the *fdhF* mRNA (C. Baron and A. Böck, unpublished data). Complex formation was not observed when the mRNA contained a base change in the loop region of the hairpin.

THE MODEL OF UGA DECODING

Based on the results described above, the following model for site-specific insertion of selenocysteine is considered: It is proposed that translation factor SELB forms a complex with selenocysteyl-tRNA^{Sec} and GTP at the secondary structure of the *fdhF* mRNA and that this preformed complex is moved into the decoding site of the ribosome. It is further assumed that the helical part of the structure is "melted" by the approaching ribosome, possibly in two steps—first at the "lower part" of the helix "up" to the bulged, unpaired region, and then in a final step also at the top of the paired region, resulting in the release of the SELB × selenocysteyl-tRNA × GTP complex into the ribosomal A-site. Preformation of the complex is thought to lead to an increased local concentration of the cognate tRNA and thereby to an effective competition with noncognate aminoacyl-tRNAs. This mechanism would explain why there is a minimal distance requirement between the UGA codon and the mRNA recognition element at the top of the hairpin (40). It also meets the observation that SELB mainly protects the loop region and the "upper" part of the helix and not the base of the stem against chemical modification (C. Baron and A. Böck, unpublished results).

The lack of termination at the UGA codon could then be visualized as a hindrance of the binding of release factor 2 to the UGA codon. This explanation is supported by the observation that none of the three termination codons (UGA, UAA, UAG) in that particular mRNA position functions as a termination signal as long as the tRNA^{Sec} carries a complementary anticodon (40). What is required apparently is (1) a match between codon and anticodon and (2) an mRNA recognition element in the correct geometrical context.

SELB appears to bind to the ribosome in the same position as EF-Tu. This conclusion can be drawn from the fact that an exchange of the UGA in the message by a serine codon (UCA) results in the insertion of L-serine when wild-type tRNA^{Sec} (with an anticodon not matching UCA) is present. However, when the anticodon is changed to UGA (complementary to UCA), selenocysteine insertion effectively competes with serine incorporation (42).

A search of mRNAs coding for selenoproteins for putative secondary structures revealed considerable diversity (20). Several of them display structures similar to that present in the *E. coli fdhF* mRNA, but other ones differ greatly (43). It may well be that the recognition between the mRNA and SELB is a specific property of the system in one organism; in other words, different SELBs may have coevolved with the recognition element of one particular mRNA. It will be interesting to see the cross-compatibility of SELB factors from different organisms.

Structure—Function Relationships

The cellular numbers of tRNA^{Sec}, selenocysteine synthase monomer, and translation factor SELB are about 400, 1,000–1,200, and 1,100, respectively (23,36,44). As a consequence, there are sufficient binding sites (~550) for seryl-tRNA^{Sec} available at the biosynthetic enzyme to scavenge the charged tRNA from the free state, and there is a surplus of SELB to act as a sink for selenocysteyl-tRNA liberated from selenocysteine synthase. Moreover, the flux of L-serine into the biosynthetic pathway is limited by the poor substrate properties of tRNA^{Sec} for the seryl-tRNA ligase (25). Consequently, there should be no considerable pool of free seryl-tRNA^{Sec} or selenocysteyl-tRNA^{Sec} in the cell, even under conditions of selenium deficiency. The possibility of binding to EF-Tu and of subsequent misincorporation, therefore, is minimized not only by the low affinity of EF-Tu to this tRNA but also by its complex formation with either selenocysteine synthase or SELB.

A structure—function analysis has been carried out by Li and Yarus (45) and by Baron and Böck (25) to elucidate structural properties contributing to the specificity of tRNA^{Sec} in its interaction with seryl-tRNA ligase, selenocysteine synthase, and SELB. The combined results of these studies were that specificity is an additive phenomenon to which most of the unusual structural features of tRNA^{Sec} contribute. The length of the aminoacyl-acceptor stem seems to play a particularly important role since shortening to the 7-base-pair consensus abolished binding to SELB but—in turn—permitted interaction with EF-Tu (25).

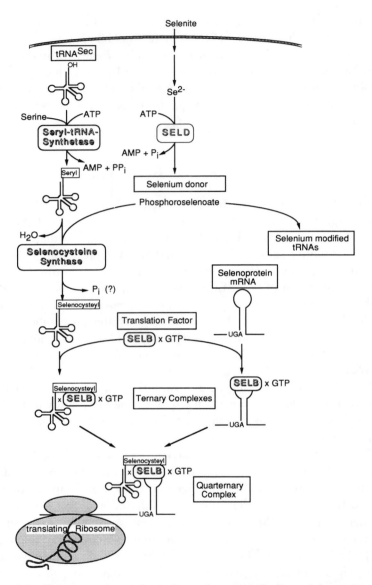

FIGURE 1.1. Selenoprotein synthesis by prokaryotes. Outline of the pathway by which prokaryotes metabolize selenium from its inorganic form to seleno-cysteine and then incorporate the amino acid into a growing polypeptide chain.

CONCLUSIONS

Study of the pathway of selenocysteine incorporation into proteins (Fig. 1.1) has revealed a number of exciting new biological phenomena: Selenocysteine insertion is coded in the DNA and, therefore, occurs cotranslationally; there is a specific translation factor; biosynthesis occurs at an adaptor molecule; and selenium is activated by phosphorylation. Future research now will be concerned with the detailed analysis of the mechanisms of these processes and, above all, with whether selenium biochemistry in eukaryotes follows the path elucidated for *E. coli*.

REFERENCES

1. Pinsent, J. The need for selenite and molybdate in the formation of formic dehydrogenase by members of the *Coliaerogenes* group of bacteria. Biochem J 57:10–16; 1954.
2. Sawers, G, Heider, J, Zehelein, E, Böck, A. Expression and operon structure of the *sel* genes of *Escherichia coli* and identification of a third selenium-containing formate dehydrogenase isoenzyme. J Bacteriol 173:4983–4993; 1991.
3. Enoch, HG, Lester, RL. The purification and properties of formate dehydrogenase and nitrate reductase from *Escherichia coli*. J Biol Chem 250:6693–6705; 1975.
4. Peck, HD, Gest, H. Formic dehydrogenase and the hydrogenlyase enzyme complex in coli-aerogenes bacteria. J Bacteriol 73:706–721; 1957.
5. Cox, JC, Edwards, ES, DeMoss, JA. Resolution of distinct selenium-containing formate dehydrogenases from *Escherichia coli*. J Bacteriol 145:1317–1324; 1981.
6. Schlindwein, C, Giordano, G, Santini, C-L, Mandrand, M-A. Identification and expression of the *Escherichia coli fdhD* and *fdhE* genes, which are involved in the formation of respiratory formate dehydrogenase. J Bacteriol 172:6112–6121; 1990.
7. Pecher, A, Zinoni, F, Böck, A. The selenopolypeptide of formic dehydrogenase (formate-hydrogen-lyase-linked) from *Escherichia coli*: genetic analysis. Arch Microbiol 141:359–363; 1985.
8. Andreesen, JR, Ljungdahl, LG. Formate dehydrogenase of *Clostridium thermoaceticum*, incorporation of selenium-75, and the effect of selenite,

molybdate, and tungstate on the enzyme. J Bacteriol 116:867–873; 1973.

9. Jones, JB, Stadtman, TC. Selenium-dependent and selenium-independent formate dehydrogenases of *Methanococcus vannielii.* J Biol Chem 256:656–663; 1981.

10. Stadtman, TC, Davis, JN, Ching, W-M, Zinoni, F, Böck, A. Amino acid sequence analysis of *Escherichia coli* formate dehydrogenase (FDH$_H$) confirms that TGA in the gene encodes selenocysteine in the gene product. BioFactors 3:21–27; 1991.

11. Arkowitz, RA, Abeles, RH. Mechanism of action of clostridial glycine reductase: isolation and characterization of a covalent acetyl enzyme intermediate. Biochemistry 30:4090–4097; 1991.

12. Cone, JE, Martin del Rio, R, Davis, JN, Stadtman, TC. Chemical characterization of the organoselenium moiety. Proc Natl Acad Sci USA 73:2659–2663; 1976.

13. Przybyla, A, Robbins, J, Menon, N, Peck Jr, HD. Structure-function relationships among the nickel-containing hydrogenases. FEMS Microbiol Rev 88:109–136; 1992.

14. Eidsness, MK, Scott, RA, Prickril, C, DerVartanian, DV, LeGall, J, Moura, I, Moura, JJG, Peck Jr, HD. Evidence for selenocysteine coordination to the active site nickel in the NiFeSe hydrogenases from *Desulfovibrio baculatus.* Proc Natl Acad Sci USA 86:147–151; 1989.

15. Voordouw, G, Menon, NK, LeGall, J, Choi, E-S, Peck Jr, HD, Przybyla, AE. Analysis and comparison of nucleotide sequences encoding the genes for [NiFe] and [NiFeSe] hydrogenases from *Desulfovibrio gigas* and *Desulfovibrio baculatus.* J Bacteriol 171:2894–2899; 1989.

16. Stadtman, TC. Selenium-dependent enzymes. Ann Rev Biochem 49: 93–110; 1980.

17. Chambers, I, Frampton, J, Goldfarb, P, Affara, N, McBain, W, Harrison, PR. The structure of the mouse glutathione peroxidase gene: the seleno-cysteine in the active site is encoded by the termination codon, TGA. EMBO J 5:1221–1227; 1986.

18. Zinoni, F, Birkmann, A, Stadtman, TC, Böck, A. Nucleotide sequence and expression of the selenocysteine containing polypeptide of formate dehydrogenase (formate-hydrogen-lyase-linked) from *Escherichia coli.* Proc Natl Acad Sci USA 83:4650–4654; 1986.

19. Leinfelder, W, Forchhammer, K, Zinoni, F, Sawers, G, Mandrand-Berthelot, M-A, Böck, A. *Escherichia coli* genes whose products are involved in selenium metabolism. J Bacteriol 170:540–546; 1988.

20. Zinoni, F, Birkmann, A, Leinfelder, W, Böck, A. Co-translational insertion of selenocysteine into formate dehydrogenase from *Escherichia*

coli directed by a UGA codon. Proc Natl Acad Sci USA 84:3156–3161; 1987.

21. Leinfelder, W, Stadtman, TC, Böck, A. Occurrence *in vivo* of selenocysteyl-tRNA$_{UCA}$ in *Escherichia coli*. J Biol Chem 264:9720–9723; 1989.

22. Haddock, BA, Mandrand-Berthelot, M-A. *Escherichia coli* formate-to-nitrate respiratory chain: genetic analysis. Biochem Soc Trans 10: 478–480; 1982.

23. Leinfelder, W, Zehelein, E, Mandrand-Berthelot, M-A, Böck, A. Gene for a novel tRNA species that accepts L-serine and cotranslationally inserts selenocysteine. Nature 331:723–725; 1988.

24. Schön, A, Böck, A, Ott, G, Sprinzl, M, Söll, D. The selenocysteine-inserting opal suppressor serine tRNA from *E. coli* is highly unusual in structure and modification. Nucleic Acids Res 17:7159–7165; 1989.

25. Baron, Ch, Böck, A. The length of the aminoacyl-acceptor stem of the selenocysteine-specific tRNA^{Sec} of *Escherichia coli* is the determinant for binding to elongation factors SELB or Tu. J Biol Chem 266:20375–20379; 1991.

26. Heider, J, Leinfelder, W, Böck, A. Occurrence and functional compatibility within Enterobacteriaceae of a tRNA species which inserts selenocysteine into protein. Nucleic Acids Res 17:2529–2540; 1989.

27. Mizutani, T, Maruyama, N, Hitaka, T, Sukenaga, Y. The detection of natural opal suppressor seryl-tRNA in *Escherichia coli* by the dot blot hybridization and its phosphorylation by a tRNA kinase. FEBS Lett 247:345–348; 1989.

28. Hatfield, D. Suppression of termination codons in higher eukaryotes. Trends Biochem Sci 10:245–250; 1985.

29. Forchhammer, K, Leinfelder, W, Boesmiller, K, Veprek, B, Böck, A. Selenocysteine synthase from *Escherichia coli*: nucleotide sequence of the gene (*selA*) and purification of the protein. J Biol Chem 266: 6318–6323; 1991.

30. Forchhammer, K, Böck, A. Selenocysteine synthase from *Escherichia coli*: analysis of the reaction sequence. J Biol Chem 266:6324–6328; 1991.

31. Reed, LJ, Cox, DJ. Macromolecular organization of enzyme systems. Ann Rev Biochem 35:57–84; 1966.

32. Brzovic, P, Litzenberger Holbrook, E, Greene, RC, Dunn, MF. Reaction mechanism of *Escherichia coli* cystathionine γ-synthase: Direct evidence for a pyridoxamine derivative of vinylglyoxylate as a key intermediate in pyridoxal phosphate dependent γ-elimination and γ-replacement reactions. Biochemistry 29:442–451; 1990.

33. Ehrenreich, A, Forchhammer, K, Tormay, P, Veprek, B, Böck, A. Selenoprotein synthesis in *E. coli*. Purification and characterisation of the enzyme catalysing selenium activation. Eur J Biochem 206: 767–773; 1992.

34. Veres, Z, Tsai, L, Scholz, TD, Politino, M, Balaban RS, Stadtman, TC. Synthesis of 5-methylaminomethyl-2-selenouridine in tRNAs: ^{31}P NMR studies show the labile selenium donor synthesized by the *selD* gene product contains selenium bonded to phosphorus. Proc Natl Acad Sci USA 89:2975–2979; 1992.

35. Engelhardt, H, Forchhammer, K, Müller, S, Engel, A, Böck, A. Structure of selenocysteine synthase from *Escherichia coli* and location of tRNA in the seryl-tRNA^{Sec}-enzyme complex. Molec Microbiol 6:3461–3467, 1992.

36. Forchhammer, K, Boesmiller, K, Böck, A. The function of selenocysteine synthase and SELB in the synthesis and incorporation of selenocysteine. Biochimie 73:1481–1486; 1991.

37. Forchhammer, K, Leinfelder, W, Böck, A. Identification of a novel translation factor necessary for the incorporation of a selenocysteine into protein. Nature 342:453–456; 1989.

38. Förster, Ch, Ott, G, Forchhammer, K, Sprinzl, M. Interaction of a selenocysteine-incorporating tRNA with elongation factor Tu from *E. coli*. Nucleic Acids Res 18:487–491; 1990.

39. Zinoni, F, Heider, J, Böck, A. Features of the formate dehydrogenase mRNA necessary for decoding of the UGA codon as selenocysteine. Proc Natl Acad Sci USA 87:4660–4664; 1990.

40. Heider, J, Baron, C, Böck, A. Coding from a distance: Dissection of the mRNA determinants required for the incorporation of selenocysteine into protein. EMBO J 11:3759–3766; 1992.

41. Berg, BL, Baron, C, Stewart, V. Nitrate-inducible formate dehydrogenase in *Escherichia coli* K-12. J Biol Chem 266:22386–22391; 1991.

42. Baron, Ch, Heider, J, Böck, A. Mutagenesis of *selC*, the gene for the selenocysteine-inserting tRNA-species in *E. coli*: effects on *in vivo* function. Nucleic Acids Res 18:6761–6766; 1990.

43. Garcia, GE, Stadtman, TC. Selenoprotein A component of the glycine reductase complex from *Clostridium purinolyticum*: nucleotide sequence of the gene shows that selenocysteine is encoded by UGA. J Bacteriol 173:2093–2098; 1991.

44. Forchhammer, K, Rücknagel, K-P, Böck, A. Purification and biochemical characterisation of SELB, a translation factor involved in selenoprotein synthesis. J Biol Chem 265:9346–9350; 1990.

45. Li, W-Q, Yarus, M. Bar to normal UGA translation by the selenocysteine tRNA. J Mol Biol 223:9–15; 1992.

Chapter
2

Selenocysteine tRNA[Ser]Sec Isoacceptors as Central Components in Selenoprotein Biosynthesis in Eukaryotes

DOLPH L. HATFIELD, IN SOON CHOI, TAKESHI OHAMA,
JAE-EON JUNG, AND ALAN M. DIAMOND

INTRODUCTION

In recent years, a variety of experimental results have led to the surprising conclusion that under certain circumstances the UGA termination codon signals the translational insertion of selenocysteine into protein. These studies include the demonstration that (1) a TGA codon (that corresponds to a selenocysteine moiety in the resulting gene products [Cone et al., 1976; Günzler et al., 1984]) occurs in the open reading frame of genes for formate dehydrogenase in *E. coli* (Zinoni et al., 1986) and glutathione peroxidase (GPx) in mammals (Chambers et al., 1986; Sukenaga et al., 1987; Mullenbach et al., 1988) and (2) a selenocysteyl-tRNA that decodes UGA occurs in *E. coli* (Leinfelder et al., 1989) and mammals (Lee et al., 1989b). The genes that utilize UGA for selenocysteine (for review see Stadtman, 1991) and the tRNAs that serve as carrier molecules for the biosynthesis of selenocysteine and donate selenocysteine to protein have been observed in a wide variety of organisms as described below. This phenomenon has evolved in all life kingdoms and thus the universal genetic code has been expanded to include selenocysteine as the 21st encoded amino acid (Hatfield et al., 1992b; Hatfield and Diamond, 1993).

Despite the conservation of function for selenocysteyl-tRNA in both prokaryotes and eukaryotes, significant differences in structure and biological regulation exist. Using genetic and biochemical approaches in bacteria, much has been learned about the prokaryotic selenocysteyl-tRNA and this work is presented elsewhere in this book. (See chapter 1.) Within this chapter, we will describe eukaryotic features of the translational machinery for selenocysteine incorporation into protein and emphasize the apparent differences between prokaryotes and eukaryotes.

DISCOVERY OF SELENOCYSTEYL-tRNAS IN EUKARYOTES

It was over 20 years ago when the first evidence was presented that UGA may serve a function in addition to that of translational termination in eukaryotes. As part of the efforts to investigate the codon specificity of mammalian tRNAs, studies utilizing a ribosome binding assay indicated the presence of a low-abundance seryl-tRNA from bovine and chicken livers that recognized the nonsense codon UGA (Hatfield and Portugal, 1970). In addition, two different groups reported that deacylation of seryl-tRNA from either rooster liver or bovine lactation mammary glands revealed a molecule that was identified as phosphoserine (Mäenpää and Bernfield, 1970; Sharp and Stewart, 1977). Since both the UGA-recognizing and phosphoseryl-tRNAs exhibited similar chromatographic properties, we purified these molecules in order to further characterize them (Diamond et al., 1981; Hatfield et al., 1982). The purified tRNA responded only to the UGA codon, and not to any of the six serine codons, in ribosome-binding experiments. Additional work on the purified tRNA demonstrated that it read UGA in an *in vitro* suppression assay (Diamond et al., 1981) and that it formed phosphoseryl-tRNA (Hatfield et al., 1982). As it became apparent that the TGA codon in the glutathione peroxidase gene corresponded to selenocysteine in the gene product (see Introduction), it was shown that the minor seryl-tRNA that recognized UGA (Hatfield and Portugal, 1970; Diamond et al., 1981) and the corresponding phosphoseryl-tRNA (Hatfield et al., 1982; Mizutani and Hashimoto, 1984) were in fact a selenocysteyl-tRNA (Lee et al., 1989b) that is now designated selenocysteine tRNA[Ser]Sec (Lee et al., 1990). As noted in the Introduction and further discussed below, the biosynthesis of selenocysteine occurs on tRNA[Ser]Sec.

Is Phosphoserine an Intermediate in the Biosynthesis of Selenocysteine?

While it has been experimentally established that mammalian seryl-tRNA[Ser]Sec can be converted to phosphoseryl-tRNA, it remains unproven whether the latter form of the tRNA represents an intermediate in the biosynthesis of selenocysteyl-tRNA. The first reports of phosphoseryl-tRNA being detected in chicken liver (Mäenpää and Bernfield, 1970) and bovine lactating mammary glands (Sharp and Stewart, 1977) prompted speculation that perhaps there were circumstances under which phosphoserine was cotranslationally inserted into a growing peptide. Phosphoserine is one of three phosphorylated amino acids detectable in protein, sometimes representing as much as 50% of the serine content of a particular protein. Yet, to date, there exist no compelling data to indicate that any phosphoserine residues are inserted in response to any particular coding triplet. In fact, the data indicate that phosphoserine in protein arises as a post-translational modification of existing serine residues encoded by the six serine codons. Whether phosphoseryl-tRNA may serve a role other than functioning in protein synthesis has also been considered (Diamond et al., 1981; Stewart and Sharp, 1984). However, the clear demonstration that selenocysteine is biosynthesized on tRNA$^{[Ser]Sec}$ and that it is encoded in protein by UGA makes it more likely that the occurrence of phosphoserine on tRNA$^{[Ser]Sec}$ is due to the fact that it is an intermediate in the selenocysteine biosynthetic pathway.

Studies on the synthesis of selenocysteyl-tRNA$^{[Ser]Sec}$ clearly have shown that the serine ester of tRNA$^{[Ser]Sec}$ is converted to phosphoseryl-tRNA *in vivo* (Lee et al., 1989b). Furthermore, phosphoseryl-tRNA$^{[Ser]Sec}$ can bind to ribosomes in response to the UGA triplet (Hatfield et al., 1982). Partially purified preparations of a seryl-tRNA kinase have been reported (Mizutani and Hashimoto, 1984) and greater than 50% conversion of seryl-tRNA$^{[Ser]Sec}$ to phosphoseryl-tRNA$^{[Ser]Sec}$ can occur (Hatfield et al., 1982). Given the necessary specificity of serine kinases that function in the posttranslational modification of protein, it seems unlikely that the same enzyme(s) would recognize a serine residing on a tRNA. It therefore remains the most likely hypothesis that phosphoseryl-tRNA$^{[Ser]Sec}$ is a biosynthetic intermediate. It should be noted that based on earlier studies Mizutani et al. concluded that phosphoseryl-tRNA is an intermediate in selenocysteyl-tRNA biosynthesis in eukaryotes (Mizutani and Hitaka, 1988; Mizutani, 1989) and in prokaryotes (Mizutani et al., 1989), but more recently these investigators concluded that phosphoseryl-tRNA is not an intermediate in eukaryotes (Mizutani et al., 1991, 1992).

In *E. coli*, biosynthesis of selenocysteyl-tRNA occurs by the initial aminoacylation of procaryotic tRNA$^{[Ser]Sec}$ with serine as in eukaryotic cells, but then proceeds via a pyridoxyl-phosphate-dependent dehydration step prior to the addition of selenium (Leinfelder et al., 1990; Forchhammer and Böck, 1991). Interestingly, the labile selenium donor molecule in this reaction has recently been shown to be a compound containing selenium bonded directly to phosphorus (Veres et al., 1992). This compound, selenophosphate, is formed from adenosine triphosphate (ATP) and selenide by selenophosphate synthetase (Z. Veres and T.C. Stadtman, personal communication).

Resolution of the comparable steps in eukaryotes awaits further biochemical characterization.

MULTIPLE tRNA[Ser]Sec ISOACCEPTORS IN MAMMALIAN TISSUES

Multiple, chromatographically distinct forms of tRNA[Ser]Sec have been observed in mammalian cells (Hatfield, 1972). In bovine liver, two distinct tRNA species have been purified and their primary sequences have been determined (Diamond et al., 1981; Hatfield et al., 1982). These tRNAs differed from each other in both primary sequence and modified base content. It was therefore surprising that only a single genetic locus was observed by Southern blot analysis of genomic bovine DNA (Diamond et al., 1990). Isolation of this locus by molecular cloning indicated that the two observed tRNAs differed not only from each other, but from the single gene from which they must be transcribed. Similarly, multiple tRNA[Ser]Sec isoacceptors have been observed by reverse-phase chromatography in the tRNA population of all higher eukaryotic organisms examined, yet only a single functional gene has been detected in chicken, rabbit, *Drosophila*, *Xenopus*, *Caenorhabditis elegans*, and man (Hatfield et al., 1990; Lee et al., 1990). The human tRNA[Ser]Sec gene has been mapped to chromosome 19 and the pseudogene to chromosome 22 (McBride et al., 1987). Furthermore, the human gene was localized on chromosome 19 to bands q13.2−q13.3 by *in situ* hybridization and ordered with respect to other genes in this region by linkage analysis (Mitchell et al., 1992). The selenocysteine tRNA[Ser]Sec gene is closely linked to cytochrome P450 IIB and IIF, to apolipoprotein C-II, and to muscle creatine kinase.

More recently, the primary sequences of two selenocysteine tRNAs were determined from rat liver (Diamond et al., 1993). The structures of these isoacceptors are colinear with the corresponding gene from rat DNA and they differ from each other by a single 2'-O-methylated ribose of the nucleoside (5-methylcarboxymethyluridine) in the wobble position of the anticodon. The tRNA[Ser]Sec sequenced from bovine liver (Diamond et al., 1981) may represent a subpopulation of selenocysteine tRNAs as discussed in Diamond et al. (1993).

Multiple tRNA[Ser]Sec species have been observed in higher vertebrates as two distinct isoacceptors that elute late from reverse-phase chromatographic columns (Hatfield, 1972; Hatfield et al., 1990). The relative abundance of these two species is different in different tissues, and we have shown that selenium influences both their abundance and distribution (Hatfield et al., 1991a). We chose human HL-60 promyelocytic leukemia cells and rat mammary tumor cells for study as both these very different cell types can be grown in the absence of selenium without any significant change in morphology. Our data indicated that shifting either cell type from selenium-deficient to selenium-proficient culture media resulted in both an increase in the steady-state levels of these isoacceptors and in a shift toward the slightly more hydrophobic form of tRNA[Ser]Sec. Similar results have been obtained in whole animals maintained on either selenium-deficient or -proficient diets (Diamond et al., 1993). In the latter studies, rats fed a selenium-proficient diet had increased steady-state levels of the tRNA[Ser]Sec isoacceptors with most organs demonstrating a significant shift to the more hydrophobic species. Other recent data have provided strong evidence that the earlier-eluting species is a precursor of the later (Choi et al., 1993a). Since selenium influences the distribution of tRNA[Ser]Sec isoacceptors toward the later-eluting species, it is tempting to speculate that this form of the tRNA is the significant donor of selenocysteine to protein.

EVOLUTIONARY CHANGES IN tRNA[Ser]Sec GENE AND UNUSUAL NATURE OF THE CLOVERLEAF STRUCTURE

The tRNA[Ser]Sec gene has been sequenced from a number of animals including human (O'Neill et al., 1985), rabbit (Pratt et al., 1985), cow (Diamond et al., 1990), chicken (Hatfield et al., 1983), *Xenopus*, *Drosophila*, and *C. elegans* (Lee et al., 1990). The gene has been highly conserved in higher vertebrates, where it has been found to be identical in humans and rabbits and differs from those in chickens and *Xenopus* by a single pyrimidine transition at position 11 (Fig. 2.1). As shown in the figure, the gene has undergone numerous evolutionary changes between vertebrates and lower animal forms. There are 22 base changes between *Drosophila* and vertebrates, 18

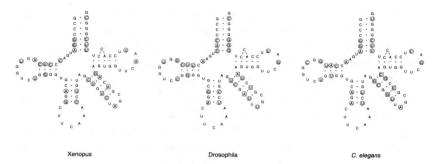

Xenopus   Drosophila   C. elegans

FIGURE 2.1. Cloverleaf models of transcripts of and evolutionary changes in *Xenopus*, *Drosophila*, and *C. elegans* tRNA[Ser]Sec genes. Circled letters designate that a single base change occurred in evolution between the three organisms; boxed letters designate that a base change occurred between all three organisms. The chicken gene is identical to that of *Xenopus* but differs from those of humans and rabbits by a single pyrimidine transition at position 11. (The figure is taken from Lee et al. [1990] with the permission of the American Society of Microbiology, Washington, D.C.)

between *C. elegans* and vertebrates, and 20 between *Drosophila* and *C. elegans* (Lee et al. 1990). The bacterial (see chapter 1) and animal selenocysteine tRNA genes, however, manifest little significant sequence conservation.

The cloverleaf model presented in Figure 2.1 probably represents the more stable secondary structure of these tRNAs. This conclusion is supported by the fact that the *C. elegans* tRNA does not fully base pair in the dihydrouracil stem in other cloverleaf representations. It should be noted that the two bases within the dihydrouracil loop that are closest to the stem of each tRNA can also base pair, leaving a six-membered loop instead of an eight-membered loop as shown.

Selenocysteine tRNAs exhibit several unique structural features. These may account for the dual role of the tRNAs, serving as carrier molecules for the synthesis of selenocysteine as well as adaptors for the incorporation of selenocysteine into protein. One such feature is the presence of four unpaired nucleotides between the acceptor and dihydouracil stems compared to other eukaryotic tRNAs that typically contain from zero to three unpaired nucleotides in this region. Another unique feature is the occurrence of an unpaired nucleotide, residue 77, in the TψC stem in a region that normally shows perfect base-pairing. The two nucleotides at positions 14 and 15 that reside in the dihydrouracil stem of the cloverleaf are extra nucleotides within the selenocysteine tRNA gene. They occur in the conserved A box, that, along with the conserved B box, is an internal control region that governs transcription of all eukaryotic genes. (See below.) These extra nucleotides are likely to contribute to the unusual roles that are unique to the selenocysteine tRNAs. Clearly, a single base change in the dihydrouracil stem of *E. coli* tRNA[Trp] alters its codon recognition properties (Hirsh, 1971) and thus the changes seen in the dihydrouracil stem of tRNA[Ser]Sec may also influence its recognition properties. It should also be noted that an alternative cloverleaf model of tRNA[Ser]Sec has recently been published (Sturchler et al., 1993). An interesting feature of this model is that the acceptor stem contains 8 base pairs similar to that reported in the prokaryotic tRNA[Ser]Sec (see also Chapter 1 and references therein).

Transcriptional Regulation and Biosynthesis of the tRNA[Ser]Sec Isoacceptors

Although two or more forms of selenocysteine tRNA[Ser]Sec can be identified by chromatographic procedures in mammalian tissues, these molecules arise from a single gene. (For review see Hatfield et al., 1990). A pseudogene of tRNA[Ser]Sec exists in human (O'Neill et al., 1985) and rabbit (Pratt et al., 1985) genomes, but bovine (Diamond et al., 1990), rat (Diamond et al., 1992), avian (Hatfield et al., 1983), and *Xenopus*, *Drosophila*, and *C. elegans* (Lee et al., 1990) DNA contain only a single gene. As noted above, these isoacceptors manifest many unique features that set them apart from other tRNAs. What then are the regulatory mechanisms that govern the expression of these unique tRNAs?

The expression of tRNA[Ser]Sec was initially examined *in vitro* in HeLa-cell extracts and *in vivo* in *Xenopus oocytes* (Lee et al., 1989a).

At least three upstream regulatory elements were identified by deletion analysis *in vivo* in the *Xenopus* gene that contribute to the regulation of transcription of tRNA[SerISec. One of these is a TATA box near −30 and a second, that is immediately upstream of the TATA box, is a GC-rich region. A third regulatory site consists of an AT-rich region that is located slightly further upstream of the GC-rich region. Only the two regulatory sites closest to the gene were shown to influence transcription in *in vitro* studies.

Carbon and collaborators have also examined the expression of the *Xenopus* gene in *Xenopus* oocytes (Carbon and Krol, 1991; Myslinski et al., 1992). Their data indicated that both the TATA box and a proximal segment element (PSE) corresponding approximately to the GC-AT-rich region of Lee et al. (1989a) are required for maximal tRNA[SerISec expression. In addition, they reported that the internal B box region plays a role in obtaining maximal transcription (Carbon and Krol, 1991). Both the A and B box internal control regions appear to have a role in processing the 3′ trailer sequence (Choi et al., 1993b). Myslinski et al. (1992) have also reported a 15-bp region that occurs upstream at position −195 to −209 that functions as a transcriptional activator element (AE). The AE, that binds to a nuclear protein, functions in stimulating the expression of a number of different genes including that of tRNA[SerISec.

Transcription of selenocysteine tRNA[SerISec occurs by a unique pathway. Unlike any known tRNA, tRNA[SerISec begins transcription at the first nucleotide within the gene and thus does not contain a 5′ leader sequence (Lee et al., 1987). The 5′ terminal triphosphate remains intact on the primary transcript through 3′ terminal processing and through subsequent transport from the nucleus to the cytoplasm. Once in the cytoplasm, the processed primary transcript undergoes further conversion to two additional forms that behave chromato-graphically very similarly to those observed in mammalian tissues and in *Xenopus* liver (Choi et al., 1993a). Thus, we are likely to have reconstituted the pathway of biosynthesis of the tRNA[SerISec isoacceptors in *Xenopus* oocytes. The pathway, from the processed primary transcript to the mature tRNA, has been duplicated using either RNA generated *in vitro* from an expression vector encoding the selenocysteine tRNA gene or from the direct injection of the gene (Choi et al., 1993a).

INCORPORATION OF SELENOCYSTEINE INTO PROTEIN

Selenocysteyl-tRNA[Ser]Sec donates selenocysteine to the growing poly-peptide chain in response to certain UGA codons but not to UGA codons serving as termination codons. Clearly, there must be specific safeguards that guarantee that selenocysteine is correctly inserted and not serine or phosphoserine. *In vitro* studies with glutathione peroxidase mRNA indicated that the "coding" UGA codon can serve as a terminator (Jung et al., 1993). Rabbit reticulocyte lysates programmed with glutathione peroxidase mRNA directed the synthesis of a small amount of peptide spanning the sequence from the initiation codon to the UGA codon. A small amount of "readthrough" of the UGA codon also occurred, generating a full-length glutathione peroxidase product. Supplementing the lysate with an authentic UGA suppressor tRNA or with unacylated tRNA[Ser]Sec resulted in an increased amount of full-length glutathione peroxidase synthesis. Programming wheat-germ extracts with glutathione peroxidase mRNA resulted in the generation of significant amounts of the truncated peptide and a much smaller amount of the read-through product. As in the case of the reticulocyte lysate, read-through (of the glutathione peroxidase UGA codon) in the wheat-germ system was stimulated by addition of authentic UGA suppressor tRNA (Jung et al., 1993). These results demonstrate that the UGA codon that *in vivo* encodes selenocysteine can also serve as a stop signal.

How then does the cell distinguish between UGA codons that designate selenocysteine incorporation and the vast majority of UGA codons that signal the cessation of protein synthesis? At least part of the answer to this critical question lies within the secondary structure of selenoprotein mRNA. It has been reported that a stem-loop structure in the mRNAs for formate dehydrogenase and glycine reductase immediately 3' to the selenocysteine encoding UGA is both necessary and sufficient for selenocysteine incorporation (Zinoni et al., 1990). Structurally similar sequences were shown to exist at the same location in glutathione peroxidase mRNAs (Zinoni et al., 1990). Surprisingly, of the 10 UGAs that encode selenocysteine in mammalian selenoprotein P mRNA, only one of these is near the amino terminus, as is the UGA in glutathione peroxidase mRNA, which may suggest similar functions for the selenocysteine moieties in the corresponding gene products (Hill et al., 1991). Stem-loop structures in other parts of mRNAs for selenoproteins seem to be important for distinguishing between UGA functions as well. Stem-loop structures of high negative free energy in the 3′ untranslated region of both type I iodothyronine 5′ deiodinase and glutathione peroxidase mRNAs are required for selenocysteine incorporation (Berry et al., 1991). This study also indicated that these structures are functionally interchangeable between the iodinase and glutathione peroxidase mRNAs despite little or no similarity in sequence.

The means by which these regions of secondary structure in selenocysteine encoding mRNAs affect the coding properties of upstream codons is unknown. One possibility, however, is they may serve as recognition sequences for cellular components involved in selenocysteine incorporation. Such a component may be an elongation factor specific for selenocysteyl-tRNA[Ser]Sec. A factor specific for selenocysteine incorporation into protein has been described in *E. coli* which is the product of the *selB* gene (Forchhammer et al., 1989, 1990).

A Central Role for tRNA[Ser]Sec in Mammalian Selenium Biology

Although selenium was once considered only because of its toxicity at high doses, it has received much attention over more recent years for its role in the chemoprevention of a variety of maladies. Low dietary consumption of selenium is causative of Keshan disease, a clinical problem endemic in China that is a cardiomyopathy. The role of selenium in Keshan disease has been well established as the supplementation of children with selenium results in prevention of the disease. Other studies have suggested a link between low selenium consumption and ischemic heart disease (Salonen and Huttunen, 1986) and the vulnerability of hepatocytes to alcohol toxicity (Aaseth et al., 1986). However, most studies have focused on the role of selenium in the chemoprevention of cancer. Human studies have indicated a statistically significant inverse correlation between cancer incidence and selenium either in the soil or the diet or in plasma (Salonen and Huttunen, 1986; Medina and Morrison, 1988). Animal studies have shown decreases in carcinogen-induced tumor incidence when rodents receive dietary supplementation of selenium a few-fold higher than the normal dietary requirement (Ip, 1986).

The means by which selenium might serve a chemopreventive role are not known. However, the existence of multiple, distinct selenoproteins suggests the possibility that some of these proteins account for the above-described effects. A candidate selenoprotein for at least some of these effects is glutathione peroxidase. Glutathione peroxidase represents a family of related selenoproteins that detoxify lipid and hydrogen peroxides using reducing equivalents from glutathione (Burk, 1991). This antioxidant activity may account for some of the bioprotective functions of selenium, although it has been suggested that the levels of selenium at which a protective effect occurs in animals apparently do not affect glutathione peroxidase levels (Lane and Medina, 1983; Lane et al., 1984). It is very likely that other selenoproteins, perhaps selenoprotein P and/or other yet-unidentified selenoproteins, account for protection associated with selenium.

As described in this chapter, tRNA[Ser]Sec isoacceptors provide the dual functions of selenocysteine biosynthesis and translational incorporation. These tRNAs will therefore be of central importance in selenoprotein regulation. This concept is already supported by the data indicating the unusual way in which the tRNA[Ser]Sec gene is transcribed and the observation that both the steady-state levels and distribution of the selenocysteyl-tRNA isoacceptors are responsive to selenium.

UBIQUITY OF SELENOCYSTEINE IN NATURE

Once the selenocysteine tRNA that decodes UGA was identified in *E. coli* (Leinfelder et al., 1989) and in mammals (Lee et al., 1989b), it was of considerable importance to determine how widespread this phenomenom was in nature. Subsequently, a selenocysteine tRNA gene was detected throughout the subkingdom Eubacteria (Heider et al., 1989) and a tRNA[Ser]Sec gene and/or its product was shown to be ubiquitous within the animal kingdom (Lee et al., 1990). Selenocysteyl-tRNAs that decode UGA were also observed in a higher plant, *Beta vulgaris*, in a filamentous fungus, *Gliocladium virens*, and

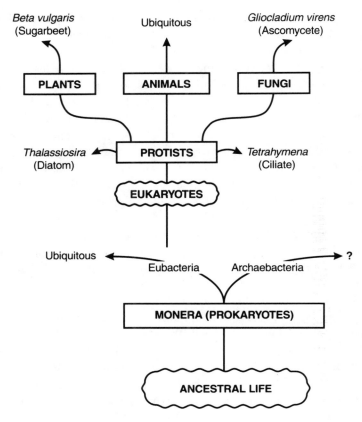

FIGURE 2.2. Evolutionary tree showing the distribution of selenocysteyl-tRNAs in Nature.

in two quite diverse protists, *Thalassiosira pseudonana* and *Tetrahymena borealis* (Hatfield et al., 1991b, 1992a). Thus, as shown in Figure 2.2, selenocysteine tRNA occurs in representatives of all five of the life kingdoms—i.e., monera, protist, plant, animal, and fungi (Margulis and Schwartz, 1988).

It would seem from the studies described above that UGA most certainly has a split personality in the universal genetic code, coding for selenocysteine and signaling the termination of translation (Fig. 2.3). The bifunctionality of AUG as a codon for the initiation of

Middle Base / 5' Base	U	C	A	G	Middle Base / 3' Base
U	Phenylalanine	Serine	Tyrosine	Cysteine	U
	Phenylalanine	Serine	Tyrosine	Cysteine	C
	Leucine	Serine	*Terminator*	Selenocysteine } *Terminator*	A
	Leucine	Serine	*Terminator*	Tryptophan	G
C	Leucine	Proline	Histidine	Arginine	U
	Leucine	Proline	Histidine	Arginine	C
	Leucine	Proline	Glutamine	Arginine	A
	Leucine	Proline	Glutamine	Arginine	G
A	Isoleucine	Threonine	Asparagine	Serine	U
	Isoleucine	Threonine	Asparagine	Serine	C
	Isoleucine	Threonine	Lysine	Arginine	A
	Methionine } *Initiator*	Threonine	Lysine	Arginine	G
G	Valine	Alanine	Aspartic acid	Glycine	U
	Valine	Alanine	Aspartic acid	Glycine	C
	Valine	Alanine	Glutamic acid	Glycine	A
	Valine	Alanine	Glutamic acid	Glycine	G

FIGURE 2.3. The universal genetic code, 1993. (From Hatfield and Diamond [1993] with permission of Elsevier Trends Journals, Cambridge, United Kingdom.)

protein synthesis and as a codon for methionine at internal positions of protein has been known for many years (Nirenberg et al., 1966; Khorana et al., 1966). However, expanding the universal genetic code to include selenocysteine is the first addition to the code since the time that it was deciphered (Nirenberg et al., 1966; Khorana et al., 1966) and shown to be universal in the mid-1960s (Nirenberg et al., 1966; Marshall et al., 1967).

REFERENCES

Aaseth, J, Smith-Kielland, A, Thomassen, Y. Selenium, alcohol and liver diseases. Ann Clin Res 18:43–47; 1986.

Berry, MJ, Banu, L, Larsen, PR. Type I iodothyronine deiodinase is a selenocysteine-containing enzyme. Nature 349:438–440; 1991.

Burk, RF. Molecular biology of selenium with implications for its metabolism, FASEB 5:2274–2279; 1991.

Carbon, P, Krol, A. Transcription of the *Xenopus laevis* selenocysteine tRNA[Ser]Sec gene: a system that combines an internal B box and upstream elements also found in U6 snRNA genes. EMBO J 10:599–606; 1991.

Chambers, I, Frampton, J, Goldfarb, P, Affara, N, McBain, W, Harrison, PR. The structure of the mouse glutathione peroxidase gene; the seleno-cysteine in the active site is encoded by the termination codon, TGA. EMBO J 5:1221–1227; 1986.

Choi, IS, Diamond, AM, Crain, PF, Kolker, JC, McCloskey, JA, Hatfield, D. Reconstitution of the biosynthetic pathway of selenocysteine tRNAs in *Xenopus* oocytes. Submitted for publication; 1993a.

Choi, IS, Lee, BJ, Kang, SG, Kim, YS, Hatfield, D. Site specific mutations in the regulatory regions of the selenocysteine tRNA[Ser]Sec gene. Manu-script in preparation; 1993b.

Cone, JE, Del Rio, RM, Davis, JM, Stadtman, TC. Chemical characterization of the selenoprotein component of clostridial glycine reductase: identifi-cation of selenocysteine as the organoselenium moiety. Proc Natl Acad Sci USA 73:2659–2663; 1976.

Diamond, AM, Dudock, B, Hatfield, D. Structure and properties of a bovine liver UGA suppressor serine tRNA with a tryptophan anticodon. Cell 25:497–506; 1981.

Diamond, AM, Montero-Puerner, Y, Lee, BJ, Hatfield, D. Selenocysteine inserting tRNAs are likely generated by tRNA editing. Nucleic Acids Res 18:6727; 1990.

Diamond, AM, Choi, IS, Crain, PF, Hashizume, T, Pomerantz, SC, Cruz, R, Steer, C, Hill, KE, Burk RF, McCloskey, JA, Hatfield, D. Dietary selenium affects methylation of the wobble nucleoside in the anticodon of selenocysteine tRNA[Ser]Sec. J Biol Chem 268:14215–14223; 1993.

Forchhammer, K, Leinfelder, W, Böck, A. Identification of a novel trans-lation factor necessary for the incorporation of selenocysteine into protein. Nature 342:453–456; 1989.

Forchhammer, K, Rücknagel, K-P, Böck, A. Purification and biochemical characterization of SELB, a translation factor involved in selenoprotein synthesis. J Biol Chem 265:9346–9350; 1990.

Forchhammer, K, Böck, A. Selenocysteine synthase from *Escherichia coli*: analysis of the reaction sequence. J Biol Chem 266:6324–6328; 1991.

Günzler, WA, Steffens, GT, Grossman, A, Kim, S-M, Otting, F, Wendel, A, Flohé, L. The amino-acid sequence of bovine glutathione peroxidase. Hoppe-Seyler's Z. Physiol Chem 365:195–212; 1984.

Hatfield, D, Portugal, FH. Seryl-tRNA in mammalian tissues: chromatographic differences in brain and liver and a specific response to the codon, UGA. Proc Natl Acad Sci USA 67:1200–1206; 1970.

Hatfield, D. Recognition of nonsense codons in mammalian cells. Proc Natl Acad Sci USA 67:3014–3018; 1972.

Hatfield, D, Diamond, AM, Dudock, B. Opal suppressor serine tRNAs from bovine liver form phosphoseryl-tRNA. Proc Natl Acad Sci USA 79:6215–6219; 1982.

Hatfield, D, Dudock, B, Eden, F. Characterization and nucleotide sequence of a chicken gene encoding an opal suppressor tRNA and its flanking DNA segments. Proc Natl Acad Sci USA 80:4940–4944; 1983.

Hatfield, DL, Smith, DWE, Lee, BJ, Worland, PJ, Oroszlan, S. Structure and function of suppressor tRNAs in higher eukaryotes. Crit Rev Biochem Mol Biol 25:71–96; 1990.

Hatfield, D, Lee, BJ, Hampton, L, Diamond, AM. Selenium induces changes in the selenocysteine tRNA[Ser]Sec population of mammalian cells. Nucleic Acids Res 19:939–943; 1991a.

Hatfield, DL, Lee, BJ, Price, NM, Stadtman, TC. Selenocysteyl-tRNA occurs in the diatom *Thalassiosira* and in the ciliate *Tetrahymena*. Mol Microbiol 5:1183–1186; 1991b.

Hatfield, D, Choi, IS, Mischke, S, Owens, LD, Selenocysteyl-tRNAs recognize UGA in *Beta vulgaris*, a higher plant, and in *Gliocladium virens*, a filamentous fungus. Biochem Biophys Res Comm 184:254–259; 1992a.

Hatfield, D, Choi, IS, Lee, BJ, Jung, J-E. Selenocysteine, a new addition to the universal genetic code. In: Hatfield, D, Lee, BJ, Pirtle, R, eds. Transfer RNA in Protein Synthesis. Boca Raton, FL CRC Press, Inc.; 1992b, pp 265–274.

Hatfield, D, Diamond, AM. UGA: A split personality in the universal genetic code. Trends Genet 9:69–70; 1993.

Heider, J, Leinfelder, W, Böck, A. Occurrence and functional compatibility within Enterobacteriaceae of a tRNA species that inserts selenocysteine into protein. Nucleic Acids Res 17:2529–2540; 1989.

Hill, KE, Lloyd, RS, Yang, J-G, Reed, R, Burk, RF. The cDNA for rat selenoprotein P contains 10 TGA codons in the open reading frame. J Biol Chem 266:10050–10053; 1991.

Hirsh, D. Tryptophan transfer RNA as the UGA suppressor. J Mol Biol 58:439–458; 1971.

Ip, C. Selenium and experimental cancer. Ann Clin Res 18:22–29; 1986.

Jung, J-E, Karoor, V, Ohama, T, Choi, IS, Lee, BJ, Mullenbach, G, Wahba, A, Hatfield, D. Direct incorporation of selenocysteine into glutathione peroxidase. Manuscript in preparation; 1993.

Khorana, GH, Büchi, H, Ghosh, H, Gupta, N, Jacob, TM, Kössel, H, Morgan, R, Narang, SA, Ohtuska, E, Wells, RD. Polynucleotide synthesis and the genetic code. Cold Spring Harbor Symp Quant Biol 31:39–49; 1966.

Lane, HW, Medina, D. Selenium concentration and glutathione peroxidase activity in normal and neoplastic development of the mouse mammary gland. Cancer Res 43:1558–1561; 1983.

Lane, HW, Tracey, CK, Medina, D. Growth, reproduction rates and mammary gland selenium concentration and glutathione peroxidase activity of BALB/c female mice fed two dietary levels of selenium. J Nutr 114:323–331; 1984.

Lee, BJ, de la Pena, P, Tobian, JA, Zasloff, M, Hatfield, D. Unique pathway of expression of an opal suppressor phosphoserine tRNA. Proc Natl Acad Sci USA 84:6384–6388; 1987.

Lee, BJ, Kang, SG, Hatfield, D. Transcription of Xenopus opal suppressor phosphoserine tRNA^{Ser} (formerly designated opal suppressor phosphoserine tRNA) gene is directed by multiple 5′ extragenic regulatory elements. J Biol Chem 264:9696–9702; 1989a.

Lee, BJ, Worland, PJ, Davis, JN, Stadtman, TC, Hatfield, DL. Identification of a selenocysteyl-tRNA^{Ser} in mammalian cells that recognizes the non-sense codon, UGA. J Biol Chem 264:9724–9727; 1989b.

Lee, BJ, Rajagopalan, M, Kim, YS, You, K-H, Jacobson, KB, Hatfield, D. Selenocysteine tRNA$^{[Ser]Sec}$ gene is ubiquitous within the animal kingdom. Mol Cell Biol 10:1940–1949; 1990.

Leinfelder, W, Stadtman, TC, Böck, A. Occurrence in vivo of selenocysteyl-tRNA$_{UCA}$ in Echerichia coli. J Biol Chem 264:9720–9723; 1989.

Leinfelder, W, Forchhammer, K, Veprek, B, Zehelein, E, Böck, A. In vitro synthesis of selenocysteinyl-tRNA$_{UCA}$ from seryl-tRNA$_{UCA}$: involvement and characterization of the selD gene product. Proc Natl Acad Sci USA 87:543–547; 1990.

Mäenpää, PH, Bernfield, MR. A specific hepatic transfer RNA for phosphoserine. Proc Natl Acad Sci USA 67:688–695; 1970.

Margulis, L, Schwartz, KV. Five Kingdoms, an Illustrated Guide to the Phyla of Life on Earth 2nd ed. San Francisco, WH Freeman; 1988.

Marshall, R, Caskey, T, Nirenberg, M. Fine structure of RNA codewords recognized by bacterial, amphibian and mammalian transfer RNA. Science 155:820–826; 1967.

McBride, OW, Rajagopalan, M, Hatfield, D. Opal suppressor phosphoserine tRNA gene and pseudogene are located on human chromosomes 19 and 22, respectively. J Biol Chem 262:11163–11166; 1987.

Mitchell, A, Bale, AE, Lee, BJ, Hatfield, D, Harley, H, Rundle, S, Fan, YS, Fukushima, Y, Shows, TB, McBride, OW. Regional localization of the selenocysteine tRNA gene (TRSP) on human chromosome 19. Cytogenet Cell Genet 61:117–120; 1992.

Medina, D, Morrison, DG. Current ideas on selenium as a chemopreventive agent. Pathol Immunopathol Res 7:187–199; 1988.

Mizutani, T, Hashimoto, A. Purification and properties of suppressor seryl-tRNA: ATP phosphotransferase from bovine liver. FEBS Lett 169:319–322; 1984.

Mizutani, T, Hitaka, T. Stronger affinity of reticulocyte release factor than natural suppressor tRNA[Ser] for the opal termination codon. FEBS Lett 226:227–231; 1988.

Mizutani, T. Some evidence of the enzymatic conversion of bovine suppressor phosphoseryl-tRNA to selenocystyl-tRNA. FEBS Lett 250:142–146; 1989.

Mizutani, T, Maruyama, N, Hitaka, T, Sukenaga, Y. The detection of natural opal suppressor seryl-tRNA in *Echerichia coli* by the dot blot hybridization and its phosphorylation by a tRNA kinase. FEBS Lett 247;345–348; 1989.

Mizutani, T, Kurata, H, Yamada, K. Study of mammalian selenocysteyl-tRNA synthesis with [75Se] HSe⁻. FEBS Lett 289:59–63; 1991.

Mizutani, T, Kurata, H, Yamada, K, Totsuka, T. Some properties of murine selenocysteine synthase. Biochem J 284:827–834; 1992.

Mullenbach, GT, Tabrizi, A, Irvine, BD, Bell, GI, Hallewell, RA. Seleno-cysteine's mechanism of incorporation and evolution revealed in cDNAs of three glutathione peroxidases. Protein Eng 2:239–246; 1988.

Myslinski, E, Krol, A, Carbon, P. Optimal tRNA[Ser]Sec gene activity requires an upstream SPH motif. Nucleic Acids Res 20:203–209; 1992.

Nirenberg, M, Caskey, T, Marshall, R, Brimacombe, R, Kellog, D, Doctor, B, Hatfield, D, Levin, J, Rottman, F, Pestka, S, Wilcox, M, Anderson, F. The RNA code and protein synthesis. Cold Spring Harbor Symp Quant Biol 31:11–24; 1966.

O'Neill, VA, Eden, FC, Pratt, K, Hatfield, D. A human opal suppressor tRNA gene and pseudogene. J Biol Chem 260:2501–2508; 1985.

Pratt, K, Eden, FC, You, KH, O'Neill, VA, Hatfield, D. Conserved sequences in both coding and 5′ flanking regions of mammalian opal suppressor tRNA genes. Nucleic Acids Res 13:4765–4775; 1985.

Salonen, JT, Huttunen, JK. Selenium in cardiovascular diseases. Ann Clin Res 18:30–35; 1986.

Sharp, SJ, Stewart, TS. The characterization of phosphoseryl tRNA from lactating bovine mammary gland. Nucleic Acids Res 4:2123–2136; 1977.

Stadtman, TC. Biosynthesis and function of selenocysteine-containing enzymes. J Biol Chem 266:16257–16260; 1991.

Stewart, TS, Sharp, SJ. Characterizing the function of O^{β}-phosphoseryl-tRNA. Methods Enzymol 106:157–161; 1984.

Sturchler, C, Westhof, E, Carbon, P, Krol, A. Unique secondary and tertiary structural features of the eucaryotic selenocysteine tRNA^{Sec}. Nucleic Acids Res 21:1073–1079; 1993.

Sukenaga, Y, Ishida, K, Takeda, T, Takagi, K. cDNA sequence coding for human glutathione peroxidase. Nucleic Acids Res 15:7178; 1987.

Veres, Z, Tsai, L, Scholz, TD, Politino, M, Balaban, RS, Stadtman, TC. Synthesis of 5-methylaminomethyl-2-selenouridine in tRNAs: ^{31}P NMR studies show the labile selenium donor synthesized by the *selD* gene product contains selenium bonded to phosphorus. Proc Natl Acad Sci USA 89:2975–2979; 1992.

Zinoni, F, Birkmann, A, Stadtman, TC, Böck, A. Nucleotide sequence and expression of the selenocysteine-containing polypeptide of formate dehydrogenase (formate-hydrogen-lyase-linked) from Escherichia coli. Proc Natl Acad Sci USA 83:4650–4654; 1986.

Zinoni, F, Heider, J, Böck, A. Features of the formate dehydrogenase mRNA necessary for decoding of the UGA codon as selenocysteine. Proc Natl Acad Sci USA 87:4660–4664; 1990.

Chapter 3

Intracellular Glutathione Peroxidases—Structure, Regulation, and Function

Roger A. Sunde

Glutathione peroxidase (glutathione: H_2O_2 oxidoreductase E.C. 1.11.1.9) was discovered by Mills (1) in 1957 in his search for the factors that function in the protection of erythrocytes against oxidative hemolysis. Similarly, John Rotruck, working in Professor Hoekstra's laboratory, focused on GPX in his search for an enzymatic function that made selenium (Se) an antioxidant (2). The unraveling of the Se/GPX story has fascinated a generation of scientists, and it has led to the use of GPX activity as one of the best indicators of Se status as well as to its use as the index of choice for the determination of Se requirements. The form of Se in GPX and the mechanism of Se insertion into the enzyme have become, together, an academic subject matter of their own; the study of this enzyme has now moved into the exciting world of molecular biology, and these investigations are helping us learn much more about the regulation of GPX and Se. This research suggests that the important function of classical GPX in some tissues is to regulate Se metabolism and Se flux to selenoproteins.

There have been many new and exciting discoveries in the past few years, and thus this review will build on the information presented in previous reviews. These include the comprehensive report from the Fourth International Symposium on Selenium and Biology and Medicine (3) as well as earlier (4,5) and more recent reviews (6–9).

The focus of this review is on cellular glutathione peroxidases, including the classical GPX discovered by Mills (1) and the monomeric phospholipid hydroperoxide glutathione peroxidase (PHGPX) discovered by Ursini (10). The purpose is to review the recent discoveries and new concepts for each of these two cellular selenoenzymes and then to discuss the functional role of these enzymes in cellular metabolism. Finally, the review turns to the exciting implication that the regulation of classical GPX by Se status may serve as a "biological selenium buffer" that regulates Se metabolism.

Glutathione Peroxidase

GPX Structure

Cytosolic glutathione peroxidase (GPX) was initially discovered because it could protect erythrocytes against H_2O_2 or ascorbate-induced hemoglobin oxidation (1). It is unique with respect to other peroxidases because it is not inhibited by azide or cyanide (11) and it reduces lipid hydroperoxides (12). The kinetics and substrate specificity of this enzyme were elaborated on by Flohé and colleagues over 20 years ago (13,14). GPX is a tetrameric protein with four identical subunits each with an M_r of approximately 23,000 daltons (Da) and each containing one Se atom per subunit. The bovine erythrocyte enzyme has been crystallized (15), and it consists of four spherical subunits, each with a diameter of 3.8 nm, arranged in an almost flat, square-planar configuration ($9 \times 11 \times 6$ nm). The Se atoms, located in slight depressions, are no closer than 2 nm, strongly suggesting that each Se functions independently. Thus it is not unlikely that a related monomeric selenium peroxidase could possess activity.

Following the cloning of murine GPX by Chambers et al. (16) from a mouse genomic DNA library, the enzyme has been cloned by numerous investigators from a variety of tissues and species. A list of these sequences is shown in Table 3.1. In general, GPX proteins consist of 201 amino acids and the selenocysteine residue is located 47 residues from the N-terminal end of the protein. Crystallography indicates that the selenocysteine is located at the end of an α-helix associated with two parallel β strands in a βαβ structure. The novel and exciting discovery by Chambers and Harrison (16) was that the selenocysteine residue was specified by a UGA codon located in-frame in the mRNA.

Cloned GPXs

Table 3.1 shows the increasing information that has accrued about GPX. In general there is about 85% amino acid sequence identity and 80% nucleotide sequence identity within the coding region. The 5'-UTRs are less conserved (~35%) than the 3'-UTRs (~70%), apparently reflecting the 3' structures important for selenocysteine incorporation and perhaps mRNA stability. The list includes the androgen-regulated epididymal secretory proteins (17,18) that have about 50% amino acid sequence identity to GPX (67% identity without the 21 amino acid putative signal peptide) but that do not contain UGA, and a gene with 33% amino acid homology to GPX from the tobacco plant that also lacks the UGA codon (19). Also included is a TGA-containing GPX gene in the parasitic worm *Schistosoma*

TABLE 3.1. Cloned GPXs, PHGPXs, and GPX-related proteins.

Species	Tissue	Clone type	Amino acids[1]	[Se] Cys codon	Authors (ref)
Glutathione peroxidase (GPX)					
Mouse	—	Genomic	201/47	TGA	Chambers et al. 1986 (16)
Human	Kidney	cDNA	201/47	TGA	Mullenbach et al. 1987 (101)
Human	Liver	cDNA	201/47	TGA	Sukenaga et al. 1987 (102)
Rat	Liver	cDNA	201/47	TGA	Ho et al. 1988 (100)
Bovine	Pituitary	cDNA	205/52	TGA	Mullenbach et al. 1988 (103)
Human	Kidney	cDNA	201/47	TGA	Mullenbach et al. 1988 (103)
Mouse	Placenta	cDNA	201/47	TGA	Mullenbach et al. 1988 (103)
Rat	Liver	cDNA	201/47	TGA	Yoshimura et al. 1988 (52)
Rabbit	Liver	cDNA	200/46	TGA	Akasaka et al. 1989 (104)
Rat	—	Genomic	201/47	TGA	Ho et al. 1992 (28)
Human	—	Genomic	202/48	TGA	Moscow et al. 1992 (27)
Phospholipid hydroperoxide glutathione peroxidase (PHGPX)					
pig	Heart	cDNA	155*/31	TGA	Schuckelt et al. 1991 (74)
pig	Blastocyst	cDNA	170/46	TGA	Sunde et al. 1993 (75)
Glutathione peroxidase-GI (GPX-GI)					
human	Liver	cDNA	190/39	TGA	Akasaka et al. 1990 (23)
human	HepG2 cells	cDNA	190/40	TGA	Chu et al. 1993 (24)
Androgen-related epididymal secretory protein					
Mouse	Epididymis	cDNA	175*/27	TGC	Ghyselinck et al. 1991 (17)
Rat	Epididymis	cDNA	221/73	TGT	Perry et al. 1992 (18)
Monkey	Epididymis	cDNA	221/73	TGT	Perry et al. 1992 (18)
GPX-like proteins					
S. mansoni	—	cDNA	169*/43	TGA	Williams et al. 1991 (20)
Tobacco	Protoplast	cDNA	169/43	TGT	Criqui et al. 1992 (19)

[1] Polypeptide length/[Se]Cys position from N-terminal end.
* Clone is missing some of the 5'-coding region, including the start ATG, and thus the polypeptide is not full length.

mansoni with 38% amino acid sequence identity with human GPX (20). Interesting GPXs not on the list include an immunologically identified tetrameric Se-containing GPX in *Chlamydomonas reinhardtii* with subunit M_r of 17,000 Da (21), and a Se-independent GPX (M_r of 130,000 Da) with enzyme activity from *Euglena gracilis* (22). The retention of GPX-like proteins with activity strongly suggests that this is one of evolution's solutions to an oxidant-filled environment.

GPX-GI

An apparent new GPX (indicated as GPX-GI) was first identified as a TGA-containing cDNA sequence from a human liver cDNA library with 66% amino acid sequence identity and 61% nucleotide sequence identity to GPX (23). Recent work has confirmed the existence of this species (24), demonstrated that it could be expressed in GPX-GI-transfected MCF-7 cells, and used in northern blotting to demonstrate expression of GPX-GI in human liver and colon, but not kidney, heart, lung, placenta, or uterus. Rat GPX-GI mRNA was found only in gastrointestinal cells in the rat. Chu and co-workers have thus proposed that this is a fourth GPX (third intracellular GPX) and that it be called GPX-GI (24). This exciting additional GPX may be a tissue-specific GPX with important peroxidase activity.

GPX has been mapped to human chromosome 3 (25) as well as to two intron-less pseudogenes on chromosomes 21 and X. The selenocysteine tRNA gene has been localized on human chromosome 19 (26), suggesting that Se-related genes are not located in a operon-like configuration in higher animals.

The consensus gene for GPX (mouse [16], human [27], rat [28]) thus consists of a 5'-untranslated region (5'-UTR), a 246-bp first exon that contains the in-frame TGA, an approximately 215–270-bp exon, and a 357-bp second intron followed by an approximately 200-bp 3'-UTR that includes one or more AATAAA polyadenylation signal sequences. The gpx gene apparently does not have a "TATA" or "CAAT" box upstream from the transcription start site. Potential transcriptional regulatory sites, indicated by the presence of consensus sequence homologies for Sp1, Ap2, Ap1, and SV40 binding proteins, are found in the 5'-UTR, the 3'-UTR, and/or the intron. It may be that transcriptional regulation is consistent with other "housekeeping" genes with tissue-specific regulatory sites in the 3'-UTR. (See below.)

SELENIUM INCORPORATION

The mechanism used by eukaryotes to insert Se into GPX and other selenoenzymes was outlined by the discovery that an in-frame UGA encoded the position of selenocysteine (16) in combination with studies showing that inorganic Se was more readily incorporated into GPX than was preformed selenocystine (29), that serine provided the carbon skeleton for selenocysteine (30), and that several unique opal sup-pressor tRNA$_{UCA}^{Ser}$s (31,32) linked serine with the UGA codon (UCA anticodon). It is now apparent that eukaryotic selenocysteine synthe-sis and incorporation is a cotranslational process mediated by the selenocysteinyl-tRNA$_{UCA}^{Ser}$ (6,32).

Much of the detailed mechanism can be inferred from corresponding prokaryotic mechanisms used to insert Se into formate dehydrogenase and glycine reductase at the UGA-specified position. Briefly, the 37-kDa *selD* gene product in bacteria is a selenophosphate kinase that synthesizes selenophosphate from ATP and selenide (33–35). Serine, the source of the carbon skeleton for selenocysteine is esterified by the usual cellular seryl-tRNA synthetases to a unique tRNA$_{UCA}^{Ser}$ that is the transcription product of the *selC* gene (36). The *selA* gene product is a selenocysteine synthase, with a subunit M_r of 51 kDa that contains pyridoxal phosphate and that has a native M_r of approximately 600 kDa. It catalyzes the dehydration of L-serine followed by a 2,3-addition of Se to form selenocysteine (37,38). Recognition of UGA as a selenocysteine codon rather than a stop codon in bacteria requires a stem-loop RNA secondary structure, immediately downstream from the UGA, and a 68-kDa *selB* gene product (SELB) that is similar to the elongation factor EF-Tu. SELB binds GTP and forms an mRNA-SELB-GTP-[Se]Cys-tRNA$_{UCA}^{Ser}$ complex that incorporates selenocysteine into the peptide backbone at the position specified by UGA (39). The analogous mammalian mechanism is not known in detail although preliminary evidence suggests the four comparable components are necessary (40).

A critical component in eukaryotic insertion of selenocysteine into selenoproteins is a stem-loop RNA secondary structure located in the 3′-UTR. Insight as well as experimental proof for the importance of this structure was provided by Berry and Larson (41), working with fusion chimera of GPX and Se-dependent 5′-deiodinase. The rat GPX 3′-UTR was equally effective as the native deiodinase 3′-UTR in catalyzing insertion of Se into deiodinase. An eight-base deletion in the loop of the stem-loop structure was sufficient to eliminate seleno-cysteine insertion. Thus, in mammalian cells a 3′-UTR region is essential for incorporation of Se. In mouse and rat GPX, the analogous loop is 540 bp from the UGA. Two similar 3′-UTR structures have been reported in plasma selenoprotein P, further suggesting that the distance between the UGA and the 3′-UTR stem-loop is important (41,42).

SELENIUM REGULATION OF GPX ACTIVITY AND PROTEIN

The dramatic impact of Se status on mammalian GPX activity has been known since 1973 (43,44). (For review, see ref. 45.) Erythrocyte GPX values fall to about 20% of Se-adequate values but liver GPX can fall to undetectable levels (43,46). This occurs without significant impact on the growth of weanling male or female rats, suggesting that this fall to undetectable levels is not essential for normal liver function; nor does the concomitant decrease in GPX activity in other tissues significantly impact the animal. Just as importantly, GPX activity reaches a plateau at dietary concentrations of $0.1\,\mu g\,Se/g$ diet in all tissues except red blood cell. Further modest increases in dietary Se (to 0.2 or $0.5\,\mu g\,Se/g$ diet) do not incrementally raise GPX activity above the plateau breakpoint achieved at $0.1\,\mu g\,Se/g$ diet. Observed apparent increases in GPX activity (expressed as EU/mg protein) in animals fed near-toxic levels of Se (e.g., $2\,\mu g/g$) can be due to a decrease in tissue protein, presumably due to Se toxicity (47).

Similar regulation of GPX protein levels by Se status are also observed (46,48,49). Thus a decline in Se status does not just reduce the percentage of GPX molecules with the Se cofactor; GPX protein also disappears. Importantly, short-term repletion studies indicate a 12-hour delay between the increase in liver Se status and the rise in GPX protein (48), suggesting that more than an increase in intracellular Se is necessary for the increases in GPX protein and activity.

SE REGULATION OF GPX mRNA

The cloning of GPX gave us the ability to further study the effect of Se status on GPX expression by determining the effect of dietary Se on steady-state levels of GPX mRNA. We first isolated total liver RNA from Se-adequate rats ($0.2\,\mu g\,Se/g$ diet) or Se-deficient rats (fed a torula-yeast-based diet containing $<0.02\,\mu g\,Se/g$ for >135 days). We showed that the 96% drop in liver GPX activity in long-term Se-deficient rats was accompanied by an 83–93% drop in GPX mRNA

(50). The effect of Se deficiency is not a general effect on mRNA, as we have observed that Se status has little or no effect on mRNA levels for β-actin, carbonic anhydrase, or PEP carboxykinase. (In spite of routine use of β-actin as a standard by molecular biologists, this cytoskeletal protein seems especially unsuited to dietary studies because of potential variability.)

We next evaluated the change in GPX expression as Se deficiency developed by determining the changes in GPX activity, protein, and mRNA levels in male weanling rats fed a Se-deficient diet for up to 28 days (44). In $0.2\,\mu g\,Se/g$ diet-supplemented controls, liver GPX activity and GPX protein increased about 50% over the 28 days, an apparent developmental change, and GPX mRNA levels remained unchanged. In Se-deficient liver, GPX activity and mRNA levels declined exponentially with a half-life of just over 3 days. In these young rats, GPX activity fell to zero by 21 days after the start of the experiment, and GPX mRNA levels declined to 6% of that observed in Se-adequate animals at 28 days. This experiment clearly indicates that Se status can exert a more than 15-fold effect on liver GPX mRNA. These dramatic changes in steady-state GPX mRNA level are similar to the order of magnitude changes elicited by hormones.

Short-term Se repletion experiments also shed light on this regulation. A single iv injection of $44\,\mu g$ of Se into 300-g Se-deficient rats did not significantly raise liver GPX mRNA levels for 6 hours, but then GPX mRNA rose at 18 hours to 60% of Se-adequate control levels before falling again at 24 hours. In contrast, GPX activity only increased to 10% of control levels by 24 hours (51). This illustrates that the amplitude of the initial GPX mRNA response to Se repletion is much greater than the GPX activity response.

We have also examined the effect of excess Se on GPX mRNA of rats. Feeding a $2.0\,\mu g\,Se/g$ diet did not raise GPX mRNA levels in liver, kidney, heart, lung, muscle, and testes above the levels observed in rats fed $0.2\,\mu g\,Se/g$ diet (47).

The observation that GPX mRNA levels fall dramatically in Se deficiency has been confirmed and extended by several investigators (52–54). In contrast, Reddy and co-workers have reported that liver GPX mRNA levels either increased twofold or remained unchanged in Se-deficient rats as compared to Se-adequate rats (55–57). The explanation for this discrepancy is unclear, but it may involve the quantity of mRNA applied to the membrane as well as the specific nature of the GPX probe used. We have specifically investigated this situation (Dyer and Sunde, unpublished) using our usual 700-bp *Eco*RI probe from the 3' half of the murine genomic GPX and the complete 800-bp *Xba*I/*Eco*RI 5' half as well as probes from the 5'-UTR (250 bp *Xba*I/*Apa*I), the 5'-coding region (230 bp *Apa*I/*Pst*I), and even the intron (300 bp *Pst*I/*Eco*RI). And we've used 5' 330-bp and 3' 560-bp portions of our own rat liver cDNA GPX clone. In all cases the GPX mRNA levels declined to less than 20% of that observed in adequate animals.

USE OF GPX mRNA LEVELS TO DETERMINE Se REQUIREMENTS

Because GPX activity has been used very successfully to determine Se requirements, and because Se status controls GPX mRNA levels, we next studied levels of Se, GPX activity, and GPX mRNA in male and female weanling rats (58,59) fed graded levels of Se for 33–35 days. In both groups, supplementation of the basal diet (0.008 µg Se/g) with 0.02 µg Se/g had little impact on GPX activity or mRNA levels; the Se was going somewhere else. In both groups, GPX activity and GPX mRNA levels plateaued at or near 0.1 µg Se/g. Higher dietary Se levels (0.2 µg/g for males and 0.3 µg/g diet for females) did not raise GPX mRNA significantly. Graphical analysis indicated that the relative change in GPX mRNA level occurs prior to the change in GPX activity. Furthermore, the relationship between GPX mRNA and activity breaks down above 0.1 µg Se/g diet, indicating that Se status is no longer tightly regulating GPX. This work clearly shows that Se regulation of GPX activity is mediated by the Se regulation of GPX mRNA.

MECHANISM OF Se REGULATION

We next used nuclear runoff transcription assays (60,61) to investigate the effect of Se status on initiated transcription complexes in nuclei isolated from Se-adequate and Se-deficient rats. In deficient rats, liver Se declined to 2% of that found in Se-adequate animals, and GPX activity was virtually undetectable. Se status had no effect on *in vitro* ^{32}P incorporation from [^{32}P]UTP into total RNA. Hybridization selection using a linearized murine GPX fragment showed no impairment of the ability of Se-deficient nuclei to synthesize GPX mRNA, demonstrating that Se-deficient nuclei can readily make GPX mRNA. Isolation of hnRNA from isolated nuclei followed by slot-blot analysis with ^{32}P-labeled GPX probe showed equivalent levels of GPX mRNA in the nuclei. These experiments indicate that Se deficiency does not impair transcription of the GPX gene, nor does it impair translocation of GPX RNA from the nucleus. The process whereby Se regulates GPX mRNA levels must occur outside the nucleus. Christensen and Burgener (53) also elegantly compared the effect of Se status on GPX transcription in Se-deficient and Se-adequate rat $(0.5 \mu g \, Se/g$ diet) liver and showed that there was no effect on runoff transcription rates. Interestingly, northern blotting of total RNA revealed a faint, approximately 18S species that hybridizes with a 248-bp probe from the 5'-coding region of GPX. The identity of this species is unknown. The implication of these results is that Se-deficient rats readily are able to transcribe the GPX gene, to process GPX hnRNA, and to translocate the completed mRNA to the cytosol. This strongly suggests that the site of Se regulation of GPX expression is extranuclear and involves mRNA stabilization.

The mechanism for GPX mRNA stabilization is unclear at present, but the transferrin receptor mRNA model may provide insight into the mechanism. The regulation of transferrin receptor expression by iron status is mediated by mRNA stability, which in turn is conferred by the presence of several (at least three) 35-bp IREs (iron response elements) that form stem-loop structures in a 250-bp 3'-UTR (62,63). It now appears that a cytosolic aconitase with a labile fourth iron in the 4Fe:4S cluster is the IRE-binding protein responsible for this regulation (64). A similar protein might cover and uncover portions of the GPX 3'-UTR and confer mRNA stability vs. degradation. This hypothetical regulatory protein might bind selenide or selenophosphate to change its affinity for a "selenium response element" region. And this regulation might or might not coincide with the interaction of a SELB-like elongation factor with the 3' stem-loop shown to be essential for selenocysteine incorporation (41).

NONSELENIUM REGULATION OF GPX

Se is not the only factor that regulates GPX. Each cell has the same genes, and there is wide tissue-to-tissue variation in the same organism, and there is wide species variation in spite of the similar

Se regulation of GPX in higher animals (dietary Se requirement of about 0.1 μg Se/g diet [45]). Clearly tissue-specific and development-specific regulation has a dramatic impact. For instance, testes GPX activity and mRNA levels are less than 5% of liver levels in Se-adequate rats (47) even though the testes has an appreciable level of Se (65). Female rats have been known to have higher GPX activity than male rats for over 20 years (66); Prohaska and Sunde found twofold-higher GPX mRNA in female liver as compared to male rat liver to explain this difference (67). This suggests that steroid-response elements may enhance GPX transcription in rats. These differences, however, are not present in mice (68), and human GPX transcription in cultured cells is apparently not enhanced by steroids (27). Paul Harrison has recently found evidence that the increase in reticulocyte GPX is due to up-regulation of erythroid GPX transcription by a tissue-specific enhancer (69). Copper deficiency down-modulates GPX activity (70) and mRNA (67). It thus becomes apparent that other factors set the maximal level of GPX expression (transcription?) in a cell, and then Se status modulates this expression by regulating GPX mRNA stability.

PHOSPHOLIPID HYDROPEROXIDE GLUTATHIONE PEROXIDASE

The diversity of Se-dependent GPXs began to be apparent in the 1980s. Purification and preparation of antibodies against cytosolic GPX (71) demonstrated the existence of an antigenically distinct extracellular GPX. Similarly, a purified 20-kDa protein with GPX activity exhibited activity with a phosphatidyl choline hydroperoxide, which is not a substrate for (classical) GPX (72). In 1985 Ursini and co-workers (10) reported that this protein was an Se-dependent phospholipid hydroperoxide GPX (PHGPX). The enzyme functions as a monomer and catalyzes the reduction of hydroperoxides and H_2O_2 to the corresponding alcohol, using GSH as the reducing substrate. The enzyme uses a ter uni Ping-Pong mechanism (10), the same as GPX (13). The addition of detergent such as Triton X-100 stimulates the activity of this enzyme, suggesting to the discoverers that this enzyme may work the interface between the membrane and the aqueous phases in the cell. This detergent effect may be the source of "cryptic" activity observed in GPX assays that use hydroperoxide.

PHGPX Structure

PHGPX appeared to be distinct from GPX because the amino acid composition is different, the monomer is active, and β-mercaptoethanol will inhibit the enzyme (73). Comparison of the apparent rate constants for peroxide substrates indicate that PHGPX is approximately 1/15th as active as GPX against hydrogen peroxide, and 1/10th as active against tertiary butyl hydroperoxide. PHGPX, however, can reduce phosphatidyl choline hydroperoxide, which is not a substrate for GPX. In fact, PHGPX is 3.5 times more reactive against phosphatidyl choline hydroperoxide than against hydrogen peroxide (73). The cause of these substrate preferences is not fully established, but the monomeric nature of PHGPX may allow reaction with substrates that are sterically hindered when bulky substrates interact with the more protected active site of GPX.

Irrefutable evidence that PHGPX is distinct from GPX was reported in 1991 by Ursini's group (74). Degenerate oligonucleotide primers were prepared from the amino acid sequences of several of the proteolytic polypeptides and used to polymerase chain-reaction (PCR) amplify a commercial pig heart cDNA library. A 200-bp product was identified. Additional steps identified overlapping 300-bp and 480-bp fragments that resulted in a 689-bp sequence that included an estimated 75% of the coding region plus an approximate 200-bp 3'-UTR including polyadenylation site and poly-A tail. Importantly, a TGA corresponded to the 31st amino acid encoded by the nucleotide sequence (34th amino acid of the tryptic peptide-determined sequence) and the base sequence corresponded to 155 amino acids. The authors estimated the sequence identity between PHGPX and GPX species at about 35% vs. 85% amongst mammalian GPX species and the nucleotide sequence identity between PHGPX and the GPX at about 45%.

We have recently isolated a full-length cDNA clone of pig PHGPX from a pig embryo cDNA library (75) using degenerate primers prepared from the published partial nucleotide sequence (74). Our sequence of 932 bp encodes a PHGPX molecule that matches exactly

PHGPX AND GPX AMINO ACID SEQUENCES

```
PHGPX   - MCASRDDWRCARSMHEFSAKDIDG-HMVNLDKYRGYVCIVTNVASQXGKT -49
            | | |      | | |          | | |    | |     | | | | *| |
GPX     - MSAARLSAVAQSTVYAFSARPLAGGEPVSLGSLRGKVLLIENVASLXGTT -50

PHGPX   - EVNYTQLVDLHARYAECGLRILAFPCNQFGRQEPGSDAEIKEF------A -93
            | |    | |   |      | |   | |||||||| || |     | |
GPX     - TRDYTEMNDLQKRLGPRGLVVLGFPCNQFGHQENGKNEEILNSLKYVRPG -100

PHGPX   - AGYNVKFDMFSKICVNGDDAHPLWKWMK--VQPKGRGMLG---------- -131
            |     | | |  | |||  ||||
GPX     - GGFEPNFTLFEKCEVNGEKAHPLFTFLRNALPAPSDDPTALMTDPKYIIW -150

PHGPX   - -----NAIKWNFTKFLIDKNGCVVKRYGPMEEPQVIEKDL-------PCY -169
               | | ||| |||     | | ||        || |        |
GPX     - SPVCRNDISWNFEKFLVGPDGVPVRRYSRRFRTIDIEPDIEALLSKQPSN -200

PHGPX   - L -170

GPX     - P -201
```

FIGURE 3.1. Amino acid sequences for rat liver GPX (100) and for pig PHGPX (74,75). The conserved residues (39% sequence homology) are linked with a |, and an * is used to highlight the selenocysteine (X) residues at position 46.

with the published C-terminal amino acid sequence and includes an apparent 15-amino-acid N-terminal portion beginning with an AUG start site at bp 131 (Fig. 3.1). The resulting polypeptide would be 170 amino acids long with a calculated M_r of 19,492 Da, and the selenocysteine residue is located 46 amino acids from the N-terminal. The full-length amino-acid sequence is 39% homologous with rat GPX. An alternative AUG start site at bp 50 would result in a 197-amino-acid polypeptide, but the amino acid composition does not agree as well with the published amino acid composition (74), and the M_r (calculated 22,338 Da) would be decidedly larger than the estimated M_r. An apparent 3'-UTR stem-loop structure, analogous but different from the GPX 3'-UTR, is located 461 bp downstream from the UGA. Thus it is clear that a second cellular Se-dependent peroxidase exists with decidedly different characteristics than the classical GPX.

Similarly, we have obtained two apparent full-length clones of rat PHGPX by screening a commercial rat liver cDNA library using our pig PHGPX as a probe. Preliminary sequence analysis indicates that rat PHGPX is also an 170-amino-acid protein with 95% amino acid sequence identity and 80% nucleotide sequence identity to pig PHGPX (Sunde, Dyer, and Moran, unpublished).

SE REGULATION OF PHGPX ACTIVITY

Weitzel et al. (76) used Se deficiency and repletion to evaluate the Se regulation of PHGPX in mice. GPX activity was rapidly lost in most tissues of mice fed the Se-deficient diet and reached undetectable levels within 130 days in liver, kidney, and lung. In contrast, heart GPX decreased only to 25% of control GPX activity. PHGPX activity, however, was less affected by Se deficiency. After 130 days liver, heart, lung, and kidney PHGPX activities were 45, 11, 41, and 29% of the levels found in animals supplemented with 0.5 μg Se/g diet. Importantly, PHGPX activity levels started out lower but did not reach zero levels in liver, lung, and kidney. Heart, however, was disproportionally reduced. A clue to PHGPX function is that PHGPX accounted for 20% of the total peroxidase activity in heart, and Se deficiency lowered both GPX and PHGPX in heart such that the two enzyme activities approached comparable levels. Longer periods of deficiency (250 days) had negligible additional effect on PHGPX activity.

Interestingly, mice injected 5 days previously with 10 μg Se/kg later showed negligible effects of the single Se injection on either GPX or PHGPX activity (76). A large Se dose (500 μg/kg), however, completely restored heart PHGPX but not GPX activity. Lung and liver PHGPX were restored to control levels, but GPX only increased to 50–66% of control values. The authors suggested that either PHGPX retains Se much more tightly than GPX, or, alternatively, residual Se is preferentially reutilized for PHGPX synthesis as compared to GPX. Thus changes in PHGPX activity with Se status are consistent with Behne's proposal (77) that large decreases in GPX occur only in major organs whereas other tissues, such as endocrine tissues, have lower GPX activities but retain their Se.

PHGPX has also been identitied as an apparent 18-kDa selenoprotein that was expressed in seven different cell lines, whereas GPX "H_2O_2" activity was barely detectable in four of the cell lines (78). Se supplementation (100 nM) raised assayed PHGPX as well as GPX activity in all cells where significant amounts of activity were present. The H_2O_2 activity in the four low-GPX cell lines may be due to PHGPX. Differential patterns of expression were noted with adriamcin-resistant MCF-7 cells that had high levels of GPX activity as compared to standard MCF-7 cells with negligible levels of classical GPX and no detectable ^{75}Se-labeled GPX subunits.

In a recent report, Roveri et al. (79) showed that PHGPX is present at high levels in rat testes. The presence of PHGPX activity was confirmed by cross-reactivity with antibodies raised against pig-heart PHGPX. Furthermore, the PHGPX activity was not detected until 3 weeks after birth, and then it increased linearly for the next 7–8 weeks, especially in nuclei and mitochondria. Hypophysectomy reduced PHGPX and this reduction was partially restored by gonadotropin treatment. PHGPX activity in testes was twice that found in liver whereas GPX activity in testes was 5% of that found in liver (79). This observation is exciting because it suggests that PHGPX is a major testes selenoprotein.

The nature of the 17–18-kDa selenoprotein in testis and sperm, however, remains confused. Calvin (80) identified this species as Se-dependent mitochondrial capsule protein ([Se]MCP), and Karimpour (81) recently reported that a cDNA clone of [Se]MCP cDNA contains three in-frame TGAs in the coding region. The increase in PHGPX activity, beginning at day 20 (79), is different than the sharp increase in testes Se that Behne (65) reported at day 40. It may be that PHGPX is the major selenoprotein in testes and [Se]MCP is the major selenoprotein in sperm mitochondria.

Se Regulation of PHGPX mRNA

We have begun to use our newly cloned pig and rat PHGPX cDNAs to evaluate the effect of Se status on liver PHGPX mRNA levels in Se-deficient rats (75). It appears that liver PHGPX mRNA levels are little affected by changes in Se status that dramatically reduce GPX activity and that reduce GPX mRNA levels to <10% of Se-adequate levels. Preliminary work with our rat PHGPX clone confirms this observation. Thus PHGPX does not appear to be regulated by the same mechanism that regulates GPX mRNA. This is not surprising, as PHGPX activity does not decrease as much as GPX activity in Se deficiency (76), and because ^{75}Se is readily incorporated into the 19-kDA selenoprotein (presumably PHGPX) in liver and heart in Se-deficient rats (82).

Function of PHGPX

PHGPX thus does not appear to be regulated by Se status in a manner similar to GPX. Activity falls in most tissues to 40–50% of adequate values, except in heart, and mRNA levels appear to be little affected by Se deficiency. This regulation pattern is more characteristic of cofactor-mediated modulation of enzyme activity rather than hormonelike processes with specific mechanisms that result in order-of-magnitude changes in expression. This suggests that PHGPX activity is necessary for the well-being of the organism. It appears that PHGPX activity falls most dramatically in the heart, an organ sensitive to Se deficiency in the human, the pig, and the mouse. Thus we have good but only circumstantial evidence that PHGPX functions as a peroxidase "antioxidant" that is critical to certain tissues. It would be interesting to use combined vitamin E- and Se-deficient diets, and to follow changes in PHGPX and GPX activity and mRNA in mouse or pig heart and in rat liver to see if pathological signs of Se deficiency appear when PHGPX drops below a threshold level.

What Is the Role/Function of GPX?

It does not make sense that tissue GPX activity levels can fall to undetectable levels without impairing growth and normal function in rats. If classical GPX is such an essential enzymatic activity, why would evolution select and preserve Se regulation of GPX mRNA if GPX is so critical to most cells? Is there an alternative hypothesis?

GPX was first discovered because it was an antioxidant factor, and the search for a functional role for Se focused on antioxidant functions because of the apparent coincidence of the roles of Se and vitamin E. Thus Hoekstra (83) summarized the logical role of GPX in metabolism as an antioxidant enzyme. Numerous enzymes and cofactors with antioxidant activity such as superoxide dismutase, glutathione-S-transferase, ascorbate, α-tocopherol, ceruloplasmin, etc., are all implicated as having important roles in protecting against oxidant damage. A recent analysis of 1990-to-present MEDLINE-listed journal articles under the "glutathione peroxidase" mesh heading indicates that over 14% of the articles were cross-listed with "antioxidants." A comprehensive discussion of this field is beyond the scope of this review, but it is clear that GPX is considered one of the primary antioxidant enzymes.

Obviously, an enzyme that reduces peroxides to alcohols can have antioxidant function. The important question, however, is whether peroxidase activity is the primary function of GPX in the major organs, such as liver, where it can account for much of the total cell Se. It is very difficult to separate changes in GPX activity alone from increases or changes in Se status or in other Se-dependent factors. Thus a recent report on paraquat-resistant HeLa cells suggests that superoxide dismutases are important at concentrations of paraquat up to 40 µM but that GPX becomes important in concentrations above 40 µM (84). In contrast, in transgenic and transfected mouse fibroblasts, there appears to be no correlation between resistance to paraquat toxicity and the level of GPX activity (85). It is likely that specific differences in exposure to the toxicants in these series of experiments as well as differences in the endogenous level of other factors, including GPX, are important in modulating these protective effects.

Recent work by Mirault and co-workers (86) showed that overexpression in stable GPX transfectants raised GPX activity 40-fold relative to controls and conferred increased resistance to acute levels of oxidants. (The transfected GPX contained 41 nucleotides of the 5'-UTR and 126 nucleotides of the 3'-UTR and the complete coding cDNA sequence of human GPX.) It should be noted that GSH levels were also increased two or three times relative to controls in cells that had higher levels of GPX activity. Cells with higher levels of GPX activity showed increasing resistance to higher concentrations of hydrogen peroxide (200 µM), cumene hydroperoxide (200 µM), and menadione (100 µM). Of special note, however, is that there was no significant increase in resistance of GPX-transfected cells that were *chronically* exposed to these oxidants (86). The full role of Se and GPX in these specific transgenic systems as well as normal cells remains to be established. The study by Mirault and co-workers, however, illustrates that specific elevation of GPX may protect in acute or *in vitro* situations but may not be effective under chronic conditions.

GPX AND PLASMA SELENOPROTEIN P

A number of researchers over the past 15 years have been convinced that Se's critical roles lie outside of the realm of (classical) GPX. Burk et al.'s (87) pioneering work on Se's protective role in paraquat and diquat toxicity in rats illustrated that a modest Se injection would protect rats against diquat toxicity without appreciable changes in measured GPX activity. They targeted a plasma selenoprotein that is rapidly labeled (maximally at 3−4 hours) following ^{75}Se injection, and cloned and characterized plasma selenoprotein P (88). One of the postulated roles for selenoprotein P is as an extracellular antioxidant.

GPX AND GLUTATHIONE-S-TRANSFERASE

Wendel demonstrated that multiple enzymatic changes occur in liver enzymes, both up and down, only after liver GPX is fully depleted (89). Glutathione-S-transferase, which has Se-independent glutathione peroxidase activity (90,91), is one of the proteins that increases in Se deficiency only after liver GPX activity is fully depressed, and it is clear that Se-deficient liver can destroy bulky hydroperoxides using either glutathione-S-transferase (92) or PHGPX.

GPX AND 5′-DEIODINASE

Arthur and colleagues looked at the impact of severe Se deficiency, observed that T3 was reduced and T4 elevated, and discovered that 5′-deiodinase activity was reduced in Se deficiency (93). Injection of 10 μg Se/kg reduced the high plasma pyruvate kinase activity and lowered the elevated GSH-S-transferase activity with negligible effect on tissue GPX activity (94). Higher doses of Se (200 μg/kg) completely reversed the effects of Se deficiency on changes in T3 and T4 metabolism but only partially restored tissue GPX activity. Behne, using ^{75}Se, found that a 28-kDa selenoprotein was high in thyroid, liver, and kidney and proposed a role for Se in thyroid hormone metabolism (77). The work of Arthur (95) and of Behne (96) has resulted in the identification of type I 5'-iodothyronine deiodinase as a selenoenzyme, which Berry and Larson (97) demonstrated contained a UGA-specified selenocysteine. Thus there clearly are additional selenoenzymes that are labeled with Se prior to the labeling of GPX.

Few nutrient cofactors regulate the expression of the protein portion of an enzyme by an order of magnitude or more, unless the protein is involved in the metabolism of the nutrient. Striking examples of metal regulation of expression do occur for proteins that are involved in the metabolism of the metal. Zinc administration increases the level of metallothionein by increasing the transcription of metallothionein mRNA, apparently by interacting with upstream metal-regulatory elements (MREs). (For recent update, see ref. 98.) Iron loading of rats leads to an increase in ferritin levels, but the increase is due to increased translatability of existing mRNA rather than *de novo* transcription of ferritin mRNA. This is mediated by a single iron IRE in the 5'-UTR (99). Iron regulation of transferrin receptor is the opposite of ferritin regulation, and is accomplished via at least three IREs on the 3'-UTR. Increasing iron status results in decreased affinity of the IRE-binding 4Fe:4S-aconitase to these three IREs, which elicits increased degradation of transferrin receptor mRNA (62,63).

These examples thus suggest that Se regulation of GPX mRNA is functionally important to the organism as a mechanism that regulates Se metabolism and Se flux to other selenoproteins. In liver and most other tissues, up-regulation of GPX does not appear to be the metabolically critical effect of an increase in Se status, although an increase in GPX activity may have beneficial effects as well. These secondary benefits may be what we measure in acute oxidant challenges such as paraquat-treated animals or cells, when increased GPX activity is correlated with protection.

GPX as a Biological Selenium Buffer

I thus propose that GPX mRNA regulation by Se status is an evolutionarily conserved mechanism that cells use to sense the Se status and to control Se metabolism. In Se-deficient animals, GPX mRNA levels are very low and thus free Se will be diverted to other selenoproteins whose mRNA levels are not significantly reduced during Se deficiency. It appears that PHGPX is one such selenoenzyme. Because plasma selenoprotein P also is readily labeled with Se soon after injection in Se-deficient animals, plasma selenoprotein P is a second example, although we do not know its biological function. The 5'-deiodinase mRNA levels are also apparently less significantly reduced in Se deficiency, and thus the Se-dependent 5'-deiodinase is a third example.

Once these important metabolic needs for Se are satisfied, intracellular Se concentrations can rise, stabilize GPX mRNA, and, after a delay, lead to additional incorporation of Se into GPX. This would keep free and presumably toxic selenide concentrations low in a cell. Only after Se incorporation into GPX is maximized would the free or "labile" Se concentrations increase.

Thus GPX in the liver, and perhaps other tissues, serves not as an important antioxidant enzyme, but as a homeostatic mechanism that keeps free concentrations of Se low, that diverts Se to more important biological functions of Se in times of deficiency, and that absorbs excess Se over the deficient-to-adequate range. It buffers the internal environment. This buffering capacity would effectively expand the dietary range between deficiency and toxicity. I have elected to call this a "biological Se buffer" rather than an "Se thermostat" or "Se store" or "Se sink" to indicate its dynamic, homeostatic nature and to indicate its active role in modulating Se flux between incorporation into other selenoenzymes and incorporation into GPX.

I have been illustrating this biological Se buffer hypothesis since 1988 using the hypothetical diagram in Figure 3.2A. This figure shows the Se concentrations that would be present in a system that contains 1 μM of a high-affinity protein (effective K_m of 0.005 μM) and 5 μM of lower-affinity protein ($K_m = 0.5$ μM). These K_m values describe processes, presumably binding or incorporation, that are half-saturated at the indicated K_m concentration of Se. The resulting distribution of Se as the total concentration increases is shown in Figure 3.2A: (1) Se initially associates only with the high-affinity protein; (2) Se begins to associate with the low-affinity protein only after the high-affinity protein is saturated; (3) free or labile Se rises only after the low-affinity protein is saturated. Can we obtain experimental proof for analogous distribution of Se *in vivo*?

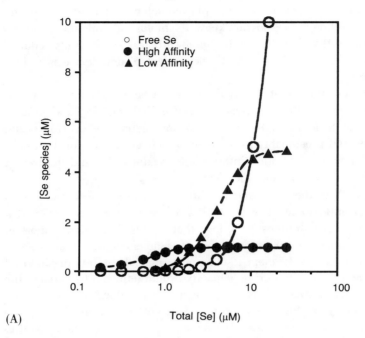

(A)

FIGURE 3.2. Figures showing hypothetical (A) and experimental data (B) illustrating the hypothesis that GPX functions as a biological selenium buffer. A: Distribution of Se amongst a high-affinity component (K_m 0.005 µM), a lower-affinity component (K_m 0.5 µM), and free Se, as total Se increases from 0.1 to 100 µM. B: Distribution of ^{75}Se in rat liver cytosol amongst PHGPX, GPX, and the labile Se pool, as determined by sodium dodecyl sulfate/ polyacrylamide gel electrophoresis (SDS/PAGE). Rats were fed the indicated levels of Se and injected with 100 µCi [^{75}Se] selenite 6 hours prior to sacrifice.

^{75}SE DISTRIBUTION IN LIVER

To directly test the Se buffer hypothesis, we used our previous experience (58) to set GPX mRNA levels in rats by feeding diets ranging between 0 and 0.2 µg Se/g diet to rats for 35 days. Rats were then injected intraperitoneally with 100 µCi of ^{75}Se as selenite and

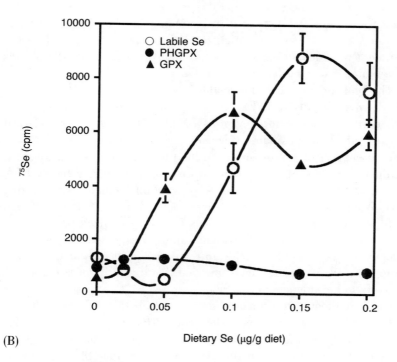

(B)

FIGURE 3.2. *Continued*

killed 3, 6, or 24 hours after Se injection. Se incorporation into various selenoproteins was determined using our SDS/PAGE procedure (82). In addition, we determined the free or labile Se in the cytosol by quantitating the ^{75}Se that was no longer bound to protein after the SDS/PAGE. We have assumed that the detected 19-kDa selenoprotein is PHGPX (82). The result at 6 hours is shown in Figure 3.2B. Under these conditions ^{75}Se incorporation into PHGPX was maximized between 0.02 and 0.05 µg Se/g diet, and at higher dietary Se concentrations the dietary Se diluted out radioactive incorporation of Se into PHGPX. In contrast there was little ^{75}Se incorporation into GPX at 0 and 0.02 µg Se/g as mRNA levels were low. ^{75}Se incorporation into GPX was maximized at 0.1 µg/g, and it declined at higher dietary Se levels, indicating that dietary Se diluted out ^{75}Se incorporation into GPX above $0.1\,\mu g/g$ diet. Labile or free Se in the cytosol only increased above $0.1\,\mu g\,Se/g$ diet, indicating that this pool only was elevated after ^{75}Se incorporation into GPX was maximized. This experiment provides strong support for our hypothesis that GPX serves as a biological Se buffer at least in liver.

The biological Se buffer hypothesis was further strengthened with the discovery of PHGPX. Expression of this enzyme is little regulated by Se status relative to classical GPX; PHGPX may be the critical Se-dependent "antioxidant" enzyme. And this enzyme may be the critical enzyme that is important in the protection of the heart against cardiomyopathy such as in Keshan disease or mulberry heart. GPX was first cloned because it is expressed at higher levels during erythrogenesis just at a time when mitochondria are being destroyed in a peroxide-mediated process. This is one specialized tissue where GPX functions in an "antioxidant" role. Tissue-specific enhancer regions are responsible for the up-regulation of erythroid GPX transcription (69), however, suggesting that this transcriptional regulation is likely to be independent of Se.

Gene duplication presumably gave rise to both GPX and PHGPX. The low homology between GPX and PHGPX suggests that this occurred long ago, giving evolution time to modify the role of each protein. It may be that unregulated PHGPX provides the usual intracellular protection against hydroperoxides, in combination with other protective systems like vitamin E and superoxide dismutase. In certain cells, like reticulocytes and perhaps continuing on in erythrocytes, GPX's enzymatic activity may still be an important function of Se. Lastly, in major organs such as liver, Se regulation of GPX mRNA levels may be a highly conserved mechanism that ensures that PHGPX, 5'-deiodinase, and plasma selenoprotein P activities are not limited by day-to-day variation of Se status.

Thus GPX's role in metabolism may be to serve as the sensor and effector in a feedback mechanism that directs Se flux toward critical functions, toward short-term storage in GPX, or toward excretion, depending on Se status. This homeostatic role would serve effectively as a biological buffer, smoothing out the variations due to changes in dietary Se intake. More careful study is needed to characterize fully the role of Se-dependent GPX—the use of recombinant GPXs in transfection experiments may be the opportunity we need to establish GPX's full role in metabolism.

ACKNOWLEDGMENTS

This research was supported by the University of Missouri Agricultural Experiment Station and the Food for the 21st Century program. Grant support was provided by NIH #DK 43491 and #CA 45164 and by a Hughes Undergraduate Internship (to J.A.D). The author would like to thank Phebe Lauffer for her proficient assistance in the preparation of this manuscript.

REFERENCES

1. Mills, GC. Hemoglobin catabolism. I. Glutathione peroxidase, an erythrocyte enzyme which protects hemoglobin from oxidative breakdown. J Biol Chem 229:189–197; 1957.
2. Rotruck, JT, Pope, AL, Ganther, HE, Swanson, AB, Hafeman, DG, Hoekstra, WG. Selenium: biochemical role as a component of glutathione peroxidase. Science 179:588–590; 1973.
3. Wendel, A. Selenium in Biology and Medicine. Heidelberg: Springer-Verlag; 1989.
4. Sunde, RA, Hoekstra, WG. Structure, synthesis and function of glutathione peroxidase. Nutr Rev 38:265–273; 1980.
5. Sunde, RA. The biochemistry of selenoproteins. J Am Oil Chem Soc 61:1891–1990; 1984.
6. Sunde, RA. Molecular biology of selenoproteins. Annu Rev Nutr 10:451–474; 1990.
7. Stadtman, TC. Selenium biochemistry. Annu Rev Biochem 59:111–127; 1990.
8. Böck, A, Forchhammer, K, Heider, J, Leinfelder, W, Sawers, G, Veprek, B, Zinoni, F. Selenocysteine: the 21st amino acid. Mol Microb 5:515–520; 1991.
9. Burk, RF. Molecular biology of selenium with implications for its metabolism. FASEB J 5:2274–2279; 1991.
10. Ursini, F, Maiorino, M, Gregolin, C. The selenoenzyme phospholipid hydroperoxide glutathione peroxidase. Biochim Biophys Acta 839:62–70; 1985.

11. Mills, GC. The purification and properties of glutathione peroxidase of erythrocytes. J Biol Chem 234:502–506; 1959.

12. Little, C, O'Brien, PJ. An intracellular GSH peroxidase with a lipid peroxide substrate. Biochem Biophys Res Commun 31:145–150; 1968.

13. Flohé, L, Loschen, G, Günzler, WA, Eichole, E. Glutathione peroxidase. V. The kinetic mechanism. Hoppe-Seyler's Z. Physiol Chem 353:987–999; 1972.

14. Günzler, WA, Vergin, H, Müller, I, Flohé, L. Glutathion-peroxidase VI die Reaktion der Glutathion-peroxidase mit verschiedenen Hydroperoxiden. Hoppe-Seyler's Z. Physiol Chem 353:1001–1004; 1972.

15. Epp, O, Ladenstein, R, Wendel, A. The refined structure of the selenoenzyme glutathione peroxidase at 0.2-nm resolution. Eur J Biochem 133:51–69; 1983.

16. Chambers, I, Frampton, J, Goldfarb, P, Affara, N, McBain, W, Harrison, PR. The structure of the mouse glutathione peroxidase gene: the selenocysteine in the active site is encoded by the "termination" codon, TGA. EMBO J 5:1221–1227; 1986.

17. Ghyselinck, NB, Jimenez, C, Dufaure, JP. Sequence homology of androgen-regulated epididymal proteins with glutathione peroxidase in mice. J Reprod Fertil 93:461–466; 1991.

18. Perry, CF, Jones, R, Niang, LSP, Jackson, RM, Hall, L. Genetic evidence for an androgen-regulated epididymal secretory glutathione peroxidase whose transcript does not contain a selenocysteine codon. Biochem J 285:863–870; 1992.

19. Criqui, MC, Jamet, E, Parmentier, Y, Marbach, J, Durr, A, Fleck, J. Isolation and characterization of a plant cDNA showing homology to animal glutathione peroxidases. Plant Mol Biol 18:623–627; 1992.

20. Williams, DL, Pierce, RJ, Cookson, E, Capron, A. Molecular cloning and sequencing of glutathione peroxidase from *Schistosoma mansoni*. Mol Biochem Parasitol 52:127–130; 1991.

21. Shigeoka, S, Takeda, T, Hanaoka, T. Characterization and immunological properties of selenium-containing glutathione peroxidase induced by selenite in *Chlamydomonas reinhardtii*. Biochem J 275:623–627; 1991.

22. Overbaugh, JM, Fall, R. Characterization of a selenium-independent glutathione peroxidase from *Euglena gracilis*. Plant Physiol 77:437–442; 1985.

23. Akasaka, M, Mizoguchi, J, Takahashi, K. A human cDNA sequence for a novel glutathione peroxidase-related protein. Nucleic Acids Res 18:4619; 1990.

24. Chu, FF, Doroshow, JH, Esworthy, RS. Expression, characterization, and tissue distribution of a new cellular selenium-dependent glutathione peroxidase, GSH-Px-GI. J Biol Chem 268:2571–2576; 1993.

25. McBride, OW, Mitchell, A, Lee, BJ, Mullenbach, G, Hatfield, D. Gene for selenium-dependent glutathione peroxidase maps to human chromosomes 3, 21 and X. Biofactors 1:285–292; 1988.

26. Mitchell, A, Bale, AE, Lee, BJ, Hatfield, D, Harley, H, Rundle, SA, Fan, YS, Fukushima, Y, Shows, TB, McBride, OW. Regional localization of the selenocysteine tRNA gene (TRSP) on human chromosome 19. Cytogenet Cell Genet 61:117–120; 1992.

27. Moscow, JA, Morrow, CS, He, R, Mullenbach, GT, Cowan, KH. Structure and function of the 5′-flanking sequence of the human cytosolic selenium-dependent glutathione peroxidase gene (hgpxl). J Biol Chem 267:5949–5958; 1992.

28. Ho, Y-S, Howard, AJ. Cloning and characterization of the rat glutathione peroxidase gene. FEBS Lett 301:5–9; 1992.

29. Sunde, RA, Hoekstra, WG. Incorporation of selenium from selenite and selenocystine into glutathione peroxidase in the isolated perfused rat liver. Biochem Biophys Res Commun 93:1181–1188; 1980.

30. Sunde, RA, Evenson, JK. Serine incorporation into the selenocysteine moiety of glutathione peroxidase. J Biol Chem 262:933–937; 1987.

31. Hatfield, D, Diamond, A, Dudock, B. Opal suppressor serine tRNA from bovine liver form phosphoseryl-tRNA. Proc Natl Acad Sci USA 79:6215–6219; 1982.

32. Hatfield, D, Lee, BJ, Hampton, L, Diamond, AM. Selenium induces changes in the selenocysteine tRNA[Ser]Sec population in mammalian cells. Nucleic Acids Res 19:939–943; 1991.

33. Ehrenreich, A, Forchhammer, K, Tormay, P, Veprek, B, Böck, A. Selenoprotein synthesis in *E-Coli*—purification and characterisation of the enzyme catalysing selenium activation. Eur J Biochem 206:767–773; 1992.

34. Veres, Z, Tsai, L, Scholz, TD, Politino, M, Balaban, RS, Stadtman, TC. Synthesis of 5-methylaminomethyl-2-selenouridine in tRNAs: 31P NMR studies show the labile selenium donor synthesized by the selD gene product contains selenium bonded to phosphorus. Proc Natl Acad Sci USA 89:2975–2979; 1992.

35. Kim, IY, Veres, Z, Stadtman, TC. *Escherichia coli* mutant SELD enzymes. J Biol Chem 267:19650–19654; 1992.

36. Leinfelder, W, Zehelein, E, Mandrand-Berthelot, M-A, Böck, A. Gene for a novel tRNA species that accepts L-serine and cotranslationally inserts selenocysteine. Nature 331:723–725; 1988.

37. Forchhammer, K, Leinfelder, W, Boesmiller, K, Veprek, B, Böck, A. Selenocysteine synthase from *Escherichia coli*: nucleotide sequence of the gene (*selA*) and purification of the protein. J Biol Chem 266: 6318–6323; 1991.

38. Forchhammer, K, Böck, A. Selenocysteine synthase from *Escherichia coli*: analysis of the reaction sequence. J Biol Chem 266:6324–6328; 1991.

39. Heider, J, Baron, C, Böck, A. Coding from a distance: dissection of the mRNA determinants required for the incorporation of selenocysteine into protein. EMBO J 11:3759–3766; 1992.

40. Mizutani, T, Kurata, H, Yamada, K, Totsuka, T. Some properties of murine selenocysteine synthase. Biochem J 284:827–834; 1992.

41. Berry, MJ, Banu, L, Chen, Y, Mandel, SJ, Kieffer, JD, Harney, JW, Larsen, PR. Recognition of a UGA as a selenocysteine codon in Type I deiodinase requires sequences in the 3' untranslated region. Nature 353:273–276; 1991.

42. Hill, KE, Lloyd, RS, Burk, RF. Conserved nucleotide sequences in the open reading frame and 3' untranslated region of selenoprotein P mRNA. Proc Natl Acad Sci USA 90:537–541; 1993.

43. Hafeman, DG, Sunde, RA, Hoekstra, WG. Effect of dietary selenium on erythrocyte and liver glutathione peroxidase in the rat. J Nutr 104:580–587; 1974.

44. Sunde, RA, Saedi, MS, Knight, SAB, Smith, CG, Evenson, JK. Regulation of expression of glutathione peroxidase by selenium. In: Wendel, A, ed. Selenium in Biology and Medicine. Heidelberg: Springer-Verlag; 1989, pp 8–13.

45. Selenium in Nutrition. Washington, DC. National Academy of Science; 1983.

46. Knight, SAB, Sunde, RA. The effect of progressive selenium deficiency on anti-glutathione peroxidase antibody reactive protein in rat liver. J Nutr 117:732–738; 1987.

47. Sunde, RA, Schwartz, JK, Johnson, AW, Foley, NF. Glutathione peroxidase mRNA levels in selenium-deficient, Se-adequate and high-selenium rats. FASEB J 5:A714; 1991.

48. Knight, SAB, Sunde, RA. Effect of selenium repletion on glutathione peroxidase protein in rat liver. J Nutr 118:853-858; 1988.

49. Takahashi, K, Newburger, PE, Cohen, HJ. Glutathione peroxidase protein. Absence in selenium deficiency states and correlation with enzymatic activity. J Clin Invest 77:1402–1404; 1986.

50. Saedi, MS, Smith, CG, Frampton, J, Chambers, I, Harrison, PR, Sunde, RA. Effect of selenium status on mRNA levels for glutathione

peroxidase in rat liver. Biochem Biophys Res Commun 153:855–861; 1988.

51. Smith, CG, Saedi, MS, Sunde, RA. The effect of selenium repletion on glutathione peroxidase mRNA and activity in rats. FASEB J 3:A451; 1989.

52. Yoshimura, S, Takekoshi, S, Watanabe, K, Fujii-Kuriyama, Y. Determination of nucleotide sequence of cDNA coding rat glutathione peroxidase and diminished expression of the mRNA in selenium deficient rat liver. Biochem Biophys Res Commun 154:1024–1028; 1988.

53. Christensen, MJ, Burgener, KW. Dietary selenium stabilizes glutathione peroxidase messenger RNA in rat liver. J Nutr 122:1620–1626; 1992.

54. Hill, KE, Lyons, PR, Burk, RF. Differential regulation of rat liver selenoprotein mRNAs in selenium deficiency. Biochem Biophys Res Commun 185:260–263; 1992.

55. Li, NQ, Reddy, PS, Thyagaraju, K, Reddy, AP, Hsu, BL, Scholz, RW, Tu, CP, Reddy, CC. Elevation of rat liver mRNA for selenium-dependent glutathione peroxidase by selenium deficiency. J Biol Chem 265:108–113; 1990.

56. Reddy, AP, Hsu, BL, Reddy, PS, Li, N-Q, Thyagaraju, K, Reddy, C, Tam, MF, Tu, CP. Expression of glutathione peroxidase I gene in selenium-deficient rats. Nucleic Acids Res 16:5557–5568; 1988.

57. Reddy, CC, Li, NQ, Reddy, PS, Reddy, AP, Hsu, B, Scholz, RW, Tu, C-PD. Evidence for cotranslational insertion of selenium into glutathione peroxidase from rat liver. FASEB J 2:A765; 1988.

58. Sunde, RA, Weiss, SL, Thompson, KM, Evenson, JK. Dietary selenium regulation of glutathione peroxidase mRNA—implications for the selenium requirement. FASEB J 6:A1365; 1992.

59. Weiss, SL, Evenson, JK, Thompson, KM, Sunde, RA. Dietary selenium regulation of glutathione peroxidase expression in female rats. FASEB J 7:A289; 1993.

60. Zhou, X, Sunde, RA. Effect of selenium status on glutathione peroxidase gene transcription in isolated rat liver nuclei. FASEB J 4:A1061; 1990.

61. Sugimoto, M, Sunde, RA. In vivo and in vitro nuclear transcription indicates selenium regulation of glutathione peroxidase occurs post-transcriptionally. FASEB J 6:A1366; 1992.

62. Mullner, E, Kuhn, LC. A stem-loop in the 3' untranslated region mediates iron-dependent regulation of transferrin receptor mRNA stability in the cytoplasm. Cell 53:815–825; 1988.

63. Casey, JL, Koeller, DM, Ramin, VC, Klausner, RD, Harford, JB. Iron regulation of transferrin receptor mRNA levels requires iron-responsive

elements and a rapid turnover determinant in the 3′ untranslated region of the mRNA. EMBO J 8:3693–3699; 1989.

64. Haile, DJ, Rouault, TA, Harford, JB, Kennedy, MC, Blondin, GA, Beinert, H, Klausner, RD. Cellular regulation of the iron-responsive element binding protein: disassembly of the cubane iron-sulfur cluster results in high-affinity RNA binding. Proc Natl Acad Sci USA 89: 11735–11739; 1993.

65. Behne, D, Duk, M, Elger, W. Selenium content and glutathione peroxidase activity in the testis of the maturing rat. J Nutr 116: 1442–1447; 1986.

66. Pinto, RE, Bartley, W. The effect of age and sex on glutathione reductase and glutathione peroxidase activities and on aerobic glutathione oxidation in rat liver homogenates. Biochem J 112:109–115; 1969.

67. Prohaska, JR, Sunde, RA, Zinn, KR. Livers from copper-deficient rats have lower glutathione peroxidase activity and mRNA levels but normal liver selenium levels. J Nutr Biochem 3:429–436; 1992.

68. Prohaska, JR, Sunde, RA. Comparison of liver glutathione peroxidase activity and mRNA in female and male mice and rats. Comp Biochem Physiol 105B:111–116; 1993.

69. O'Prey, J, Ramsey, S, Chambers, I, Harrison, PR. Transcriptional up-regulation of the mouse cytosolic glutathione peroxidase gene in erythroid cells is due to a tissue-specific 3′ enhancer containing functionally important CACCC/GT motifs and binding sites for GATA and its transcription factors. Mol Cellular Biol (submitted) 1993.

70. Jenkinson, SG, Lawrence, RA, Burk, RF, Williams, DM. Effects of copper deficiency on the activity of the selenoenzyme glutathione peroxidase and on excretion and tissue retention of ^{75}Se-selenite. J Nutr 112:197–204; 1982.

71. Takahashi, K, Avissar, N, Whitin, J, Cohen, H. Purification and characterization of human plasma glutathione peroxidase: A selenoglycoprotein distinct from the known cellular enzyme. Arch Biochem Biophys 256:677–686; 1987.

72. Maiorino, M, Ursini, F, Leonelli, M, Finato, N, Gregolin, C. A pig heart peroxidation inhibiting protein with glutathione peroxidase activity on phospholipid hydroperoxides. Biochem Int 5:575–583; 1982.

73. Maiorino, M, Gregolin, C, Ursini, F. (47) Phospholipid hydroperoxide glutathione peroxidase. Methods Enzymol 186:448–457; 1990.

74. Schuckelt, R, Brigelius-Flohé, R, Maiorino, M, Roveri, A, Reumkens, J, Strassburger, W, Flohé, L. Phospholipid hydroperoxide glutathione peroxidase is a selenoenzyme distinct from the classical glutathione

peroxidase as evident from cDNA and amino acid sequencing. Free Radic Res Commun 14:343–361; 1991.

75. Sunde, RA, Dyer, JA, Moran, T, Evenson, JK, Sugimoto, M. Phospholipid hydroperoxide glutathione peroxidase: Full-length pig blastocyst cDNA sequence and regulation by selenium status. Biochem Biophys Res Commun 193:905–911; 1993.

76. Weitzel, F, Ursini, F, Wendel, A. Phospholipid hydroperoxide glutathione peroxidase in various mouse organs during selenium deficiency and repletion. Biochim Biophys Acta 1036:88–94; 1990.

77. Behne, D, Hilmert, H, Scheid, S, Gessner, H, Elger, W. Evidence for specific selenium target tissues and new biologically important selenoproteins. Biochim Biophys Acta 966:12–21; 1988.

78. Maiorino, M, Chu, FF, Ursini, F, Davies, KJ, Doroshow, JH, Esworthy, RS. Phospholipid hydroperoxide glutathione peroxidase is the 18-kDa selenoprotein expressed in human tumor cell lines. J Biol Chem 266:7728–7732; 1991.

79. Roveri, A, Casasco, A, Maiorino, M, Dalan, P, Calligaro, A, Ursini, F. Phospholipid hydroperoxide glutathione peroxidase of rat testis. Gonadotropin dependence and immunocytochemical identification. J Biol Chem 267:6142–6146; 1992.

80. Calvin, HI, Cooper, GW, Wallace, E. Evidence that selenium in rat sperm is associated with a cysteine-rich structural protein of the mitochondrial capsule. Gamete Res 4:139–149; 1981.

81. Karimpour, I, Cutler, M, Shih, D, Smith, J, Kleene, K. Sequence of the gene encoding the mitochondrial capsule selenoprotein of mouse sperm: identification of three in-phase TGA selenocysteine codons. DNA Cell Biol 11:693–699; 1992.

82. Evenson, JK, Sunde, RA. Selenium incorporation into selenoproteins in the Se-adequate and Se-deficient rat. Proc Soc Exp Biol Med 187:169–180; 1988.

83. Hoekstra, WG. Biochemical function of selenium and its relation to vitamin E. Fed Proc 34:2083–2089; 1975.

84. Krall, J, Speranza, MJ, Lynch, RE. Paraquat-resistant HeLa cells: increased cellular content of glutathione peroxidase. Arch Biochem Biophys 286:311–315; 1991.

85. Huang, T-T, Carlson, EJ, Leadon, SA, Epstein, CJ. Relationship of resistance to oxygen free radicals to CuZn-superoxide dismutase activity in transgenic, transfected, and trisomic cells. FASEB J 6:903–910; 1992.

86. Mirault, M-E, Tremblay, A, Beaudoin, N, Tremblay, M. Overexpression of seleno-glutathione peroxidase by gene transfer enhances

the resistance of T47D human breast cells to clastogenic oxidants. J Biol Chem 266:20752–20760; 1991.

87. Burk, RF, Lawrence, RA, Lane, JM. Liver necrosis and lipid per-oxidation in the rat as the result of paraquat and diquat administration. Effect of selenium deficiency. J Clin Invest 65:1024–1031; 1980.

88. Hill, KE, Lloyd, RS, Yang, JG, Read, R, Burk, RF. The cDNA for rat selenoprotein P contains 10 TGA codons in the open reading frame. J Biol Chem 266:10050–10053; 1991.

89. Reiter, R, Wendel, A. Selenium and drug metabolism—II. Independence of glutathione peroxidase and reversibility of hepatic enzyme modulations in deficient mice. Biochem Pharmacol 33:1923–1928; 1984.

90. Lawrence, RA, Burk, RF. Glutathione peroxidase activity in selenium-deficient rat liver. Biochem Biophys Res Commun 71:952–958; 1976.

91. Prohaska, JR, Ganther, HE. Glutathione peroxidase activity of glutathione-S-transferase purified from rat liver. Biochem Biophys Res Commun 76:437–445; 1977.

92. Burk, RF, Nishiki, K, Lawrence, RA, Chance, B. Peroxide removal by selenium-dependent and selenium-independent peroxidases in hemoglobin-free perfused rat liver. J Biol Chem 253:43–46; 1978.

93. Beckett, GJ, Beddows, SE, Morrice, PC, Nicol, F, Arthur, JR. Inhibition of hepatic deiodination of thyroxine is caused by selenium deficiency in rats. Biochem J 248:443–447; 1987.

94. Arthur, JR, Nicol, F, Boyne, R, Allen, KGD, Hayes, JD, Beckett, GJ. Old and new roles for selenium. In: Hemphill, D.D, ed. Trace Substances in Environmental Health XXI. Columbia: University of Missouri; 1987, pp. 487–498.

95. Arthur, JR, Nicol, F, Beckett, GJ. Hepatic iodothyronine 5′ deiodinase: the role of selenium. Biochem J 272:537–540; 1990.

96. Behne, D, Kyriakopoulos, A, Meinhold, H, Köhrle, J. Identification of type I iodothyronine 5′-deiodinase as a selenoenzyme. Biochem Biophys Res Commun 173:1143–1149; 1990.

97. Berry, MJ, Banu, L, Larsen, PR. Type I iodothyronine deiodinase is a selenocysteine-containing enzyme. Nature 349:438–440; 1991.

98. Koizumi, S, Yamada, H, Suzuki, K, Otsuka, F. Zinc-specific activation of a HeLa cell nuclear protein which interacts with a metal responsive element of the human metallothionein-IIA gene. Eur J Biochem 210: 555–560; 1992.

99. Rouault, TA, Hentze, MW, Caughman, SW, Harford, JB, Klausner, RD. Binding of a cytosolic protein to the iron-responsive element of human ferritin messenger RNA. Science 241:1207–1210; 1988.

100. Ho, Y-S, Howard, AJ, Crapo, JD. Nucleotide sequence of a rat glutathione peroxidase cDNA. Nucl Acids Res 16:5207; 1988.
101. Mullenbach, GT, Tabrizi, A, Irvine, BD, Bell, GI, Hallewell, RA. Sequence of a cDNA coding for human glutathione peroxidase confirms TGA encodes active site selenocysteine. Nucleic Acids Res 15:5484; 1987.
102. Sukenaga, Y, Ishida, K, Takeda, T, Takagi, K. cDNA sequence coding for human glutathione peroxidase. Nucl Acids Res 15:7178; 1987.
103. Mullenbach, GT, Tabrizi, A, Irvine, BD, Bell, GI, Tainer, JA, Hallewell, RA. Selenocysteine's mechanism of incorporation and evolution revealed in cDNAs of three glutathione peroxidases. Protein Eng 2:239–246; 1988.
104. Akasaka, M, Mizoguch, J, Yoshimura, S, Watanabe, K. Nucleotide sequence of cDNA for rabbit glutathione peroxidase. Nucleic Acids Res 17:2136; 1989.

Chapter
4

Extracellular Glutathione Peroxidase: A Distinct Selenoprotein

Harvey J. Cohen and Nelly Avissar

INTRODUCTION

Disease states in animals and humans have been attributed to selenium deficiency because they can be prevented or reversed by the addition of selenium to the diet (1–7). In patients undergoing chronic parenteral nutrition, selenium deficiency has been associated with heart failure (5–7) muscle pain (8) and muscle weakness (9). A role for selenium in intracellular metabolism of mammals was first realized in 1973 with the discovery that selenium was part of the enzyme glutathione peroxidase (10) and was essential for its activity (11). Selenium in this protein is in the form of selenocysteine (12), which gets specifically incorporated in response to the opal suppressor codon UGA (13,14). Except for the recent description of (type 1) 5' iodothyronine deiodinase as a selenocysteine-containing enzyme (15), the only other selenoprotein with a known function in mammalian tissue is the selenium-dependent glutathione peroxidase. At least three different glutathione peroxidases have been described: A cytoplasmic cellular form found within all cells tested (16), a membrane form described in porcine heart (17) and rat liver (18), and an extracellular form described by us and others (19–21). The enzymes are structurally, functionally, and antigenically distinct from each other. This manuscript will describe the studies that led to the recognition of the extracellular form of glutathione peroxidase as a distinct protein and current information as to its structure, sites of synthesis and secretion, and potential role in extracellular metabolism.

GLUTATHIONE PEROXIDASE ACTIVITY IN PLASMA AND CELLS

All cells and all plasmas tested contain glutathione peroxidase (16,22). In selenium-deficient animals (23) and humans (24) both plasma and cellular glutathione peroxidase activities decreased, and with replacement of selenium, both plasma and cellular enzyme activities returned to normal. Neither activity could be augmented by an excess of selenium. It was, thus, felt that the plasma glutathione peroxidase reflected the cellular enzyme activity. During the 1970s, plasma glutathione peroxidase activity and red blood cell (RBC) glutathione peroxidase activity were both used as indices of the selenium status of animals and humans (16,22). Since both enzymes utilize only reduced glutathione as a reductant and could oxidize both organic hydroperoxides and hydrogen peroxide, they were felt to be due to the same protein (16,23).

Plasma Glutathione Peroxidase as a Distinct Entity

The first indication that plasma glutathione peroxidase may not be just a representation of the cellular enzyme activity was obtained during repletion studies with selenium in individuals who were on chronic intravenous hyperalimentation (24). It was found that RBC glutathione peroxidase activity was low in these individuals and remained unchanged for up to 2 weeks after selenium replacement was started. RBC glutathione peroxidase activity returned to normal after approximately 3–4 months. This was consistent with the appearance of new RBC, made in the presence of selenium. Granulocyte and platelet glutathione peroxidase activities also returned to normal with time courses that were very similar to the time necessary for synthesizing new cells. However, in patients with very low glutathione peroxidase activities and selenium contents in both their RBCs and plasma, within 6 hours after initiation of selenium supplementation, there was a detectable increase in plasma glutathione peroxidase activity, with normal values reappearing within 7 to 10 days (25). These kinetics were inconsistent with the plasma enzyme being representative of either the RBCs or other blood-cell-enzyme activities.

In an attempt to determine whether glutathione peroxidase activity and protein content were equally affected by selenium depletion, polyclonal antibodies against purified human RBC glutathione peroxidase were obtained from immunized rabbits. These antibodies precipitated 100% of the RBC glutathione peroxidase activity and greater than 90–95% of the granulocyte and platelet glutathione peroxidase activities (26). This antibody also precipitated 70% of the liver glutathione peroxidase activity when this activity was measured with organic hydroperoxides and almost 100% of the activity when hydrogen peroxide was the substrate (26). An unexpected finding was that this antibody could precipitate none of the plasma glutathione peroxidase activity. That this was not due to an inhibitor in the plasma was determined by adding purified RBC enzyme to plasma and demonstrating that the antibody could precipitate that component of the glutathione peroxidase activity that was due to the RBC enzyme that was added. This demonstrated that the two enzymes had dissimilar antigenic properties (26).

PURIFICATION AND CHARACTERIZATION OF PLASMA GLUTATHIONE PEROXIDASE

Glutathione peroxidase from human plasma was purified to homogeneity utilizing ammonium sulfate precipitation, diethylaminoethyl (DEAE) cellulose, hydroxyapatite, and Sephadex G-200 chromatography (19). The protein had a molecular weight of approximately 92,000 and a subunit molecular weight of 23,000, slightly greater than the cellular protein. It was found to contain four seleniums per molecule. These results were similar to that found for the cellular enzyme (27). The specific activity of the purified plasma enzyme was only 10% that of the cellular enzyme. It was also found to be more heat stable and to have altered mobility in sodium doderyl sulfate (SDS) gels under nonreducing conditions (19–28). In addition, unlike the cellular enzyme, the purified plasma enzyme bound iodinated concanavalin A, and this binding was inhibited by pretreatment of the purified protein with glycopeptidase F (19). Polyclonal antibodies were made against the purified plasma enzyme and were found to precipitate >90% of the plasma glutathione peroxidase activity and none of the cellular glutathione peroxidase activity (29). Thus, these two proteins were found to be immunologically non-cross-reactive. While investigating fatty-acid hydroperoxide-reducing activity of human plasma, Maddipati and Marnett purified an enzyme utilizing ammonium sulfate precipitation, hydrophobic interaction chromatography on phenyl sepharose, and anion-exchange chromatography and gel filtration (20). This purified peroxidase had similar specific activity and subunit molecular mass and Se content as did the protein purified by our laboratory (19). In both their description and in our investigations, the K_m for glutathione was 4.5 mM (19,20). Broderick also purified the same enzyme from human plasma (21). SDS-(PAGE) polyacrylamide gel electrophoresis of the purified human plasma enzyme showed it to have a different mobility constant than the cellular enzyme (19,20). Partial amino acid sequencing of the plasma enzyme also showed that there were different amino acid sequences from that of the cellular enzyme (30). Thus, functionally, antigenically, and structurally, these two enzymes were different.

Sources of Synthesis and Secretion of Extracellular Glutathione Peroxidase

Since plasma glutathione peroxidase was found to be a distinct entity and a glycoprotein, it was logical to assume that it might be synthesized in liver as are most plasma proteins. Immunopurification techniques examining both selenium-75 metabolically labeled cells and extracellular media of endothelial cells, myeloid leukemic cells, and a hepatocellular carcinoma cell line showed that all cells made the cellular form of glutathione peroxidase but that only the liver cell line made and secreted extracellular glutathione peroxidase, since only the extracellular form of glutathione peroxidase was found in the medium (28). The addition of monensin, an inhibitor of protein processing, to the cell-culture system resulted in an increase in the amount of the extracellular protein found in the cells, indicating that secretion of extracellular glutathione peroxidase was an active process (28). That the extracellular glutathione peroxidase was not localized specifically to plasma was determined by examining breast milk. It had been known for some time that breast milk contains selenium and glutathione peroxidase (31). Utilizing the non-cross-reacting antibodies to the two forms of glutathione peroxidase, it was determined that over 90% of the breast milk glutathione peroxidase was the extracellular form of the enzyme (30). Recently we have found that pulmonary lavage fluid also contains glutathione peroxidase activity and that at least 50–75% of this activity is due to the extracellular form of the enzyme (unpublished results). Although glutathione peroxidase activity has been found in other extracellular fluids such as bile (32), saliva (33), semen (34), and cerebrospinal fluid (35), it is not yet known how much of the activity in these fluids is due to extracellular glutathione peroxidase.

In another investigation utilizing the non-cross-reacting antibodies, it was found that 15% of the selenium in RBCs could be accounted for by the cellular glutathione peroxidase and 12% of the selenium in plasma could be accounted for by the extracellular glutathione peroxidase (29). In breast milk, up to 14% of the selenium could be accounted for by the extracellular glutathione peroxidase (30). Because of the demonstration that a liver-tumor cell line made and secreted extracellular glutathione peroxidase, we attempted to clone the cDNA for this protein from a human-liver library. We were unsuccessful in that endeavor. Takahashi et al. were able to clone the cDNA for extracellular glutathione peroxidase from a placenta library (36), and although they were able to demonstrate the mRNA for glutathione peroxidase in the same liver-tumor cell line that we showed could make and secrete the protein, they were not able to find the mRNA in normal human liver. Thus, it became apparent that human liver might not be the source for the plasma enzyme activity. The cDNA for extracellular glutathione peroxidase was also cloned from rat placenta and partially cloned from human kidney, and the various tissues were assessed for the extracellular glutathione peroxidase mRNA content. Of all the tissues studied, rat and mouse kidney had the highest content of this specific mRNA (38). Other tissues that were found to have high mRNA content were heart and lung. Rodent, but not human, liver was devoid of this mRNA (37,38). We found that human kidney had the highest expression of extra-cellular glutathione peroxidase mRNA and that skeletal muscle, pancreas, and brain also express this mRNA (Avissar et al., manuscript in preparation).

It had previously been shown that patients undergoing chronic dialysis had low levels of cellular and plasma glutathione peroxidase activities (39). They also were found to be selenium deficient. When their selenium status was corrected, the RBC glutathione peroxidase activity returned to normal (39). However, the plasma glutathione peroxidase activity remained below normal (39). In a recent in-vestigation on patients undergoing chronic dialysis, and in anephric patients, we were able to demonstrate that their plasma glutathione peroxidase activity was only 40% and 23% of normal, respectively, despite the fact that the patients had normal plasma selenium content (40). After renal transplantation of the anephric patients, the plasma glutathione peroxidase activity increased to up to 200% of normal. Thus, it appears that the kidney is a major, if not the sole, source of plasma glutathione peroxidase (Avissar et al., manuscript in preparation). The source for this enzyme in the lung lavage fluid and in breast milk is as yet unknown, although we have shown that primary bronchial cells in culture are capable of synthesizing and secreting extracellular glutathione peroxidase (41).

FUNCTION OF EXTRACELLULAR GLUTATHIONE PEROXIDASE

Glutathione peroxidase has the ability to reduce hydrogen peroxide and organic hydroperoxides. It only utilizes reduced glutathione as a reductant. It is controversial whether it can also reduce phospholipid hydroperoxides (32,42). Also, as mentioned above, glutathione peroxidase is the sole source of lipid peroxide-reducing activity in plasma (29). Thus, it is intriguing to postulate that plasma glutathione peroxidase serves as an antioxidant for oxygen-radical-produced organic hydroperoxides and hydrogen peroxide. A major problem with this hypothesis is that there is very little reduced glutathione in plasma (less than 20 µM) (43) and that the K_m for glutathione for this enzyme is 4.5 mM (19,20). Thus, although plasma glutathione peroxidase can function as a glutathione-dependent lipid hydroperoxide-reducing enzyme, it is not clear whether it does function as such in plasma. Of note, glutathione content in the lung lavage fluid is 400 µM (44), and it is possible that the glutathione peroxidase activity in lung lavage fluid can function as a peroxide reducing enzyme. Since plasma glutathione peroxidase is made and secreted by kidney, it is possible that its site of action is not in the plasma but in the renal extracellular space. It is known that kidney utilizes a great deal of oxygen during intermediary metabolism, especially the proximal convoluted tubule cells (45), and mesangial cells within the kidney can make oxygen radicals (46). It is, thus, possible that the function for this extracellular enzyme may not be in the plasma, but in the local tissue enviromment.

Conclusion

Extracellular glutathione peroxidase is a distinct selenoglycoprotein with immunological, structural, and functional differences from the cellular enzymes. Although it appears to be a good indicator of selenium status, its role in the body is as yet unknown. Since the extracellular enzyme is found not only in plasma but also in breast milk and lung lavage fluid, and since the source of the plasma enzyme appears to be primarily the kidney, it is possible that the role for this enzyme as an antioxidant is not in the plasma, where there is very little glutathione, but in extracellular fluid. Future investigations in both selenium-deficient humans and animals and in specific antibody-treated and genetically manipulated animals might help answer the important question of the function of extracellular glutathione peroxidase.

References

1. VanFleet, JF, Ferrans, VJ, Ruth, GR. Induction of lesions of selenium-vitamin E deficiency in weaning swine fed silver, cobalt, zinc, cadmium and vanadium. Am J Vet Res 42:789–799; 1981.
2. Whanger, PD, Weswig, PH, Schnitz, JA, Oldfield, JE. Effect of selenium-vitamin E on blood selenium levels, tissue glutathione peroxidase activities and white muscle disease in sheep fed purified or hay diets. J Nutr 107:1298–1307; 1977.
3. Patterson, EL, Milstrey, R, Stokstad, E. Effect of selenium in preventing exudative diathesis in chicks. Proc Soc Exp Biol Med 95:617–620; 1975.
4. Schwarz, K, Bieri, JG, Briggs, GM. Prevention of exudative diathesis in chicks by factor 3 and selenium. Proc Soc Exp Biol Med 95:621–625; 1957.
5. Ge, K, Xue, A, Bai, J, Wang, S. Keshan Disease—an endemic cardiomyopathy in China. Virchows Arch Pathol Anat 401:1–15; 1983.
6. Johnson, RA, Baker, SS, Fallon, JT, Maynard, EP, Ruskin, JN, Wen, I, Ge, K, Cohen, HJ. An occidental case of cardiomyopathy and selenium deficiency. N Engl J Med 304:1210–1212; 1981.
7. Fleming, CR, Lie, JT, McCall, JT, O'Brien, JF, Baillie, EE, Thistle, JL. Selenium deficiency and fatal cardiomyopathy in a patient on home parenteral nutrition. Gastroenterology 83:689–693; 1982.

8. Van RiJ, AM, McKenzie, JM, Thomson, CD, Robinson, MF. Selenium supplementation in total parenteral nutrition. JPEN 5:120–124; 1981.

9. Brown, MR, Cohen, HJ, Lyons, JM, Curtis, TW, Thunberg, B, Cochran, WJ, Klish, WJ. Proximal muscle weakness and selenium deficiency associated with long term parenteral nutrition. Am J Clin Nutr 43:549–554; 1986.

10. Rotruck, JT, Pope, AL, Ganther, HE, Hafeman, DG, Hoekstra, WG. Selenium biochemical role as a component of glutathione peroxidase. Science 179:588–590; 1973.

11. Smith, PJ, Tappel, AL, Chow, CK. Glutathione peroxidase activity as a function of dietary selenomethionine. Nature 247:392–393; 1974.

12. Forstrom, JW, Zakowski, JJ, Tappel, AL. Identification of the catalytic site of rat liver glutathione peroxidase as selenocysteine. Biochemistry 17:2639–2644; 1978.

13. Chambers, I, Frampton, J, Goldfarb, P, Affara, N, McBain, W, Harrison, PR. The structure of the mouse glutathione peroxidase gene: the selenocysteine in the active site is encoded by the termination codon TGA. EMBO J 5:1221–1227; 1986.

14. Mullenbach, GT, Tabrizi, A, Irvine, BD, Bell, GI, Hallewell, RA. Sequence of a cDNA coding for human glutathione peroxidase confirms TGA encodes active site selenocysteine. Nucleic Acids Res 15:5485; 1987.

15. Berry, ML, Banu, L, Larsen, PR. Type I iodothyronine deiodinase is a selenocysteine containing enzyme. Nature 349:438–440; 1991.

16. Levander, OA. A global view of human selenium nutrition. Ann Rev Nutr 7:227–250; 1987.

17. Ursini, F, Maiorino, M, Gregolin, C. The selenoenzyme phospholipid hydroperoxide glutathione peroxidase. Biochim Biophys Acta 839:62–70; 1985.

18. Duan, Y-J, Komura, S, Fiszer-Szafarz, F, Szafarz, D, Yagi, K. Purification and characterization of a novel monomeric glutathione peroxidase. J Biol Chem 263:19003–19008; 1988.

19. Takahashi, K, Avissar, N, Whitin, J, Cohen, HJ. Purification and characterization of human plasma glutathione peroxidase: a selenoglycoprotein distinct from the known cellular enzyme. Arch Biochem Biophys 256:677–686; 1987.

20. Maddipati, KR, Marnett, LJ. Characterization of the major hydroperoxide reducing activity of human plasma. J Biol Chem 262:17398–17403; 1987.

21. Broderick, SJ, Deagen, JT, Whanger, PD. Properties of the glutathione peroxidase isolated from human plasma. J Inorg Biochem 30:299–308; 1987.

22. Ganther, HE, Hafeman, DG, Lawrence, RA, Serfass, RE, Hoekstra, WG. Selenium and glutathione peroxidase in health and disease—a review. In: Prasad, AS, Oberleas, D, eds. Trace Elements in Human Health and Disease, Vol 2. New York: Academic Press; 1976, pp 165–234.

23. Hill, KE, Burk, RF, Lane, JM. Effect of selenium depletion and repletion on plasma glutathione and glutathione dependent enzymes in the rat. J Nutr 117:99–104; 1987.

24. Cohen, HJ, Chovaniac, ME, Mistrerra, D, Baker, SS. Selenium repletion and glutathione peroxidase differential effects on plasma and red blood cell enzyme activity. Am J Clin Nutr 41:735–747; 1985.

25. Cohen, HJ, Brown, MR, Hamilton, D, Lyons, JM, Patterson J, Avissar, N, Liegey, P. Glutathione peroxidase and selenium deficiency in patients receiving home parenteral nutrition, time course for development of deficiency and repletion of enzyme activity in plasma and blood cells. Am J Clin Nutr 49:132–139; 1989.

26. Takahashi, K, Cohen, HJ. Selenium dependent glutathione peroxidase protein and activity: immunological investigation on cellular and plasma enzymes. Blood 68:640–645; 1986.

27. Oh, S-H, Ganther, HE, Hoekstra, WG. Selenium as a component of glutathione peroxidase isolated from ovine erythrocytes. Biochemistry 9:1825–1829; 1974.

28. Avissar, N, Whitin, JC, Allen, PZ, Wagner, DD, Liegey, P, Cohen, HJ. Plasma selenium-dependent glutathione peroxidase: Cell of origin and secretion. J Biol Chem 264:15850–15855; 1989.

29. Avissar, N, Whitin, JC, Allen, PZ, Palmer, IS, Cohen, HJ. Anti-human plasma glutathione peroxidase antibodies: immunological investigations to determine plasma glutathione peroxidase protein and selenium content in plasma. Blood 73:318–323; 1988.

30. Avissar, N, Slemmon, JR, Palmer, IS, Cohen, HJ. Partial sequence of human plasma glutathione peroxidase and immunologic identification of milk glutathione peroxidase as the plasma enzyme. J Nutr 121:1243–1249; 1991.

31. Mannan, S, Picciano, MF. Influence of maternal selenium intake on human milk selenium concentrations and glutathione peroxidase activity. Am J Clin Nutr 46:95–100; 1987.

32. Esworthy, RS, Chu, F-F, Paxton, RJ, Akman, S, Doroshow, SH. Characterization and partial amino acid sequence of human plasma glutathione peroxidase. Arch Biochem Biophys 286:330–336; 1991.
33. Hojo, Y. Selenium and glutathione peroxidase in human saliva and other human body fluids. Sci Total Environ 65:85–94; 1987.
34. Kantola, M, Saaranen, M, Vanha-Perttula, T. Selenium and glutathione peroxidase in seminal plasma of men and bulls. J Reprod Fert 83:785–794; 1988.
35. Macdonald, RL, Weir, BKA, Runzer, TD, Grace, MGA. Malondialdehyde, glutathione peroxidase and superoxide dismutase in cerebrospinal fluid during cerebral vasospasm in monkeys. Can J Neurol Sci 19:326–332; 1992.
36. Takahashi, K, Akasaka, M, Yamamoto, Y, Kobayashi, C, Mizoguchi, J, Koyama, J. Primary structure of human plasma glutathione peroxidase deduced from cDNA sequences. J Biochem 108:145; 1990.
37. Yoshimura, S, Watanabe, K, Suemizu, H, Onozawa, T, Mizoguchi, J, Tsuda, K, Hatta, H, Moriuchi, T. Tissue specific expression of plasma glutathione peroxidase gene in rat kidney. J Biochem 109:918–923; 1991.
38. Chu, FF, Esworthy, SE, Doroshow, HK, Doan, J, Lie, X-F. Expression of plasma glutathione peroxidase in human liver in addition to kidney heart and breast in humans and rodents. Blood 79:3233–3238; 1992.
39. Saint-Georges, MD, Bonnefont, DJ, Bourely, BA, Jaudon, M-CT, Cereze, P, Chaumer, P, Gard, C, D'Auzac, CL. Correction of selenium deficiency in hemodialyzed patients. Kidney Int 36:S-274; 1989.
40. Cohen, HJ, Avissar, N, Yagil, Y, Ornt, DB, Bushinsky, DA, Palmer, IS. Effect of nephrectomy and renal transplantation on serum glutathione peroxidase activity. FASEB J 6:A1397; 1992.
41. Avissar, N, Willey, C, Kerl, EA, Frampton, MW, Cerilli, JC, Cohen, HJ. Kidney and lung cells make and secrete extracellular glutathione peroxidase. Fifth International Symposium on Selenium in Biology and Medicine, Nashville, TN, 1992, p 57.
42. Yamamoto, Y, Yoshizu, T, Katoh, M, Takahashi, K. Structure, origin and function of human plasma glutathione peroxidase. Fifth International Symposium on Selenium in Biology and Medicine, Nashville, TN, 1992, p 163.
43. Anderson, ME, Meister, A. Dynamic state of glutathione in blood plasma. J Biol Chem 255:9530–9533; 1980.
44. Cantin, AM, North, SL, Hubbard, RC, Crystal, RG. Normal alveolar epithelial fluid contains high levels of glutathione. J Appl Physiol 63:152–157; 1987.

45. Soltoff, SP. ATP and the regulation of renal cell function. Ann Rev Physiol 48:9–31; 1986.

46. Radeke, HH, Cross, AR, Hancock, JT, Jones, OTG, Nakamu, M, Kaever, V, Resch, K. Functional expansion of NADPH oxidase components (α and β subunits of cytochrome b558 and 45-kDa flavoproteins) by intrinsic human glomerular mesangial cells. J Biol Chem 266: 21025–21029; 1991.

Chapter 5

Roles of Selenium in Type I Iodothyronine 5'-Deiodinase and in Thyroid Hormone and Iodine Metabolism

John R. Arthur and Geoffrey J. Beckett

ROLES FOR SELENIUM

A biological function of selenium was first recognized when it was shown to be an essential component of factor 3, which prevented liver necrosis in rats that were also vitamin E–deficient (1). Subsequently, selenium deficiency was shown to cause several diseases in other animals, usually associated with concurrent vitamin E deficiency (2). Although some conditions that responded to selenium or vitamin E supplementation were thought to be caused by tissue fat oxidation, the biochemical basis of the involvement of selenium with vitamin E was not understood until Rotruck et al. demonstrated that selenium was essential for glutathione peroxidase activity (3). Thereafter Hoekstra proposed a scheme to explain the interaction between vitamin E in the cell membrane and selenium-containing glutathione peroxidase in the cell cytoplasm (4). Glutathione peroxidase was suggested to act in the cell cytoplasm, metabolizing a range of peroxides that were sources of free radicals, while vitamin E acted in the cell membrane as a free-radical scavenger.

As well as the cytosolic glutathione peroxidase, two other genetically and immunologically distinct selenium-containing glutathione peroxidases have been identified. One form is found in the plasma (5–7) and another is probably associated with cell membranes and is capable of metabolizing fatty-acid peroxides still attached to phospholipids (8–10). The latter reaction cannot be performed by the "classical" glutathione peroxidase. An important consequence of the identification of different selenium-dependent glutathione peroxidases was the possibility that they had differing sensitivities to selenium deficiency.

Loss of cytosolic glutathione peroxidase activity cannot explain all the effects of selenium deficiency, particularly some that occur in the presence of adequate supplies of vitamin E. Systems and enzymes whose response on repletion of selenium-deficient animals cannot be related to changes in glutathione peroxidase activity include drug-metabolizing enzymes in liver, glutathione metabolism in liver and plasma, toxicity of some herbicides, and neutrophil function (11–13). A striking feature of the glutathione-peroxidase-independent responses to selenium repletion in rats and mice was the similar sensitivity of all the affected enzymes/metabolic processes to the dose (up to 50 µg selenium/kg body weight) (12,14–16). This indicated that a common mechanism such as a hormone effect could be controlling all these apparently diverse processes. Since neutrophil function and hepatic enzyme expression can be affected by thyroid status, this prompted investigation of thyroid hormone metabolism in selenium deficiency.

THYROID HORMONE SYNTHESIS AND METABOLISM

Thyroid hormones regulate many of the metabolic processes in the body and are essential for the normal development of the brain in the foetus. The follicular cells of the thyroid provide the sole source of thyroxine (T_4) but this is thought to be a prohormone requiring 5' (outer ring) monodeiodination to produce the biologically active hormone 3,3',5-triiodothyronine (T_3). In man and the rat more than 80% of circulating T_3 is derived from deiodination of T_4 in nonthyroidal tissue, particularly in liver, kidney, and possibly skeletal muscle (17). Under normal circumstances the thyroid provides less than 20% of circulating T_3 but in iodine deficiency the thyroid becomes the most important source of circulating T_3 (18). Synthesis of T_4 and T_3 in the thyroid requires iodination of tyrosine residues on thyroglobulin, followed by coupling of the mono- and diiodotyrosines. After intracellular hydrolysis of thyroglobulin, T_3 and T_4 are released into the circulation. Although T_3 is formed on thyroglobulin, another possible source of thyroidal T_3 is intrathyroidal deiodination of T_4 but the quantitative importance of this mechanism is unclear (19).

The control of thyroid hormone production is primarily exerted by thyrotropin (TSH) released from the pituitary, but hypothalamic thyrotropin-releasing hormone (TRH) is also involved. The plasma levels of TSH are under strict negative feedback control from circulating free (nonprotein bound) T_4 and T_3; these hormones may also influence TRH release (20).

DEIODINATION

Thyroid hormones undergo stepwise deiodination in most nonthyroidal tissues (17). The 5' deiodination of T_4 leads to the production of the

DEIODINATION OF THYROXINE

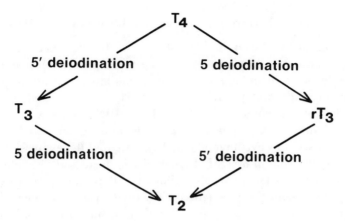

FIGURE 5.1. Pathways for deiodination of thyroxine (T_4).

active hormone T_3 but if 5 deiodination of T_4 occurs the inactive isomer 3,3′,5′-triiodothyronine (reverse T_3) is produced. Reverse T_3 and T_3 can undergo 5 and 5′ monodeiodination, respectively, to produce the inactive 3,3′-diiodothyronine (Fig. 5.1). The family of

TABLE 5.1. Characteristics of type I, II, and III iodothyronine deiodinases[1].

	I	II	III
Deiodination Reaction	$5\begin{cases} T_4 \text{ to } rT_3 \text{ (inactive)} \\ T_3 \text{ to } T_2 \text{ (inactive)} \end{cases}$ and $5'\begin{cases} T_4 \text{ to } T_3 \text{ (active)} \\ rT_3 \text{ to } T_2 \text{ (inactive)} \end{cases}$	$5'\begin{cases} T_4 \text{ to } T_3 \text{ (active)} \\ rT_3 \text{ to } T_2 \text{ (inactive)} \end{cases}$	$5\begin{cases} T_4 \text{ to } rT_3 \text{ (inactive)} \\ T_3 \text{ to } T_2 \text{ (inactive)} \end{cases}$
Tissue location	Liver, kidney (thyroid)	Brain, brown adipose tissue, pituitary	Brain, skin, placenta
Selenoenzyme	Yes	No	Unknown
Hypothyroidism	Decreased	Increased	Decreased
Hyperthyroidism	Increased	Decreased	Increased
Selenium deficiency	Decreased	Decreased	Unknown
Substrate specificity	$rT_3 \gg T_4 > T_3$	$T_4 > rT_3$	$T_3 > T_4$

[1] IDI is not present in the thyroid of all species and when present its activity is increased by TSH (see text).

microsomal iodothyronine deiodinases catalyzes these deiodination reactions and three types have been described (Table 5.1).

TYPE I IODOTHYRONINE 5'-DEIODINASE (IDI)

This enzyme is found in highest activity in the liver and kidney and its prime role is considered to be the supply of plasma T_3. IDI is a selenoprotein and enzyme activity is inhibited by gold thioglucose, iopanoic acid, and propylthiouracil (PTU). Both 5 and 5' monodeiodination reactions are catalyzed by IDI, and its activity is increased in hyperthyroidism (or administration of thyroid hormones) and decreased in hypothyroidism. In the thyroid the expression of IDI is under the control of TSH. IDI activity is decreased in nonthyroidal illness and after fasting or large drops in caloric intake with resultant decrease in both the production of T_3 from T_4 and the catabolism of reverse T_3. These changes in IDI activity result in the characteristic pattern of plasma thyroid hormone levels in illness—i.e., plasma T_3 is decreased and rT_3 increased (17).

TYPE II IODOTHYRONINE 5'-DEIODINASE (IDII)

Brain, brown adipose tissue (BAT), and pituitary contain the highest activities of IDII. This enzyme catalyzes only 5' monodeiodination, converting T_4 to T_3 or reverse T_3 to T_2. However, IDII makes little contribution to circulating T_3, with the possible exception of activity in BAT in the neonate. Thus the role of IDII is the local supply of T_3 in tissues that express the enzyme. The activity of IDII is unaffected by PTU at concentrations that inhibit IDI. Unlike IDI, its activity is decreased in hyperthyroidism or following administration of thyroid hormones and increased in hypothyroidism. In the pituitary the IDII is the major deiodinase, but mRNA for IDI has also been detected (21). This raises the possibility that different cell types in the pituitary show differential expression of the deiodinases. Intrapituitary 5' monodeiodination of T_4 appears to be an important regulator of TSH production and release, since at least 50% of T_3 bound to pituitary nuclear receptors in the pituitary is derived locally rather than from plasma T_3 (22). In BAT, IDII plays an important role in the control of thermogenesis (23). Following adrenergic stimulation of BAT through the $\alpha 1$ receptor, IDII activity increases with resultant increase in intracellular T_3 production, synthesis of the mitochondrial uncoupling protein, and thermogenesis. Although IDII has not been purified or cloned, the available evidence suggests that it is not a selenoenzyme, despite the fact that its activity is decreased in selenium deficiency (24,25).

TYPE III IODOTHYRONINE 5-DEIODINASE (IDIII)

IDIII is found in brain, skin, and placenta and can carry out only 5 monodeiodination, producing reverse T_3 from T_4 and T_2 from T_3. Under normal circumstances most of the circulatory reverse T_3 probably arises from IDIII and not IDI activity. IDIII activity is increased by hyperthyroidism, decreased by hypothyroidism, and unaffected by PTU. At present the selenium dependence of IDIII is unknown.

IDENTIFIATION OF TYPE I IODOTHYRONINE DEIODINASE AS A SELENOENZYME

IDI has proved to be extremely difficult to purify. In part, this is due to its location in cell membranes in low abundance, since it comprises, for example, <0.01% of hepatic microsomal protein in the rat. Additionally, the enzyme is labile when it is partially purified and binds tightly to the matrices of ion-exchange and affinity columns used for its purification (26). The first indication that IDI might be a selenoenzyme was the discovery of decreased hepatic T_3 production from T_4 in selenium-deficient rats. This IDI activity could not be restored by the addition of a variety of cofactors, such as pyridine nucleotides, thiols, and selenite (27). Thus the decrease in IDI activity was not mediated by changes in thiol levels, and selenium was not an essential cofactor *in vitro*; it was suggested therefore that selenium had to be present during the *de novo* synthesis of IDI. This was confirmed by the restoration of hepatic IDI activity in selenium-deficient rats when selenite was administered by intraperitoneal injection 3 days prior to sacrifice (28).

Although this evidence suggested that IDI was a selenoenzyme, Boada et al. claimed to have isolated a near-full-length cDNA clone for rat hepatic IDI with a predicted amino acid sequence that showed 99% identity with protein disulphide isomerase (PDI) (29). This prompted the suggestion that PDI and IDI were the same protein (29). However, there was no codon in the sequence to indicate selenocysteine incorporation. Using bromoacetyl [^{125}I]T$_3$ as an affinity label Schoenmakers et al. demonstrated the presence of two hepatic microsomal proteins with molecular mass 27 kDa and 55 kDa (30). By using IDI inhibitors, these proteins were identified as the substrate-binding subunit of IDI and as PDI, respectively. Further evidence for the nonidentity of IDI and PDI came from the demonstration that PDI activity and the affinity labelling of the 55-kDa hepatic microsomal protein were unaffected by selenium deficiency, whereas IDI activity and affinity labelling of the 27-kDa protein were both impaired (31).

The use of *in vivo* labelling with [^{75}Se]selenite and *in vitro* labelling with bromoacetyl [^{125}I]rT$_3$ provided conclusive evidence that IDI was a selenoenzyme (32). Following *in vivo* labelling with [^{75}Se]selenite, a partially purified rat liver microsomal fraction with IDI activity was found to contain only one ^{75}Se protein of molecular mass 27.5 kDa. This protein, which was identified by autoradiography following SDS/PAGE, could be labeled *in vitro* by a bromoacetyl [^{125}I]rT$_3$ affinity label.

Using similar techniques, Behne et al. showed that each substrate binding subunit of IDI probably contained one atom of selenium (33). Further confirmation of the role of selenium in IDI came with the cloning of the rat liver enzyme using a *Xenopus* oocyte expression system (21). The mRNA for a protein with IDI activity contained an in-frame UGA codon which, although normally a stop codon, can code for the amino acid selenocysteine. Selenocysteine had previously been detected at the active site of glutathione peroxidase (7). The similarities between IDI and glutathione peroxidase in their extreme sensitivity to iodoacetate inhibition and the assumption that they contained a hyperactive sulfur had also indicated that IDI contains selenocysteine at the active site. The recognition of UGA as a codon for selenocysteine in IDI relies on sequences in the 3' untranslated region of the mRNA, which consists of about 200 nucleotides and is found in both rat and human IDI mRNAs (34). A mutant of IDI, which has cysteine at the active site, does not require this untranslated region for expression. The mutant enzyme has very low activity and is insensitive to PTU inhibition (21,34). The untranslated region is predicted to have a stem-loop structure and any mutation within this region can decrease or prevent translation of the message to give IDI activity.

Decreases in IDI activity and protein mass occur in severe selenium deficiency, and both are modulated within the normal range of dietary selenium intakes. For example, when the dietary selenium content in rats was decreased from 0.1 mg/kg to 0.045 mg/kg, IDI activity and protein were decreased by approximately 50% (Arthur, Nicol, and Beckett, unpublished observations).

THYROIDAL DEIODINATION OF T_4

The thyroid of the rat expresses high 5′-deiodinase activity that appears from substrate specificity and inhibitor studies and from the detection of IDI mRNA to be associated with the type I enzyme (19,21). However, unlike hepatic IDI, thyroidal IDI is stimulated by TSH or the TSH-stimulating immunoglobulins that cause Graves' disease, probably through increased synthesis that is signalled by the cyclic-AMP second-messenger system (35).

Although several animal species have IDI activity in the liver, there are considerable species differences in thyroidal IDI activity. The rat

TABLE 5.2. Activities of IDI in the thyroids and livers of various species (results expressed as percentages of the activity found in rat thyroid, which was the tissue with the most active IDI.

Species	Thyroid	Liver
Rat	100	81
Guinea pig	22	ND
Mouse	6	ND
Human	4	34
Goat	<1	81
Cattle	<1	82
Rabbit	<1	ND
Sheep	<1	13
Pig	<1	22
Llama	<1	9
Deer	<1	ND

ND denotes not determined.

thyroid has the highest IDI activity, with guinea pig, mouse, and human also demonstrating significant activity. In contrast, thyroidal IDI activity in goat, cattle, rabbit, sheep, pig, llama, and deer is very low or undetectable (Table 5.2).

Thus in many animal species intrathyroidal deiodination of T_4 cannot provide a source of T_3 but in man it is possible that this pathway of T_3 production is significant. When human thyrocytes are grown in culture, they produce T_3 but not T_4 and it has been suggested that T_3 arises from release of preformed intracellular hormone (36). However, T_3 production from human thyrocytes can be stimulated by TSH and this stimulation is unaffected by methimazole, a compound that inhibits *de novo* thyroid hormone synthesis (37). T_3 production in the cultured thyrocytes is inhibited by iopanoic acid and propylthiouracil (inhibitors of IDI). This indicates that in primary culture, T_3 production in human thyrocytes arises from deiodination of T_4 and not from release of preformed T_3. In contrast, sheep thyrocytes grown in primary culture synthesize T_3 and T_4 *de novo* and thus synthesis can be inhibited by methimazole. However, since sheep thyrocytes do not have significant IDI activity, synthesis of T_3 is not affected by iopanoic acid, although PTU does inhibit since it also inhibits *de novo* synthesis (Table 5.3). The concentration of selenium in the medium has no effect on T_3 production by human thyrocytes (37). Similarly, in the rat, consumption of selenium-deficient diets for 6 weeks did not decrease thyroidal IDI activity (37). These data are consistent with the finding that the brain and

TABLE 5.3. Effect of inhibitors of thyroid hormone synthesis and IDI on T_3 production by human and sheep thyrocytes grown in primary culture: T_3 production was determined in the presence of 1 mU/L TSH and 10 μmol/L KI, which produces maximal T_3 production rates in both systems.

	Mean T_3 production (pmol/5 days)	
	Sheep	Human
No inhibitor	4.1	2.2
Methimazole (10^{-3} M)	2.5*	2.4
Propylthiouracil (10^{-3} M)	2.1**	1.4*
Iopanoic acid (10^{-4} M)	3.8	0.6**

*$P < 0.05$ significant decreases in activity from activities with no inhibitor.
**$P < 0.001$.

endocrine tissues (including the thyroid) can conserve selenium far more efficiently than liver and kidney in selenium deficiency (38). Thus intrathyroid deiodination of T_4 may provide a significant source of plasma T_3 in the rat and man, particularly when IDI activity in liver and kidney is markedly inhibited because of selenium deficiency.

TYPE II DEIODINASE

Decreases in IDII activity in the brain and BAT tissue of selenium-deficient rats indicated that this deiodinase may also be a seleno-protein or have a selenium-containing cofactor essential for activity (25). However, the decrease in activity in selenium deficiency is much less than that of IDI and the enzyme is much less sensitive to inhibition by iodoacetate than is IDI or selenium-containing glutathione peroxidase (39,40). Initial indications that IDII is not a selenoprotein came from experiments with glial cells in culture. Although a 27.5-kDa protein could be labelled with ^{75}Se in kidney cells that contained IDI activity, in glial cells a comparable protein that was identified by affinity labelling as IDII could not be labelled with ^{75}Se (24). Kinetic studies showing that IDII was much less sensitive than IDI to inhibition by gold thioglucose and PTU provided further evidence that IDII was not a selenoprotein (41). The decrease in IDII activity in brain, pituitary, and BAT of selenium-deficient rats is a reflection of the suppression of enzyme activity by the elevated T_4 concentrations. Thus in thyroidectomized rats, which have undetectable levels of circulating T_4, IDI activity in liver and kidney is markedly diminished by selenium deficiency whereas brain and pituitary IDII is unaffected by selenium. However IDII activity is increased as a result of the hypothyroidism (42).

THE EFFECT OF SELENIUM DEFICIENCY ON THYROID HORMONE METABOLISM

PLASMA AND TISSUE THYROID HORMONE LEVELS

The first indications for a role of selenium in thyroid hormone meta-bolism came with the observations that plasma total T_4 was increased and total T_3 decreased in selenium-deficient rats and cattle and that these changes could be normalized in the rat by intraperitoneal administration of 200 µg of Se/kg body weight as selenite (12,25, 27,28,43). Plasma free T_4 concentrations are increased in selenium deficiency, indicating that the changes in total thyroid hormones occur as a result of alterations in hormone production and not as a result of differences in plasma thyroid-hormone-binding proteins (42,44). The concentration of plasma reverse T_3 is unaffected by selenium deficiency (27), indicating that the effects of selenium deficiency on thyroid hormone metabolism are not a result of poor nutrition, which leads to increased concentrations of reverse T_3 (19). The possibility that the abnormal thyroid hormone metabolism resulted from increased peroxidative damage was excluded since vitamin E deficiency had no effect on plasma T_4 and T_3 (25). Similar to the changes in plasma thyroid hormones, hepatic T_3 is decreased and T_4 is increased by selenium deficiency (45).

Plasma and Pituitary Thyrotropin

Selenium deficiency for periods of up to 6 weeks in rats causes small increases in plasma TSH but has no significant effect on pituitary TSH or plasma growth hormone (44). Under normal circumstances an increase in plasma T_4 should suppress plasma TSH to undetectable concentrations. Since this does not occur in selenium deficiency, pituitary IDII may be inhibited, which, in turn, may decrease pituitary intracellular T_3.

Tissue Deiodinase Activity

In rat liver, selenium deficiency decreases both the 5 and 5' deiodination reactions catalyzed by IDI (45). In contrast, IDI activity is not decreased in the thyroid of selenium-deficient rats. The activity of IDII in BAT, brain, and pituitary is also lowered in selenium deficiency (25,46), but this is a response to increased plasma T_4 concentrations and not a direct effect of deficiency (42). As with plasma thyroid hormone levels, the abnormalities in IDI and IDII activity can be normalized by selenium repletion of selenium-deficient rats (25,28,44).

THYROID CHANGES

In the rat selenium deficiency causes decreases in thyroidal T_4, T_3, and iodine concentrations (44). At least two possible mechanisms could account for these changes. First, an increase in plasma TSH will stimulate the synthesis and release of thyroidal T_4 and T_3. Second, if selenium deficiency causes a decrease in thyroidal glutathione peroxidase activity, this may lead to an increase in intracellular hydrogen peroxide due to impaired hydrogen peroxide metabolism. Since hydrogen peroxide supply is thought to be a rate-limiting step in thyroid hormone synthesis (19), an increase in intracellular hydrogen peroxide could lead to increased thyroid hormone synthesis and release and thus to thyroidal depletion of iodine and hormone. The effects of selenium deficiency on thyroidal glutathione peroxidase, T_4, T_3, and iodine can be reversed after 5 days by a single intraperitoneal injection of $10\,\mu g\,Se/kg$ body weight as selenite, while a dose of $200\,\mu g\,Se/kg$ is required to reverse the effects of selenium deficiency on plasma thyroid hormone levels and hepatic IDI and glutathione peroxidase (28,44). This again emphasizes the diversion of limited supplies of selenium to the thyroid (38).

INTERRELATIONSHIPS BETWEEN CHANGES IN THYROID HORMONE METABOLISM AND SELENIUM DEFICIENCY

In summary, selenium deficiency decreases both IDI and IDII activities. Since 5 and 5' monodeiodination reactions of IDI are impaired by selenium deficiency, both the production of T_3 from T_4 and the catabolism of T_3 to T_2 are decreased. Thus plasma T_3 concentrations are decreased by only $10-20\%$ in selenium deficiency, despite hepatic IDI activity being less than 10% of normal. Inhibition of pituitary IDII causes increased plasma TSH, which stabilizes thyroidal T_3 production, which also tends to maintain plasma T_3 levels. Plasma T_4 increases as a result of impaired peripheral deiodination and also as a result of increased thyroidal production driven by increased TSH. The overall effect is that, on average, plasma T_4 is increased by approximately 30%, while plasma T_3; thyroidal T_4, T_3, and iodine are

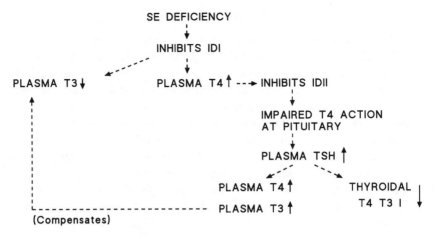

FIGURE 5.2. Changes in plasma and thyroidal hormones in selenium deficiency.

decreased by approximately 10–20%. These changes are summarized in Figure 5.2.

THE EFFECTS OF COMBINED IODINE AND SELENIUM DEFICIENCY ON THYROID HORMONE METABOLISM

Iodine deficiency remains one of the world's most serious public-health problems. Approximately one billion people live in iodine-deficient areas. Iodine deficiency is associated with hypothyroidism and goiter and severe iodine deficiency may produce cretinism (47). Iodine deficiency is accompanied by a decline in plasma T_4 but plasma T_3 is usually maintained unless the iodine deficiency is particularly severe. The fall in plasma T_4 leads to an increase in plasma TSH and this provides an important compensatory response, since the high TSH leads to increased iodide trapping by the thyroid and also increased thyroidal synthesis of T_3. Maintenance of plasma T_3 at the expense of T_4 is, however, disadvantageous to the fetus since the early stages of normal brain development are thought to require an adequate supply of maternal T_4—not of T_3 (48).

Animal Experiments

Observations that selenium status can influence thyroidal iodine levels (44), together with the suggestion that selenium deficiency is a factor in the pathogenesis of myxedematous endemic cretinism (49), led to the study of the effects of combined iodine and selenium deficiency on thyroid hormone metabolism in the rat (46,50). Rats with combined selenium and iodine deficiency had lower plasma, thyroid, and hepatic T_4 and higher plasma TSH than animals deficient only in iodine. Total thyroidal iodine and T_3 were also lower in rats with selenium and iodine deficiency than in those with iodine deficiency. Plasma T_3 was unaffected by iodine deficiency or combined selenium and iodine deficiency but hepatic T_3 levels were increased in both these dietary groups (46).

Both hepatic 5- and 5'-IDI activities and pituitary IDII activity were decreased in selenium and iodine-deficient rats compared with iodine-deficient animals. In contrast, IDII activity in the brain was higher in animals deficient in both trace elements than in control animals receiving both trace elements or in animals deficient in iodine alone (46). Thyroid weight was increased by iodine deficiency but the glands in rats with combined selenium and iodine deficiency were even heavier, their weight being two-and-a-half times that in control animals (46). Thus rats with combined selenium and iodine deficiency are able to maintain plasma and hepatic T_3 levels, despite a marked decrease in peripheral T_3 production (Fig. 5.2). The higher TSH levels, the higher brain IDII activities, the increased thyroid weight, and lower plasma and hepatic total T_4 concentrations indicate, however, that there is a greater hypothyroid stress in combined selenium and iodine deficiencies than in iodine deficiency alone. Although cerebral IDII activity is higher in the dual-deficient animal, the substrate, T_4, is strictly limited. The lower plasma T_4 levels found in dual deficiency may thus be particularly significant to the fetus, since normal brain development depends on maternal T_4.

Studies in Humans

Following the observation that in some areas of Zaire low serum selenium and plasma glutathione peroxidase activity were associated with a high incidence of endemic goiter and cretinism in children

(49,51), the effect of selenium supplementation for 2 months on thyroid hormone metabolism was studied. This did not affect plasma total T_3 and free T_4 but total T_4 fell and plasma TSH increased (52). These observations led to the suggestion that selenium deficiency could protect the population and fetus against the effects of iodine deficiency and brain damage, but this needs further confirmation. For example, it is only the free T_4 fraction and not total T_4 that is thought to be available to the brain, yet free T_4 was unaltered by selenium supplementation. These human supplementation trials are not directly comparable with the selenium/iodine-deficiency animal experiments described above, since it is only in the former that selenium and iodine deficiency also occurred *in utero*, with consequent possible effects on fetal growth and development. Nonetheless, it would seem to be inadvisable to provide only selenium supplementation to patients with both selenium and iodine deficiency where thyroid destruction may have already occurred. Such a regimen would give priority of the limited T_4 supply to tissues expressing IDI, thus depriving the brain and other critical sites. Therefore a supply of T_4 would also have to be provided to selenium- and iodine-deficient subjects before or at the same time as a selenium supplement. At present there is a dearth of reliable data describing the thyroid status of human subjects living in low-selenium areas.

BIOLOGICAL CONSEQUENCES OF ALTERED THYROID HORMONE METABOLISM IN SELENIUM DEFICIENCY

Since selenium deficiency leads to changes in thyroid hormone metabolism as well as in glutathione peroxidase activity, it is possible that certain of the biochemical and biological changes that occur in selenium deficiency when vitamin E supplies are adequate may be a consequence of altered thyroid status. However, although selenium deficiency leads to impaired conversion of T_4 to T_3 and thus to potentially marked hypothyroidism, this can be ameliorated by compensatory factors, such as diminished catabolism of T_3 to T_2, increased thyroidal T_3 production, and recycling of T_3 (45,53).

LIVER

Selenium deficiency affects the expression of several hepatic enzymes and also leads to approximately 20% diminution in hepatic T_3 content (12–16,45). However, tissue hypothyroidism does not appear to be responsible for the changes in enzyme expression. For example, selenium deficiency increases hepatic cytosolic malic enzyme and mitochondrial α-glycerophosphate dehydrogenase activities, which are normally decreased in hypothyroidism (54). The expression of glutathione-S-transferase (GST) is increased in both selenium deficiency and hypothyroidism but apparently by different mechanisms. GST mRNA and thus GST expression is increased in selenium deficiency but decreased in hypothyroidism. The increased levels of hepatic GST in hypothyroidism appear to result from a prolonged tissue half-life of the enzymes (45). Current evidence suggests that tissue hypothyroidism does not occur in the liver (54), but impaired catabolism of T_3 cannot be eliminated as a cause of some of the hepatic enzyme changes in selenium deficiency.

PITUITARY

As well as effects on TSH production, discussed above, selenium deficiency decreases pituitary growth-hormone production in the rat, probably because growth-hormone synthesis is dependent on T_3 (55) in the rat. Ewan (56) reported a decrease in pituitary growth hormone after prolonged selenium deficiency that was thought to result from changes in food intake (56). However, pituitary growth-hormone levels can decrease in selenium deficiency before there is any alteration in food intake or growth restriction, and thus these hormonal changes may be the basis of the growth retardation caused by prolonged selenium deficiency (15). Golstein et al. (57) have also reported changes in thyroid-hormone metabolism and growth abnormalities in rats maintained on a selenium-deficient diet. However, their diets did not contain added vitamin E and the results are therefore not directly comparable with ours (57).

BROWN ADIPOSE TISSUE

BAT IDII activity is of particular importance for the control of thermogenesis in neonatal animals and is induced by cold stress. This induction of IDII activity by cold stress is impaired in selenium-deficient animals (58). Levels of uncoupling protein are also decreased in BAT from rats deficient in both selenium and iodine (59). It thus seems likely that selenium-deficient animals have an impaired physiological response to cold stress and that this is mediated through impaired thyroid-hormone metabolism.

The Effect of Thyroid Status on Apparent Selenium Status as Assessed by Blood Measurements

In addition to these effects of selenium deficiency on thyroid-hormone metabolism there is evidence that selenium metabolism is disrupted in patients with abnormal thyroid-hormone metabolism. For example, in a study of 106 patients presenting to a thyroid clinic, glutathione peroxidase activity and selenium concentrations in blood were lower in subjects with hyperthyroidism than in euthyroid patients. Normal levels were restored when the hyperthyroidism was successfully treated (60). Thus hyperthyroidism results in a lowering of blood selenium and glutathione peroxidase rather than the converse—i.e., low selenium status does not predispose to hyperthyroidism. The apparent decrease in selenium status in hyperthyroidism probably arises from increased turnover of selenoproteins in blood, but this has yet to be confirmed.

Conclusion

Selenium plays a crucial role in the control of thyroid hormone homeostasis. In selenium deficiency, compensatory mechanisms, particularly increased thyroidal T_3 production, operate to ameliorate the disturbances in thyroid hormone metabolism, but if thyroidal hormone production is also impaired—e.g., as is found in combined selenium and iodine deficiency—then a hypothyroid stress may occur. The combined action of selenium and iodine in preventing abnormal thyroid hormone metabolism is analogous to the synergistic effects of selenium and vitamin E in protecting against oxidative damage in the cell.

REFERENCES

1. Schwarz, K, Foltz, CM. Selenium as an integral part of factor 3 against dietary necrotic liver degeneration. J Am Chem Soc 79:3292–3293; 1957.

2. Combs, GF, Combs, SB. The Role of Selenium in Nutrition. New York: Academic Press; 1986.

3. Rotruck, JT, Pope, AL, Ganther, HE, Swanson, AB, Hafeman, DG, Hoekstra, WG. Selenium: biochemical role as a component of glutathione peroxidase. Science 179:588–590; 1973.

4. Hoekstra, WG. Biochemical function of selenium and its relation to vitamin E. Fed Proc 34:2083–2089; 1975.

5. Takahashi, K, Avissar, N, Whitin, JC, Cohen, HJ. Purification and characterization of human plasma glutathione peroxidase: a selenoglycoprotein distinct from the known cellular enzyme. Arch Biochem Biophys 256:677–686; 1987.

6. Avissar, N, Whitin, JC, Allen, PZ, Wagner, DD, Liegey, P, Cohen, HJ. Plasma selenium-dependent glutathione peroxidase—cell of origin and secretion. J Biol Chem 264:15850–15855; 1989.

7. Sunde, RA. Molecular biology of selenoproteins. Ann Rev Nutr 10: 451–474; 1990.

8. Ursini, F, Maiorino, M, Gregolin, C. The seleno-enzyme phospholipid hydroperoxide glutathione peroxidase. Biochim Biophys Acta 839:62–70; 1985.

9. Zhang, LP, Maiorino, M, Roveri, A, Ursini, F. Phospholipid hydroperoxide glutathione peroxidase—specific activity in tissues of rats of different age and comparison with other glutathione peroxidases. Biochim Biophys Acta 1006:140–143; 1989.

10. Weitzel, F, Ursini, F, Wendel, A. Phospholipid hydroperoxide glutathione peroxidase in various mouse organs during selenium deficiency and repletion. Biochim Biophys Acta 1036:88–94; 1990.

11. Burk, RF. Biological activity of selenium. Ann Rev Nutr 3:53–70; 1983.

12. Arthur, JR, Nicol, F, Boyne, R, Allen, KGD, Hayes, JD, Beckett, GJ. Old and new roles for selenium. In: Hemphill, DD ed. Trace Substances in environmental Health XXI. Columbia, MD, University of Missouri Press; 1987, pp 487–498.

13. Arthur, JR, Morrice, PC, Nicol, F, Beddows, SE, Boyd, R, Hayes, JD, Beckett, GJ. The effects of selenium and copper deficiencies on glutathione S-transferase and glutathione peroxidase in rat liver. Biochem J 248:539–544; 1987.

14. Reiter, R, Wendel, A. Selenium and drug metabolism. II. Independence of glutathione peroxidase and reversibility of hepatic enzyme modulations in deficient mice. Biochem Pharmacol 33:1923–1928; 1984.

15. Hill, KE, Burk, RF, Lane, JM. Effect of selenium depletion and repletion on plasma glutathione and glutathione dependent enzymes in the rat. J Nutr 117:99–104; 1987.

16. Burk, RF. Recent developments in trace element metabolism and function: newer roles of selenium in nutrition. J Nutr 119:1051–1054; 1989.

17. Leonard, JL, Visser, TJ. Biochemistry of deiodination. In: Hennemann, G, ed. Thyroid Hormone Metabolism. New York: Marcel Dekker; 1986, pp.189–222.

18. Hennemann, G. Thyroid hormone deiodination in healthy man. In: Hennemann, G, ed. Thyroid Hormone Metabolism. New York: Marcel Dekker; 1986, pp. 277–295.

19. Taurog, AG. Hormone synthesis: Thyroid iodine metabolism. In: Braverman, LE, Utiger, RD, eds. Werner and Ingbar's The Thyroid. New York: JB Lippincott; 1992, pp. 51–98.

20. Toft, AD. Thyrotropin: Assay, secretory physiology and testing of regulation. In: Braverman, LE, Utiger, RD, eds. Werner and Ingbar's The Thyroid. New York: JB Lippincott; 1992, pp. 287–305.

21. Berry, MJ, Banu, L, Larsen, PR. Type-I iodothyronine deiodinase is a selenocysteine-containing enzyme. Nature 349:438–440; 1991.

22. Silva, JE, Larsen, PR. Regulation of thyroid hormone expression at the pre-receptor and receptor levels. In: Hennemann, G, ed. Thyroid Hormone Metabolism. New York: Marcel Dekker; 1986, pp 441–500.

23. Silva, JE, Larsen, PR. Adrenergic activation of triiodothyronine production in brown adipose tissue. Nature 305:712–713; 1983.

24. Safran, M, Farwell, AP, Leonard, JL. Evidence that type II 5'-deiodinase is not a selenoprotein. J Biol Chem 266:13477–13480; 1991.

25. Beckett, GJ, MacDougall, DA, Nicol, F, Arthur, JR. Inhibition of type I and type II iodothyronine deiodinase activity in rat liver, kidney and brain produced by selenium deficiency. Biochem J 259:887–892; 1989.

26. Mol, JA, Van Den Berg, TP, Visser, TJ. Partial purification of the rat liver iodothyronine deiodinase I. Solubilization and ion-exchange chromatography. Mol Cell Endocrinol 55:149–157; 1988.

27. Beckett, GJ, Beddows, SE, Morrice, PC, Nicol, F, Arthur, JR. Inhibition of hepatic deiodination of thyroxine caused by selenium deficiency in rats. Biochem J 248:443–447; 1987.

28. Arthur, JR, Nicol, F, Hutchinson, AR, Beckett, GJ. The effects of selenium depletion and repletion on the metabolism of thyroid hormones in the rat. J Inorg Biochem 39:101–108; 1990.

29. Boada, RJ, Campbell, DA, Chopra, IJ. Nucleotide sequence of rat liver iodothyronine 5-monodeiodinase (5 MD): its identity with protein disulphide isomerase. Biochem Biophys Res Commun 155:1297–1304; 1988.

30. Schoenmakers, RB, Pigmans, IGAJ, Hawkins, HC, Freedman, RB, Visser, TJ. Rat liver type I iodothyronine deiodinase is not identical to protein disulfide isomerase. Biochem Biophys Res Commun 162:857–868; 1989.

31. Arthur, JR, Nicol, F, Grant, E, Beckett, GJ. The effects of selenium deficiency on hepatic type-I iodothyronine deiodinase and protein disulphide-isomerase assessed by activity measurements and affinity labelling. Biochem J 274:297–300; 1991.

32. Arthur, JR, Nicol, F, Beckett, GJ. Hepatic iodothyronine deiodinase: the role of selenium. Biochem J 272:537–540; 1990.

33. Behne, D, Kyriakopoulos, A, Meinhold, H, Köhrle, J. Identification of type-I iodothyronine 5-deiodinase as a selenoenzyme. Biochem Biophys Res Commun 173:1143–1149; 1990.

34. Berry, MJ, Banu, L, Chen, Y, Mandel, SJ, Kieffer, JD, Harney, JW, Larsen, PR. Recognition of UGA as a selenocysteine codon in type I deiodinase requires sequences in the 3' untranslated region. Nature 353:273–276; 1991.

35. Köhrle, J. Thyrotropin (TSH) action on thyroid hormone deiodination and secretion. One aspect of thyrotropin regulation of thyroid cell biology. Horm Metab Res (Suppl) 23:18–28; 1990.

36. Ollis, CA, Fowles, A, Brown, BL, Munro, DS, Tomlinson, S. Human thyroid cells in monolayer retain the ability to secrete triiodothyronine in response to thyrotropin. J Endocrinol 104:285–290; 1985.

37. Beech, S, Walker, SW, Arthur, JR, Dorrance, A, Nicol, F, Beckett, GJ. The effect of selenium deficiency on iodothyronine deiodinase in cultured human thyrocytes and rat thyroid homogenates. J Endocrinol (Suppl) 132:81; 1992.

38. Behne, D, Hilmert, H, Scheid, S, Gessner, H, Elger, W. Evidence for specific selenium target tissues and new biologically important selenoproteins. Biochim Biophys Acta 966:12–21; 1988.

39. Arthur, JR. The role of selenium in thyroid hormone metabolism. Can J Physiol Pharmacol 69:1648–1652; 1991.

40. Berry, MJ, Kieffer, JD, Harney, JW, Larsen, PR. Selenocysteine confers the biochemical properties characteristic of the type I iodothyronine deiodinase. J Biol Chem 266:14155–14158; 1991.

41. Berry, MJ, Kieffer, JD, Larsen, PR. Evidence that cysteine not seleno-cysteine is at the catalytic site of type II iodothyronine deiodinase. Endocrinology 129:550–552; 1991.

42. Chanoine, JP, Safran, M, Farwell, AP, Tranter, P, Ekenbarger, D, Dubord, S, Alex, S, Stone, S, Arthur, JR, Beckett, GJ, Braverman, LE, Leonard, JL. Selenium deficiency and type II 5'-deiodinase regulation in the euthyroid and hypothyroid rat: evidence of a direct effect of thyroxine. Endocrinology 131:479–484; 1992.

43. Arthur, JR, Morrice, PC, Beckett, GJ. Thyroid hormone concentrations in selenium-deficient and selenium-sufficient cattle. Res Vet Sci 46:226–230; 1988.

44. Arthur, JR, Nicol, F, Rae, PWH, Beckett, GJ. Effects of selenium deficiency on the thyroid gland and on plasma and pituitary thyrotropin and growth hormone concentrations in the rat. Clin Chem Enzyme Commun. 3:209–214; 1990.

45. Beckett, GJ, Russell, A, Nicol, F, Sahu, P, Wolf, CR, Arthur, JR. Effect of selenium deficiency on hepatic type I 5-iodothyronine deiodinase activity and hepatic thyroid hormone levels in the rat. Biochem J 282:483–486; 1992.

46. Beckett, GJ, Nicol, F, Rae, PWH, Beech, S, Guo, Y, Arthur, JR. Effects of combined iodine and selenium deficiency on thyroid hormone metabolism in the rat. Am J Clin Nutr (Suppl) 57:2405–2435; 1993.

47. Hetzel, BS, Mano, MT. A review of experimental studies of iodine deficiency during fetal development. J Nutr 119:145–151; 1989.

48. Silva, JE. The responses of the body to iodine deficiency and hy-pothyroxinaemia: a source of variability in the clinical presentation of endemic goitre and cretinism. In: Medeiros-Neto, G, Maciel, RMB, Halpern, A, eds. Iodine Deficiency Disorders and Congenital Hypo-thyroidism. Sao Paulo: Ach; 1985 pp. 80–88.

49. Goyens, P, Golstein, J, Nsombola, B, Vis, H, Dumont, JE. Selenium deficiency as a possible factor in the pathogenesis of myxoedematous cretinism. Acta Endocrinol 114:497–502; 1987.

50. Arthur, JR, Nicol, F, Rae, PWH, Beckett, GJ. Effects of combined selenium and iodine deficiencies on the thyroid gland of the rat. J Endocrinol (Suppl) 124:240; 1990.

51. Vanderpas, JB, Contempre, B, Duale, NL, Goossens, W, Bebe, N, Thorpe, R, Ntambue, K, Dumont, J, Thilly, CH, Diplock, AT. Iodine and selenium deficiency associated with cretinism in Northern Zaire. Am J Clin Nutr 52:1087–1093; 1990.

52. Contempre, B, Dumont, JE, Ngo, B, Thilly, CH, Diplock, AT, Vander-pas, J. Effect of selenium supplementation in hypothyroid subjects of an

iodine and selenium deficient area: the possible danger of indiscriminate supplementation of iodine-deficient subjects with selenium. J Clin Endocrinol Metab 73:213–215; 1991.

53. Chanoine, J-P, Safran, M, Farwell, AP, Dubord, S, Alex, S, Stone, S, Arthur, JR, Braverman, LE, Leonard, JL. Effects of selenium deficiency on thyroid hormone economy in rats. Endocrinology 131:1787–1792; 1992.

54. Beckett, GJ, Nicol, F, Proudfoot, D, Dyson, K, Loucaides, G, Arthur, JR. The changes in hepatic enzyme expression caused by selenium deficiency and hypothyroidism in rats are caused by independent mechanisms. Biochem J 266:743–747; 1990.

55. Koenig, RJ, Brent, GA, Warne, RL, Larsen, PR, Moore, DD. Thyroid hormone receptor binds to a site in the rat growth hormone promotor required for induction by thyroid hormone. Proc Natl Acad Sci USA 84:5670–5674; 1987.

56. Ewan, RC. Effect of selenium on rat growth, growth hormone and diet utilization. J Nutr 106:702–709; 1976.

57. Golstein, J, Corvilain, B, Lamy, F, Paquer, D, Dumont, JE. Effects of a selenium deficient diet on thyroid function of normal and perchlorate treated rats. Acta Endocrinol 118:495–502; 1988.

58. Arthur, JR, Nicol, F, Beckett, GJ, Trayhurn, P. Impairment of iodothyronine 5'-deiodinase activity in brown adipose tissue and its acute stimulation by cold in selenium deficiency. Can J Physiol Pharmacol 69:782–785; 1991.

59. Geloen, A, Arthur, JR, Beckett, GJ, Trayhurn, P. Effect of selenium and iodine deficiency on the level of uncoupling protein in brown adipose tissue of rats. Biochem Soc Trans 18:1269–1270; 1990.

60. Beckett, GJ, Peterson, FE, Choudhury, K, Rae, PWH, Nicol, F, Wu, PS-C, Toft, AD, Smith, AF, Arthur, JR. Inter-relationships between selenium and thyroid hormone metabolism in rat and man. Trace Elem Elect Health Dis 5:265–267; 1992.

Chapter 6

Selenoprotein P— An Extracellular Protein Containing Multiple Selenocysteines

KRISTINA E. HILL AND RAYMOND F. BURK

Selenoprotein P can be traced to reports in the early 1970s that demonstrated ^{75}Se incorporation into a plasma protein in the rat (Millar, 1972; Burk, 1973). Later Herrman (1977) showed that this plasma protein was distinct from glutathione peroxidase. It was referred to as selenoprotein P by Tappel's group because of its plasma location (Motsenbocker and Tappel, 1982) and as ^{75}Se-P by our group because of its incorporation of [75]Se (Burk and Gregory, 1982). All workers have now adopted the name of selenoprotein P because it has been shown to be a selenoprotein and it is present in plasma. A further name change will be necessary when its function is established.

CHARACTERIZATION OF SELENOPROTEIN P

PURIFICATION

The purification of selenoprotein P required the use of immunoaffinity chromatography (Yang et al., 1987). Efforts using conventional methods yielded preparations that were only partially pure (Motchnik and Tappel, 1989). A mouse was injected with a partially pure preparation and serum was monitored for antibodies to selenoprotein P by radioimmunoprecipitation. After antibody was detected, hybridomas were produced by fusion of spleen cells with myeloma cells. Screening of the hybridomas was carried out using ^{75}Se-labeled selenoprotein P in plasma. With this technique two hybridomas were isolated. Both produce monoclonal antibodies that precipitate native selenoprotein P (Yang et al., 1987; Read et al., 1990). These antibodies were used for a radioimmunoassay and to make an immunoaffinity column for purification. The first purification scheme employed an Affi-Gel Blue step before the immunoaffinity column. It achieved a 1,270-fold purification with a yield of 11%. The Affi-Gel Blue step can be deleted if care is taken not to overload the immunoaffinity column, although a second immunoaffinity column step has sometimes been required (Read et al., 1990).

GLYCOSYLATION, AMINO ACID COMPOSITION, AND SELENIUM CONTENT

Purified selenoprotein P was estimated to have a size of 57 kDa from its migration on sodium dodecyl sulfate–polyacrylamide gel electrophoresis (Yang et al., 1987). It stained with dansyl hydrazine−periodic acid, indicating that it contained carbohydrate. After enzymatic deglycosylation, it migrated as two Coomassie Blue−staining bands with sizes of 48 and 43 kDa (Read et al., 1990). The latter band was almost devoid of carbohydrate staining. This indicates that selenoprotein P is a glycoprotein with a peptide weight of 43 kDa or less and suggests that there is microheterogeneity of the glycosylation.

Amino acid analysis was carried out after protection of thiols and selenols by carboxymethylation (Read et al., 1990). The protein was studied in the form isolated as well as in the form produced by treatment with reducing agents. In both cases 7.5 selenocysteine residues were detected per 43-kDa peptide. This accounts for all the selenium found by direct analysis and indicates that many selenocysteine residues are present in each molecule of selenoprotein P. Moreover, it suggests that they are all in the reduced form. Reduction of the protein increased the half-cystine residues detected from approximately eight to 17. This suggests that approximately 10 cysteine residues are involved in disulfide bridges and the remaining seven are in thiol form. Limited peptide analysis has been carried out. Its results indicate that selenium-rich regions exist in selenoprotein P (Read et al., 1990).

MOLECULAR BIOLOGY

cDNAs ISOLATED FROM RAT LIVER, HUMAN LIVER, AND HUMAN HEART LIBRARIES

Using a polyclonal antibody preparation, a partial cDNA was isolated and cloned from a rat liver expression library. The cDNA was verified as a selenoprotein P clone by comparing the amino acid sequence of a peptide from the purified protein with the amino acid sequence implied by the cDNA (Hill et al., 1991). A full-length clone was obtained from a λZAP II rat liver library by screening with the partial cDNA clone. The deduced amino acid sequence of the full-length cDNA was partially confirmed by comparison with amino acid sequences of several peptides obtained from purified selenoprotein P. The rat cDNA was then used to obtain a cDNA clone from a human liver library. The human liver cDNA was used to obtain a human

TABLE 6.1. Rat and human selenoprotein P (deduced)[1].

	Amino acids in secreted protein	Peptide weight (daltons)	N-glycosylation sites[2]	Selenocysteine residues[3]
Rat	366	41,052	5	10
Human	362	41,229	6	10

[1] cDNAs from rat and human sources encode 19 amino acid signal peptides. This table does not include these peptides that are not present in the mature protein.
[2] Two of these sites are conserved.
[3] Eight of these residues occupy identical positions in both sequences.

heart cDNA clone (Hill et al., 1993). The human cDNAs from the two organ sources were essentially identical.

Comparison of the cDNAs from rat and human sources reveals many similarities. In the open reading frame, the nucleotide sequences are 69% identical and the deduced amino acid sequences are 72% identical. A 19 amino acid signal peptide is encoded, consistent with the fact that the protein is secreted. This signal peptide is encoded also in the heart cDNA, indicating that the liver is not the only organ that secretes selenoprotein P. Ten TGA codons, which code for selenocysteine, were found in the open reading frame of each cDNA (Hill et al., 1993).

Northern analysis indicates that the size of selenoprotein P mRNA is 2.2 kilobases in rat and in human tissues (Hill et al., 1992, 1993). The mRNA was detected in rat liver, kidney, heart, lung, brain, and testis.[1] In human material it was demonstrated in liver and kidney, the only tissues that were studied (Hill et al., 1993). Thus seleno-protein P is synthesized by many tissues.

DEDUCED AMINO ACID SEQUENCES OF RAT AND HUMAN PROTEINS

Mature selenoprotein P is similar between the two species in size and in number of amino acids. It contains glycosylation sites in both (Table 6.1). There is a preponderance of positively charged amino acids, which could explain the binding of selenoprotein P to heparin (Herrman, 1977).

The deduced amino acid sequence from each species contains 10 selenocysteine residues. Eight are in identical positions within the

[1] K.E. Hill, P.R. Lyons, and R.F. Burk, unpublished observations.

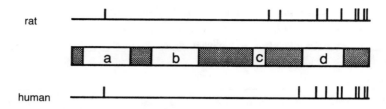

FIGURE 6.1. Comparison of deduced amino acid sequences of rat and human selenoprotein Ps. The 19 amino acid signal peptides are not represented. Positions of selenocysteine residues are indicated by vertical lines. The bar indicates four areas of higher than average (72%) conservation of sequence: a = 80%, b = 95%, c = 100%, d = 83%.

sequences (Fig. 6.1). A conserved selenocysteine is in amino acid position 40 and the rest are clustered in the carboxyl terminus of the protein. Four are in the last 15 amino acids. There is evidence that selenoprotein P is present in plasma of selenium-deficient rats in a selenium-poor form (Read et al., 1990). An explanation for this would be the early termination of translation at one of the UGA codons (TGA in DNA) that encode selenocysteine. This would lead to production of a truncated protein with a disproportionate loss of selenium.

Several regions of the amino acid sequence are conserved better than the average of 72% (Fig. 6.1). A region containing amino acids 30–74 contains the first selenocysteine and is 80% identical between the two species. The next highly conserved (95%) region is 57 amino acids long and begins at position 101. It contains no selenocysteines but there are four conserved cysteines and five conserved tyrosines in this stretch. A third region that is little changed from rat to man is the region beginning at position 225 with the run of seven histidine residues in the rat protein and four in the human protein. This stretch is 17 amino acids long in the rat and 14 long in man. It is a highly positively charged region. A final highly conserved region (83%) reaches from amino acid 287 to amino acid 338 in the human protein and contains the second through sixth selenocysteines. The functions of these conserved regions are not known but their conservation implies importance.

3′ Untranslated Region (3′utr) of cDNAs

The steps involved in the incorporation of selenocysteine into pro-karyotic selenoproteins have been elucidated by Böck and co-workers (Böck, 1993). The corresponding process in eukaryotes is under study by several groups. A distinguishing feature between prokaryotes and eukaryotes is the location of the mRNA stem-loop structure responsible for distinguishing a UGA that codes for selenocysteine incorporation from a UGA that codes for termination of translation. In prokaryotes, an essential stem loop is present immediately downstream from the UGA codon (Zinoni et al., 1990). In eukaryotes, essential stem-loop structures have been identified in the 3′utr of selenoprotein mRNAs (Berry et al., 1991b).

Studies with type I iodothyronine 5′ deiodinase (5′DI) have shown that transient expression of this activity can be achieved by trans-fection of COS-7 cells with a cDNA construct containing the 5′DI open reading frame and 3′utr (Berry et al., 1991a). Deletion of a specific portion of the 3′utr eliminated expression of the selenoenzyme. This portion of the 3′utr contains a predicted stem-loop structure. The 3′utr of cellular glutathione peroxidase also contains a predicted stem-

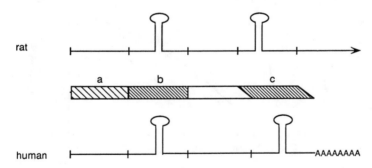

FIGURE 6.2. Comparison of 3′utr of rat and human selenoprotein P cDNAs. Shaded areas in bars indicate conserved stretches: a = 75%, b = 84%, c = 77%. Vertical line across the cDNAs correspond to these stretches. Predicted stem-loop structures are present in stretches b and c. A polyadenylation site was present at the end of the human 3′utr, but none was found on the rat 3′utr, which extended 762 bases past the end of c.

loop structure, and substitution of the 3'utr of cellular glutathione peroxidase for the 3'utr of 5'DI in the cDNA construct allowed expression of 5'DI activity by the COS-7 cells. This indicates that specific stem-loop structures are needed in the 3'utr for UGA codons in the open reading frame to be translated as selenocysteines.

Computer analysis of the 3'utr of rat and human selenoprotein P predicts the presence of two stable stem loops in each mRNA (Fig. 6.2). These stem loops are present in stretches of high conservation, indicating their likely importance (Hill et al., 1993). Because only two stem loops are present and 10 selenocysteines are encoded in the open reading frame, a simple one-to-one relation between stem loops and UGAs is excluded. It is possible that the first stem loop serves the UGA in the amino-terminal portion of the protein and the other one serves the other nine UGAs. Expression of selenoprotein P has not yet been achieved and therfore direct testing of this hypothesis has not been possible.

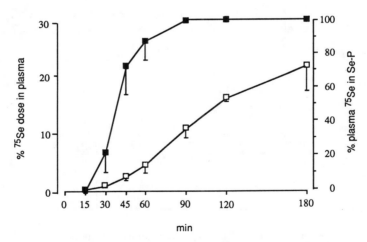

FIGURE 6.3. Incorporation of intragastrically administered ^{75}Se into plasma selenoprotein P. The open squares show the percentage of the administered dose found in the total plasma at various times. The closed squares show the percentage of the plasma ^{75}Se determined to be in selenoprotein P by radioimmunoprecipitation. Values are means ± SD, n = 4, and are from Kato et al. (1992).

PHYSIOLOGY AND FUNCTION

Selenoprotein P is the major form of selenium in rat plasma, accounting for 65% of the element there (Read et al., 1990). Plasma selenoprotein P contains 5–10% of the total body selenium. It is synthesized in the liver and secreted by that organ, but northern analysis indicates that it is made by many other tissues as well (Hill et al., 1993). It had been expected that the liver would be the sole source of selenoprotein P, so the discovery of its mRNA in other tissues has led to a rethinking of the supposition that it functions solely as a plasma protein.

PHYSIOLOGY

Synthesis and secretion of selenoprotein P appear to be very rapid. Thirty minutes after administration of ^{75}Se by stomach tube, the isotope can be found in plasma selenoprotein P (Fig. 6.3). This rapid incorporation of ^{75}Se into selenoprotein P leads to virtually all the ^{75}Se in plasma being in this protein within 90 minutes. Incorporation of label into the other major plasma selenoprotein, extracellular glutathione peroxidase, occurs more slowly (Burk and Gregory, 1982).

The half-lives of selenium in selenoprotein P and in extracellular glutathione peroxidase have been estimated (Burk et al., 1991). Partially purified preparations of these proteins, labeled with ^{75}Se, were injected intravenously into selenium-deficient and control rats. Plasma was sampled at frequent intervals and its ^{75}Se content was determined. ^{75}Se administered as selenoprotein P disappeared with a half-life of 3–4 hours while that administered as extracellular glutathione peroxidase disappeared with a half-life of approximately 12 hours. Neither protein's half-life was affected by the selenium status of the rat.

These results suggest several important conclusions. One is that selenoprotein P synthesis rate is very high. Calculations based on plasma concentration and half-life give a synthesis rate of approximately 5% of the rate of albumin synthesis. It seems inescapable that a major fraction of the selenium incorporated into protein in the rat is accounted for by selenoprotein P synthesis. Another conclusion is that the turnover of plasma selenoprotein P is not receptor mediated.

Clearance of selenoprotein P by a receptor appears to be unlikely because selenium status does not affect turnover (Burk et al., 1991). Selenium status has a large effect on the plasma concentration of selenoprotein P and therefore the specific activity of the protein would be much higher in selenium-deficient than in control animals after injection of small amounts of ^{75}Se-labeled protein. In spite of this, disappearance of ^{75}Se from plasma was similar in the two dietary groups. Had specific molecular recognition been involved in clearance, the half-life should have been shorter in selenium-deficient rats than in controls. It was not.

Many tissues synthesize selenoprotein P. Isolation from a human heart library of a cDNA that encodes selenoprotein P complete with

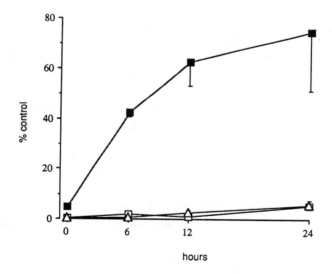

FIGURE 6.4. Effect of selenium administration on levels of selenoproteins in selenium-deficient rats. Rats were injected intraperitoneally with 100 μg selenium per kg as selenite. Rats at 0 time did not receive injections. Selenoprotein P concentration is shown by filled squares, liver glutathione peroxidase activity is shown by open triangles, and plasma glutathione peroxidase activity is shown by open squares. Values are means ± SD, n = 4. Control values were determined in animals fed a selenium-adequate diet from weaning. Results are from Burk et al. (1991).

its signal peptide is evidence that the heart synthesizes and secretes this protein (Hill et al., 1993). Northern analysis has revealed the presence of selenoprotein P mRNA in kidney and in several other tissues. Thus, synthesis of selenoprotein P is not restricted to the liver, and it seems likely that other tissues secrete the protein as well. This is supported by experiments in which rats given ^{75}Se after a total hepatectomy were able to incorporate small amounts of the isotope into plasma selenoprotein P.[2] This incorporation involved protein synthesis because treatment with cycloheximide abolished it.

Several studies have been carried out which show that, under conditions of limited selenium availability, selenoprotein P synthesis takes precedence over synthesis of glutathione peroxidase. Figure 6.4 shows that a single injection of selenium into selenium-deficient rats raises the selenoprotein P concentration to 75% of control by 24 hours. The activities of the two glutathione peroxidases measured were only increased to 6% of control. Similar results have been reported from feeding experiments (Yang et al., 1989).

Protein synthesis rate is related to the abundance of mRNA present. Selenium deficiency causes a fall in the hepatic glutathione peroxidase mRNA level (Saedi et al., 1988). A recent study reported that selenoprotein P mRNA also falls in selenium deficiency but not as severely as does the mRNA of glutathione peroxidase (Hill et al., 1992). This provides an explanation of how selenium is used for synthesis of selenoprotein P instead of glutathione peroxidase in selenium deficiency. It is not known how selenoprotein mRNA levels are regulated.

FUNCTION

Tappel's group postulated that selenoprotein P was a selenium transport protein (Motsenbocker and Tappel, 1982). They suggested that it carried selenium from the liver to other tissues. They claimed that many tissues contained receptors for the protein (Gomez and Tappel, 1989) to facilitate its uptake.

While it is difficult to rule out some role for selenoprotein P in selenium transport, we conclude that this is not likely to be its

---

[2] T. Kato and R.F. Burk, unpublished observations.

primary function. This conclusion is based on several findings. The selenium in selenoprotein P is in the form of selenocysteine, which is present in the primary structure of the protein. Thus selenium could not be removed without damaging or destroying the protein. Transport by such a mechanism would be inefficient.

Efforts have been made to determine whether tissues bind seleno-protein P *in vivo*. Tissues were removed and their ^{75}Se contents were determined in the half-life experiment described above. The only tissue that had a greater uptake of ^{75}Se given as selenoprotein P in selenium-deficient rats than in controls was the brain (Burk et al., 1991). This uptake appeared to be specific because no such difference was noted when the ^{75}Se was given as glutathione peroxidase. The percentage of ^{75}Se taken up by the brain was small, so it did not significantly affect plasma disappearance. These results suggest that a receptor for selenoprotein P is present in the brain but do not confirm the presence of receptors in other tissues. Thus, a role for seleno-protein P in transport of selenium to the brain is possible, but there is no evidence for such a role in other tissues. Evidence has recently been presented that a small molecule containing selenium is involved in transport of the element through the plasma (Kato et al., 1992).

Our group has suggested an oxidant defense role for selenoprotein P. This hypothesis is based on the appearance of selenoprotein P simultaneously with a protective effect of selenium injection against diquat-induced liver injury and lipid peroxidation in selenium-deficient rats.

Administration of sub-LD$_{50}$ doses (for selenium-adequate rats) of diquat to selenium-deficient rats causes death within a few hours (Burk et al., 1980). Severe liver necrosis occurs with transaminase values above 5,000 U/L at the time of death. Evidence of massive lipid peroxidation in the form of very high ethane exhalation is found as part of the process. Thus, it appears that diquat-related free radicals cause massive lipid peroxidation leading to liver necrosis in selenium-deficient rats. The liver necrosis and lipid peroxidation were prevented by injecting 50 μg selenium into the rats 10 hours before giving diquat. As noted above (Fig. 6.4), glutathione peroxidase is not increased at this time but selenoprotein P is. This is consistent with a protective effect by selenoprotein P. Further work will be required to determine whether this relationship is causal.

Summary and Conclusions

Selenoprotein P has been characterized in considerable detail. It has been purified and determined to be a glycoprotein. Its cDNA has been sequenced and shown to encode a protein with a signal peptide. The mature protein (deduced) contains 10 selenocysteines. Stem-loop structures are present in the 3′utr that are similar to those found in mRNAs of other selenoproteins and that are necessary for translation of in-frame UGAs as selenocysteines. Northern analysis indicates that selenoprotein P mRNA is present in a number of tissues.

Selenoprotein P contains 65% of the selenium in rat plasma. It has a shorter half-life than extracellular glutathione peroxidase and incorporates selenium within minutes of its ingestion by the rat. Under conditions of limited selenium supply, it appears to be preserved by the organism in preference to glutathione peroxidases. A cDNA representing human selenoprotein P has been cloned and sequenced. The amino acid sequence of the protein is highly conserved between the rat and man.

The function of selenoprotein P is unknown. Its extracellular location has led to speculation that it is a selenium transport protein. However, the presence of selenium in its primary structure and its synthesis by a number of tissues lessen this possibility. Appearance of selenoprotein P coincides with selenium-produced protection against diquat-induced liver injury and lipid peroxidation. This has led to suggestions that selenoprotein P serves as an oxidant defense. Selenium has long been recognized to have oxidant defense properties and thus such a function for selenoprotein P would provide an explanation for them. Further work will be necessary to evaluate this hypothesis.

Acknowledgments

The authors' work is supported by NIH grants ES 02497, ES 06093, and ES 00267.

References

Berry, MJ, Banu, L, Chen, Y, Mandel, SJ, Kieffer, JD, Harney, JW, Larsen, PR. Recognition of UGA as a selenocysteine codon in Type I deiodinase requires sequences in the 3′ untranslated region. Nature 353:273–276; 1991a.

Berry, MJ, Banu, L, Larsen, PR. Type I iodothyronine deiodinase is a selenocysteine-containing enzyme. Nature 349:438–440; 1991b.

Böck, A. Incorporation of selenium into bacterial selenoproteins. In: Burk, RF, ed. Selenium in Biology and Human Health. New York: Springer Verlag; 1993.

Burk, RF. Effect of dietary selenium on ^{75}Se binding to rat plasma proteins. Proc Soc Exp Biol Med 143:719–722; 1973.

Burk, RF, Gregory, PE. Some characteristics of ^{75}Se-P, a selenoprotein found in rat liver and plasma, and comparison of it with selenoglutathione peroxidase. Arch Biochem Biophys 213:78–80; 1982.

Burk, RF, Hill, KE, Read, R, Bellew, T. Response of rat selenoprotein P to selenium administration and fate of its selenium Am J Physiol 261: E26–E30; 1991.

Burk, RF, Lawrence, RA, Lane, JM. Liver necrosis and lipid peroxidation in the rat as the result of paraquat and diquat administration. J Clin Invest 65:1024–1031; 1980.

Gomez, B, Tappel, AL. Selenoprotein P receptor from rat. Biochim Biophys Acta 979:20–26; 1989.

Herrman, JL. The properties of a rat serum protein labelled by the injection of sodium selenite. Biochim Biophys Acta 500:61–70; 1977.

Hill, KE, Lloyd, RS, Burk, RF. Conserved nucleotide sequences in the open reading frame and 3′ untranslated region of selenoprotein P mRNA. Proc Natl Acad Sci USA 90:537–541, 1993.

Hill, KE, Lloyd, RS, Yang, JG, Read, R, Burk, RF. The cDNA for rat selenoprotein P contains 10 TGA codons in the open reading frame. J Biol Chem 266:10050–10053; 1991.

Hill, KE, Lyons, PR, Burk, RF. Differential regulation of rat liver selenoprotein mRNAs in selenium deficiency. Biochem Biophys Res Commun 185:260–263; 1992.

Kato, T, Read, R, Rozga, J, Burk, RF. Evidence for intestinal release of absorbed selenium in a form with high hepatic extraction. Am J Physiol 262:G854–G858; 1992.

Millar, KR. Distribution of ^{75}Se in liver, kidney, and blood proteins of rats after intravenous injection of sodium selenite. NZJ Agr Res 15:547–564; 1972.

Motchnik, PA, Tappel, AL. Rat plasma selenoprotein P properties and purification. Biochim Biophys Acta 993:27–35; 1989.

Motsenbocker, MA, Tappel, AL. A selenocysteine-containing selenium-transport protein in rat plasma. Biochim Biophys Acta 719:147–153; 1982.

Read, R, Bellew, T, Yang, JG, Hill, KE, Palmer, IS, Burk, RF. Selenium and amino acid composition of selenoprotein P, the major selenoprotein in rat serum. J Biol Chem 265:17899–17905; 1990.

Saedi, MS, Smith, CG, Frampton, J, Chambers, I, Harrison, PR, Sunde, RA. Effect of selenium status on mRNA levels for glutathione peroxidase in rat liver. Biochem Biophys Res Commun 153:855–861; 1988.

Yang, JG, Hill, KE, Burk, RF. Dietary selenium intake controls rat plasma selenoprotein P concentration. J Nutr 119:1010–1012; 1989.

Yang, JG, Morrison-Plummer, J, Burk, RF. Purification and quantitation of a rat plasma selenoprotein distinct from glutathione peroxidase using monoclonal antibodies. J Biol Chem 262:13372–13375; 1987.

Zinoni, F, Heider, J, Böck, A. Features of the formate dehydrogenase mRNA necessary for decoding of the UGA codon as selenocysteine. Proc Natl Acad Sci USA 87:4660–4664; 1990.

Chapter 7

The Mitochondrial Capsule Selenoprotein—A Structural Protein in the Mitochondrial Capsule of Mammalian Sperm

KENNETH C. KLEENE

A series of papers appeared between 1973 and 1983 that suggested that selenium is required for the development of the sperm mitochondrial capsule, a specialized structure associated with the outer mitochondrial membrane of spermatozoa in mammals. For example, intraperitoneal injections of ^{75}Se and autoradiography demonstrate that ^{75}Se is primarily incorporated into the midpiece of spermatozoa, the segment of the sperm tail containing the mitochondria (Brown and Burk, 1973). The levels of selenium in rat and bull spermatozoa are also unusually high, ca. 20–30 ng/mg protein or dry weight (Pallini and Bacci, 1979; Calvin et al., 1981; Behne et al., 1986). When rats and mice are maintained for prolonged periods on a selenium-deficient diet, the morphology of the tails and mitochondria is abnormal (Wu et al., 1979; Wallace et al., 1983a,b). All of these observations can be explained by the finding that selenium is present in a cysteine- and proline-rich structural protein in the mitochondrial capsule (Calvin and Cooper, 1979; Calvin et al., 1981; Pallini and Bacci, 1979). This protein has been referred to as the mitochondrial capsular protein (Calvin and Cooper, 1979), but the term "mitochondrial capsule selenoprotein" (MCS, Kleene et al., 1990) seems more appropriate to identify it as one of the very small number of selenoproteins. The purpose of this chapter is to evaluate earlier work in light of new information derived from characterization of recombinant DNAs encoding MCS.

THE MITOCHONDRIAL CAPSULE SELENOPROTEIN: SUBCELLULAR LOCALIZATION AND CHARACTERIZATION

The morphological and biochemical events of spermatogenesis have been reviewed previously (Fawcett, 1975; Bellvé and O'Brien, 1983). However, a brief description of spermatogenesis will be helpful in understanding the work described here. The entire process of spermatogenesis is divided into three main phases, each with a different function. In the mitotic phase, diploid spermatogonia divide rapidly by mitotic division, amplifying the number of cells that will eventually become spermatozoa. In the meiotic phase, spermatocytes spend most of their time in prophase I of meiosis, the period in which genetic crossing over occurs. After the reduction divisions, the haploid cells known as "spermatids" undergo a series of profound morphological changes that transform the Golgi, nucleus, mitochondria, and flagellum into the highly specialized organelles of the mature spermatozoa. The haploid phase of mice lasts about 2 weeks and can be subdivided into 16 steps and based on the cellular morphology and cell associations of the developing spermatids (Oakberg, 1956), but the duration of the haploid phase and the number of steps differ somewhat in other mammals. The flagellum of mammalian sperm is reinforced along most of its length by outer dense fibers, and the anterior portion of the flagellum and outer dense fibers, the so-called midpiece, is wrapped tightly in a sheath of mitochondria. The mitochondria in the sheath are elongated, bent into a slightly curved shape, and aligned end-to-end, forming a helix with 10 to >300 gyres in various mammals (André, 1962; Woolley, 1970; Dooher and Bennett, 1973; Fawcett, 1975).

The capsules associated with the outer membranes of sperm mitochondria have been purified by procedures that depend largely on the fact that the organelles of mammalian spermatozoa are stabilized by disulfide bridges. Pallini et al. (1979) sonicated bull spermatozoa to separate the mitochondria from the flagellum and nuclei, and the mitochondria were purified by sedimentation on sucrose density gradients. After lysing the purified mitochondria with sodium dodecyl sulfate (SDS), the capsules that sediment at $100,000\,g$ can be separated from the vast majority of mitochondrial proteins in the supernatant. Calvin and his co-workers (Calvin and Cooper, 1979; Calvin et al., 1981) used trypsin, SDS, and low concentrations of dithiothreitol to separate the mitochondrial capsules from the nuclei and fibrous tail structures in rat sperm. The capsules are separated from heavier nuclei and fibrous tail fragments by low-speed centrifugation and sucrose density centrifugation. Examination of the capsules purified in either lab with the electron microscope reveals that the capsules retain the size and extended crescent shape of the outer walls of mitochondria in the helical sheath (Pallini et al., 1979; Pallini and Bacci, 1979; Calvin, 1979; Calvin et al., 1981). The capsules dissolve upon reduction with high concentrations of β-mercaptoethanol or dithiothreitol, indicating that their integrity in SDS is maintained by disulfide bridges. Pallini et al. (1979) reported that bull sperm mitochondrial capsules contain three proteins in mass ratios of $2:1:1$ that migrate with apparent molecular weights of 20, 29, and 31 kDa in SDS−polyacrylamide gel electrophoresis (PAGE), whereas Calvin et al. (1981) reported that rat sperm mitochondrial capsules contain one major protein with a molecular weight of 15−17 kDa and small amounts of four slightly larger proteins. The reasons for the differences in composition of the capsule and size of the smallest protein are unknown but may reflect differences in species or purification techniques. Pallini et al. (1979) determined the amino acid composition of the three proteins of bull sperm mitochondrial capsules after chromatography on DEAE-Sephadex. The compositions of the 29- and 31-kDa proteins are not distinctive, whereas the 20-kDa protein contains exceptionally large amounts of cysteine (17.9%) and proline (26.5%).

Cell fractionation experiments using atomic absorption spectroscopy and ^{75}Se to monitor selenium demonstrate that 40−64% of selenium is recovered in the mitochondrial capsule fractions of bull and rat sperm (Pallini and Bacci, 1979; Calvin and Cooper, 1979; Calvin et al., 1981). Both Pallini and Bacci (1979) and Calvin et al. (1981) have argued from the concentrations of selenium and ultrastructural analyses of the structures in various fractions that essentially all of the selenium in spermatozoa is contained in the mitochondrial capsule. The selenium in the capsule is limited to the 15−20-kDa capsular protein based on SDS−PAGE and autoradiography (Calvin and Cooper, 1979; Calvin et al., 1981) and atomic absorption spectroscopy of purified MCS (Pallini and Bacci, 1979). In addition, when carboxymethylated ^{75}Se-labeled mitochondrial capsules are resolved by two-dimensional (2D) electrophoresis, the vast majority of ^{75}Se and the major stained protein coincide exactly (Calvin et al., 1987). The isoelectric point of the predominant ^{75}Se-labeled polypeptide is 4.6, although small amounts of ^{75}Se were detected at isoelectric points 4.5, 4.7, and 4.9 (Calvin et al., 1987). It should be noted that carboxymethylated MCS will be much more acidic than the native protein, and the isoelectric point variants may reflect incomplete carboxymethylation as well as posttranslational modifications. Pallini and Bacci (1979) estimate that there are 0.4 atoms of selenium per molecule of MCS and 17,000 atoms/mitochondrion, and Calvin et al. (1981) estimate 25,000−30,000 atoms per mitchondrial capsule and about 1.5×10^7 atoms/sperm cell. Unfortunately, biochemical analyses of MCS have not been performed to determine whether the selenium is associated nonspecifically with MCS or is present as selenocysteine at specific sites in the polypeptide chain.

The presence of selenium in a major structural protein in the mitochondrial sheath provides a simple explanation for the deleterious effects of dietary selenium deficiency on sperm development. In selenium-deficient rats, spermatozoa are produced in decreased numbers, and the sperm can be seen with the light microscope to be immobile and display abnormal breaks and sharp bends in or near the midpiece (Wu et al., 1979; Wallace et al., 1983a). Electron microscope studies show that the shape and arrangement of mito-chondria in the sheath are abnormal and that mitochondrial capsules isolated from selenium-deficient rats are more fragile than normal capsules (Wallace et al., 1983b). Since MCS is the predominant pro-tein in the mitochondrial capsule, it would be interesting to examine the levels and structure of MCS in selenium-deficient mammals.

A recent paper by Roveri et al. (1992) questions the conclusion that MCS is the major selenoprotein in spermatozoa. These workers report that there are high levels of a second selenoprotein in rat testis, phospholipid hydroperoxide glutathione peroxidase (PHGPX). Since the molecular weight of PHGPX is similar to MCS and a large fraction of PHGPX is found in mitochondria, Roveri et al. (1992) suggested that PHGPX might account for the selenium in sperm mitochondria. This possibility merits serious consideration in view of disagreement as to the time of synthesis of MCS (see below), but it is unlikely to explain the coincidence of ^{75}Se and the major stained protein in purified mitochondrial capsules in 2D gel electrophoresis (Calvin et al. 1987).

SEQUENCE OF THE MCS mRNA, GENE, AND PROTEIN

In 1987 my lab fortuitously isolated cDNAs from a mouse testis cDNA library that we believe encode MCS (Kleene et al., 1990). DNA sequencing revealed that the major reading frame of this cDNA encoded a 143-amino-acid protein containing ≥20% of both cysteine and proline (Kleene et al., 1990). Although mammalian sperm con-tain a fair number of cysteine-rich proteins, such large amounts of both proline and cysteine have only been reported in bull MCS (Pallini et al., 1979). Unexpectedly, the reading frame of the initial cDNAs lacked the in-phase UGA codons that signify stop in the universal genetic code but have been shown to encode selenocysteine in several selenoproteins (Chambers et al., 1986; Zinoni et al., 1986; Hill et al., 1991; Berry et al., 1991a). When we characterized the 5′ ends of the MCS mRNA by sequencing additional cDNAs, primer extension, S1 mapping, and isolating and sequencing the MCS gene (Karimpour et al., 1992), it became clear that our original cDNAs were incomplete and that mouse MCS is 54 amino acids longer at the

TABLE 7.1. Amino acid composition of bull and mouse MCS (residues/100 residues)[1].

	Mouse	Bull
Cysteine	18.3	17.9
Aspartic acid + asparagine	7.1	7.0
Aspartic acid	2.5	NM
Asparagine	4.6	NM
Threonine	6.6	3.4
Serine	9.6	8.8
Glutamic acid + glutamine	8.6	13.6
Glutamic acid	2.5	NM
Glutamine	6.1	NM
Proline	22.8	26.5
Glycine	3.0	3.5
Alanine	2.0	1.8
Valine	1.0	0.8
Methionine	1.0	0.2
Isoleucine	1.5	0.3
Leucine	2.0	2.7
Tyrosine	0.5	0.3
Phenylalanine	0.5	0.3
Histidine	0.0	0.0
Lysine	11.2	11.3
Arginine	1.5	1.5
Tryptophan	1.0	NM
Selenocysteine	1.5	NM

[1] The amino acid composition of mouse MCS is predicted from the DNA sequence in Karimpour et al. (1992) and the amino acid composition of bull MCS was determined by Pallini et al. (1979). NM, not measured.

amino terminus, including three in-phase UGA codons that presumably encode selenocysteine. The predicted molecular weight of mouse MCS, 21.1 kDa, is similar to the molecular weight of bull and rat MCS determined by SDS-PAGE, 15–20 kDa, although the electrophoretic mobility of MCS might be expected to be anomalous considering its unusual composition. The predicted isoelectric points of native and completely carboxymethylated mouse MCS are 8.08 and 3.97, respectively. Table 7.1 shows a comparison of the amino acid composition of bull MCS determined by Pallini et al. (1979) and the predicted composition of mouse MCS (Karimpour et al., 1992). The extraordinary similarity suggests not only that the sequence of MCS is conserved, but also that Pallini and his co-workers purified bull MCS to homogeneity. However, the predicted amount of selenium in mouse MCS is considerably higher than that measured by Pallini and Bacci (1979), 3 vs. 0.4 atoms selenium/molecule. The difference may reflect technical errors, species differences, inefficient translation of UGA codons, or posttranslational elimination of selenium.

The predicted amino acid sequence of mouse MCS can be divided into four distinct regions based on the distribution of selenocysteine, proline, and cysteine residues as shown in Figure 7.1. The 35 amino acids proximal to the amino terminus contain all three selenocysteine

Amino Acids

1–35	mdsldC**U**gr**p**siysiC**U**niqettfntenqvwkCUt
36–62	kks**p**rknCvarsgt**p**tlkkmsd**p**sktn
63–102	qC**ppp**CC**pp**k**p**CC**pp**k**p**CC**p**qk**pp**CC**p**ks**p**CC**pp**ks**p**CC**p**
103–126	**p**k**p**C**p**C**ppp**C**p**C**p**C**p**atC**p**C**p**lk**p**
127–157	**p**CC**p**qkCsCC**p**kkCtCC**p**q**ppp**CCaq**p**tCCs
158–197	senktesdsdtsgqtlekgsqs**p**qs**pp**gaqgnwnqkksnk

FIGURE 7.1. Distribution of proline, cysteine, and selenocysteine in mouse MCS. The amino acid sequence of mouse MCS (Karimpour et al., 1992) is shown in one-letter code. Selenocysteine residues are shown as uppercase *U* (Böck et al., 1991) in bold type; cysteine residues are shown as uppercase *C*, and proline residues are shown as lowercase *p* in bold type. All other amino acids are depicted in lowercase type.

residues, which interestingly appear as three selenocysteine-cysteine dipeptides. The presence of three selenocysteines is itself unusual because most selenoproteins are enzymes that contain one seleno-cysteine in their active site (reviewed in Böck et al., 1991), and only selenoprotein P contains multiple selenocysteines (Read et al., 1990; Hill et al., 1991). The next 27 residues are generally hydrophilic and deficient in cysteine and proline; 75% of amino acids 63–157 are either cysteine or proline. This region can be subdivided into three smaller regions: a 40-amino-acid region with six Pro-Cys-Cys-Pro tetrapeptides; a 24-amino-acid region containing seven single Cys residues, six of which are flanked on both sides by Pro; and a 31-amino-acid region containing five Cys-Cys dipeptides only one of which is flanked on both sides by Pro. The 40 amino acids proximal to the carboxy terminus are also hydrophilic and deficient in proline and cysteine. Protein sequence database searches reveal that the sequence Pro-Cys-Cys-Pro is found in fewer than 20 proteins and that it is only repeated in MCS. The sequence of MCS in other mammals might be correlated with the structure of the mitochondrial sheath such as the number of mitchondrial gyres.

It is reasonable to speculate that the selenocysteine residues in MCS have a specific function related to the formation of intermole-cular bonds that crosslink the mitochondrial capsule. Although the tail and chromatin of mammalian sperm contain a variety of cysteine-rich proteins that are crosslinked by disulfide bridges, the formation of the disulfide bonds is a progressive process: Many cysteine-rich proteins retain free sulfhydryl groups in the testis, evidently because oxidation is prevented, and only form disulfide bridges during sperm maturation in the epididymis (Calvin and Bedford, 1971; Calvin et al., 1973; Loir and Lanneau, 1984; Meistrich, 1989; Balhorn, 1989). In this context, it is important to note that the principal difference between selenocysteine and cysteine is that the proton in the selenyl group of selenocysteine dissociates much more readily at physiological pH than the proton in the sulfhydryl group of cysteine. Consequently, selenocysteine is more highly ionized and more reactive than cysteine, and the reactivity of selenocysteine has been shown to enhance the activity of enzymes in which it appears in the active site (Axley et al., 1991; Berry et al., 1992). Wallace et al. (1983b) suggested that the reactivity of selenocysteine might enable MCS to form intermolecular bridges in the testis under conditions in which oxidation of sulfhydryl groups is blocked. Alternatively, the selenocysteine might be necessary for the formation of an initial set of intramolecular selenocysteine—cysteine linkages in MCS that determine the configuration of subsequent disulfide bridges in the mitochondrial capsule. The location of these initial bonds might be dictated by the direction of translation as well as the context of the selenocysteine—cysteine residues since the selenocysteine residues are close to the amino terminus. In either case, it is relevant to note that the formation of disulfide bridges in sperm chromatin is a two-stage process in which intramolecular disulfide bonds lock protamines into a conformation that fixes the locations of intermolecular bonds (Balhorn, 1989; Balhorn et al., 1991).

A biological problem created by the alternative meanings of UGA codons is how the translational apparatus distinguishs UGA codons that should be decoded as selenocysteine from those that specify termination. In mammalian cells, Berry et al. (1991b) have determined that this signal is a stem loop in the 3′ nontranslated region that includes a small number of conserved bases. The 3′ nontranslated region of the MCS mRNA contains a similar sequence, but the activity in directing insertion of selenocysteine has not been tested experimentally.

DEVELOPMENTAL EXPRESSION OF MCS AS STUDIED WITH cDNA PROBES AND ^{75}Se LABELING

The synthesis of mouse MCS is regulated at both the transcriptional and translational levels during spermatogenesis. Northern blots demonstrate that MCS mRNA is about 1,050 bases long, that it is present at high levels in testis, and that it is not detectable in liver, kidney, thigh muscle, brain, or skin (Kleene et al., 1990; Kleene, unpublished). Northern blots using RNAs extracted from populations of spermatogenic cells purified by sedimentation on bovine serum albumin gradients further reveal that the MCS mRNA is present at high and similar levels in step-1–8 and step-12–16 spermatids (Kleene et al., 1990) and cannot be detected in spermatocytes which are meiotic cells (Shih and Kleene, 1992). *In situ* hybridizations show that the MCS mRNA is present at levels over background from step 3 to step 16 in the haploid phase (Shih and Kleene, 1992).

To determine when the MCS mRNA is translated, we have analyzed the distribution of the MCS mRNA in the polysomal and nonpolysomal fractions of sucrose gradients by sedimenting postmitochondrial extracts of purified spermatids in steps 1–8 and steps 12–16 on sucrose gradients, purifying the RNA from each fraction, and comparing the amount of MCS mRNA in each fraction by northern blots using an MCS cDNA probe referred to as HEM1050 (Kleene, 1989). MCS mRNA in step-1–8 spermatids primarily sediments slower than the single ribosomes, implying that the mRNA is translationally inactive. By comparison, about half the MCS mRNA sediments in the polysomal fractions in step-12–16 spermatids, implying that the mRNA is translationally active (Kleene, 1989). It can be inferred from these results that the mouse MCS mRNA is synthesized and stored in a translationally repressed form in early haploid cells for up to 1 week and that it is only translationally active in late haploid cells, shortly before or at the same time as the mitochondrial sheath is formed in steps 15 and 16 in mice (André, 1962; Woolley, 1970; Dooher and Bennett, 1973).

The temporal control of translation of the MCS mRNA is observed for several other mRNAs encoding testis-specific basic chromosomal proteins that are synthesized in late spermatids (Kleene, 1989) and is a logical consequence of the complete cessation of transcription in step-9 spermatids due to the chromatin condensation (reviewed in Meistrich, 1990). Since the timing of translation of mouse protamine mRNAs is thought to be regulated by transacting factors that bind to the 3' nontranslated region (Braun et al., 1989; Kwon and Hecht, 1990), the 3' nontranslated region of the MCS mRNA may contain a cis-acting element for regulation of the timing of translation in addition to a cis-acting element for selenocysteine incorporation.

Our finding that the mouse MCS mRNA is translationally active in late haploid cells disagrees generally with studies that show that ^{75}Se is incorporated during the meiotic and haploid stages of spermatogenesis of rats, rams, and bulls (Gunn and Gould, 1970; Smith et al., 1979; Pond et al., 1983). The most detailed developmental study was carried out by Calvin et al. (1987) in the rat. In one experiment, ^{75}Se was injected into the testes of sexually mature rats, and the levels of ^{75}Se were measured in whole epididymal spermatozoa at various times after injection. The stage of incorporation of ^{75}Se into MCS was deduced from the time for various stages of spermatogenesis to complete development in the testis and transport to the epididymis. The results showed that the synthesis of MCS begins in meiotic cells, increases gradually becoming maximal in step-7−12 spermatids, and decreases sharply after step 12. In another experiment, the incorporation of ^{75}Se was analyzed in the mitochondrial pellets 24 hours after injection of ^{75}Se into the testes of prepubertal rats at ages when they contain spermatogonia and spermatocytes but lack either all or late haploid cells. These results also demonstrated significant incorporation of ^{75}Se into a 15-kDa protein in one dimensional-gel electrophoresis in meiotic cells and early spermatids. Thus, the high levels of incorporation of ^{75}Se into MCS in meiotic and early haploid cells in rats is at odds with our evidence that the MCS mRNA is undetectable in meiotic cells and translationally repressed in early haploid cells in mice.

This disagreement points out several important gaps of knowledge. First, strong evidence is lacking that the protein encoded by our cDNA clone in mice, the selenoprotein synthesized in meiotic and early haploid cells, and selenoprotein in whole spermatozoa are identical. There are probably several selenoproteins in mammalian testes with electrophoretic mobility similar to MCS (McConnell et al., 1979; Behne et al., 1988; Roveri et al., 1992), and MCS can only be reliably identified at present as a constituent of the SDS-insoluble fraction of sperm mitochrondria. Second, although the proportion of an mRNA associated with polysomes is almost always an accurate indication of the rate of translation, in exceptional instances polysome-bound mRNAs may be blocked at the level of elongation (Hershey, 1991). Third, since the utilization of selenium in mammals is regulated to ensure that specific tissues receive an adequate supply (Behne et al., 1986, 1988), ^{75}Se might be incorporated into MCS long after intratesticular injection. Resolving this conflict should lead to insights into the mechanisms of utilization of selenium in the testis, the construction of the mitochondrial sheath, the identity of the selenoproteins in mammalian spermatogenesis, and the mechanisms of translational regulation in the testis.

Summary

Work in the late 1970s revealed that the most abundant protein in the mitochondrial capsule of rat and bull spermatozoa contains selenium and large amounts of cysteine and proline. The existence of this structural protein explains the requirement for selenium in the development of the midpiece of mammalian sperm. Recombinant DNAs have been isolated recently that apparently encode this protein based on similarities in deduced amino acid composition and the presence of three putative UGA selenocysteine codons near the beginning of the open reading frame.

Throughout this chapter I have pointed out a series of unresolved questions concerning such issues as the structure of the mitochondrial capsule, the identity of various selenoproteins in the testis, and the time of synthesis of MCS. Elucidation of the precise chemical location of selenium in MCS is critical and would resolve most of these questions. Further work on MCS will undoubtedly contribute to understanding spermatogenesis and selenium biochemistry.

Acknowledgments

The author is grateful to Adel Bozorgzadeh, Michael Cutler, Iman Karimpour, Deborah Shih, and Jean Smith for their work on this project. The research in the author's laboratory was supported by NSF grants DCB-8510350, DCB-8710485, and DCB-9018486.

References

André, J. Contribution à la connaissance du chondriome. Etude de ses modifications ultrastructurales pendant la spermatogénèse. J Ultrastruct Res Suppl 3:1–185; 1962.

Axley, MJ, Böck, A, Stadtman, TC. Catalytic properties of an *Escherichia coli* formate dehydrogenase mutant in which sulfur replaces selenium. Proc Natl Acad Sci USA 88:8450–8454; 1991.

Balhorn, R. Mammalian protamines: structure and molecular interactions. In: Adolph, KW, ed. Molecular Biology of Chromosome Function. New York: Springer-Verlag; 1989, pp 366–395.

Balhorn, R, Corzett, M, Mazrimas, J, Watkins, B. Identification of bull protamine disulfides. Biochemistry 30:175–81; 1991.

Behne, D, Duk, M, Elger, W. Selenium content and glutathione peroxidase activity in the testis of the maturing rat. J Nutr 116:1442–1447; 1986.

Behne, D, Hilmert, H, Scheid, S, Gessner, H, Elger, W. Evidence for specific selenium target tissues and new biologically important seleno-proteins. Biochim Biophys Acta 960:12–21; 1988.

Bellvé, AR, O'Brien, DA. The mammalian spermatozoon: structure and temporal assembly. In: Hartman, JF, ed. Mechanism and Control of Animal Fertilization, New York: Academic Press; 1983, pp 55–137.

Berry, MJ, Banu, L, Larsen, PR. Type I iodothyronine deiodinase is a selenocysteine-containing enzyme. Nature 349:438–440; 1991a.

Berry, MJ, Banu, L, Chen, Y, Mandel, SJ, Kieffer, JD, Harney, JW, Larsen, PR. Recognition of UGA as a selenocysteine codon in Type I deiodinase requires sequences in the 3′ untranslated region. Nature 353:273–276; 1991b.

Berry, MJ, Maia, AL, Kieffer, JD, Harney, JW, Larsen, PR. Substitution of cysteine for selenocysteine in type I iodothyronine deiodinase reduces the catalytic efficiency of the protein but enhances its translation. Endocrinology 131:1848–1852; 1992.

Böck, A, Forchhammer, K, Heider, J, Leinfelder, W, Sawers, G, Veprek, B, Zinoni, F. Selenocysteine: the 21st amino acid. Mol Microbiol 5:515–520; 1991.

Braun, RE, Peschon, JJ, Behringer, RR, Brinster, RL, Palmiter, RD. Protamine 3′ untranslated sequences regulate temporal translational control of growth hormone in spermatids of transgenic mice. Genes Dev 3:793–802; 1989.

Brown, DG, Burk, RF. Selenium retention in tissues and sperm of rats fed a torula yeast diet. J Nutr 103:102–108; 1973.

Calvin, HI, Bedford, JM. Formation of disulphide bonds in the nucleus and accessary structures of mammalian spermatozoa during maturation in the epididymis. J Reprod Fertil Suppl 13:65–76; 1971.

Calvin, HI, Yu, CC, Bedford, JM. Effects of epidiymal maturation zinc (II) and copper (II) on the reactive sulfhydryl content of structural elements in rat spermatozoa. Exp Cell Res 81:333–341; 1973.

Calvin, HI. Selective incorporation of selenium-75 into a polypeptide of the rat sperm tail. J Exp Zool 204:445–452; 1979.

Calvin, HI, Cooper, GW. A specific selenopolypeptide associated with the outer membrane of rat sperm mitochondria. In: Fawcett, DW, Bedford, JM, eds. The Spermatozoon. Baltimore-Munich: Urban and Schwartzenberg; 1979, pp 135–140.

Calvin, HI, Cooper, GW, Wallace, E. Evidence that selenium in rat sperm is associated with a cysteine-rich structural protein of the mitochondrial capsules. Gamete Res 4:139–149; 1981.

Calvin, HI, Grosshans, K, Musicant-Shikora, SR, Turner, SI. A developmental study of rat sperm and testis selenoproteins. J Reprod Fertil 81:1–11; 1987.

Chambers, I, Frampton, J, Goldfarb, P, Affara, N, McBain, W, Harrison, PR. The structure of mouse glutathione peroxidase gene: the selenocysteine in the active site is encoded by the "termination" codon, TGA. EMBO J 5:1221–1227; 1986.

Dooher, GB, Bennett, D. Fine structural observations on the development of the sperm head in the mouse. Am J Anat 136:339–362; 1973.

Fawcett, DW. The mammalian spermatozoon. Dev Biol 44:394–436; 1975.

Gunn, SA, Gould, TC. Cadmium and other mineral elements. In: Johnson, AD, Gomez, WR, VanDeMark, NL, eds. The Testis, vol 3. NY: Academic Press; 1970, pp 377–481.

Hershey, JWB. Translational control in mammalian cells. Ann Rev Biochem 60:717–755; 1991.

Hill, KE, Lloyd, RS, Yang, JG, Read, R, Burk, RF. The rat selenoprotein P contains 10 TGA codons in the open reading frame. J Biol Chem 266:10050–10053; 1991.

Karimpour, I, Cutler, M, Shih, D, Smith, J, Kleene, KC. Sequence of the gene encoding the mitochondrial capsule selenoprotein of mouse sperm: identification of three in-phase TGA selenocysteine codons. DNA Cell Biol 11:693–699; 1992.

Kleene, KC. Poly(A) shortening accompanies the activation of translation of five mRNAs during spermiogenesis in the mouse. Development 106:367–373; 1989.

Kleene, KC, Smith, J, Bozorgzadeh, A, Harris, M, Hahn, L, Karimpour, I, Gerstel, J. Sequence and developmental expression of the mRNA encoding the seleno-protein of the sperm mitochondrial capsule in the mouse. Dev Biol 137:395–402; 1990.

Kwon, YH, Hecht, NB. Cytoplasmic protein binding to highly conserved sequences in the 3' untranslated region of mouse protamine 2 mRNA, a translationally regulated transcript of male germ cells. Proc Natl Acad Sci USA 88:3584–3588; 1990.

Loir, M, Lanneau, M. Structural functions of basic nuclear proteins in ram spermatids. J Ultr Res 86:262–276; 1984.

McConnell, KP, Burton, RM, Kute, T, Higgins, PJ. Selenoproteins from rat testis cytosol. Biochim Biophys Acta 588:113–119; 1979.

148   K.C. Kleene

Meistrich, ML. Histone and basic nuclear protein transitions in mammalian spermatogenesis. In: Hnilica, LS, Stein, GS, Stein, JL, eds. Histones and Other Basic Nuclear Proteins. Boca Raton, FL: CRC Press; 1989, pp 165–182.

Oakberg, EF. A description of spermiogenesis in the mouse and its use in analysis of the cycle of the seminiferous epithelium and germ cell renewal. Am J Anat 99:391–409; 1956.

Pallini, V, Baccetti, B, Burrini, AG. A peculiar cysteine-rich polypeptide related to some unusual properties of mammalian sperm mitochondria. In: Fawcett, DW, Bedford, JM, eds. The spermatozoon. Baltimore-Munich: Urban and Schwartzenberg; 1979, pp 141–151.

Pallini, V, Bacci, E. Bull sperm selenium is bound to a structural protein of mitochondria. J Submicr Cytol 11:165–170; 1979.

Pond, FR, Tripp, MJ, Wu, ASH, Whanger, PD, Schmitz, JA. Incorporation of selenium-75 into semen and reproductive tissues of bulls and rams. J Reprod Fertil 69:411–418; 1983.

Read, R, Bellew, T, Yang, JG, Hill, KE, Palmer, IS, Burk, RF. Selenium and amino acid composition of selenoprotein P, the major selenoprotein in rat serum. J Biol Chem 265:17899–17905; 1990.

Roveri, A, Casasco, A, Maiorino, M, Dalan, P, Calligaro, A, Ursini, F. Phospholipid hydroperoxide glutathione peroxidase of rat testis. Gonadotropin dependence and immunocytochemical identification. J Biol Chem 267:6142–6146; 1992.

Shih, DM, Kleene, KC. A study by *in situ* hybridization of the stage of appearance and disappearance of the transition protein 2 and mitochondrial capsule seleno-protein mRNA during spermatogenesis in the mouse. Mol Reprod Dev 33:222–227; 1992.

Smith, DG, Senger, PL, McCutchan, JF, Landa, CA. Selenium and glutathione peroxidase distribution in bovine semen and selenium-75 retention by the tissues of the reproductive tract in the bull. Biol Reprod 20:377–383; 1979.

Wallace, E, Calvin, HI, Cooper, GW. Progressive defects observed in mouse sperm during the course of three generations of selenium deficiency. Gamete Res 4:377–387; 1983a.

Wallace, E, Cooper, GW, Calvin, HI. Effects of selenium deficiency on the shape and arrangement of rodent sperm mitochondria. Gamete Res 4:389–399; 1983b.

Woolley, DM. The midpiece of the mouse spermatozoon: its form and development as seen by surface replication. J Cell Sci 6:865–879; 1970.

Wu, SH, Oldfield, JE, Shull, LR, Cheeke, PR. Specific effect of selenium deficiency on rat sperm. Biol Reprod 20:793–798; 1979.

Zinoni, F, Birkmann, A, Stadtman, TC, Böck, A. Nucleotide sequence and expression of the selenocysteine-containing polypeptide of formate dehydrogenase (formate-lyase-linked) from *Escherichia coli*. Proc Natl Acad Sci USA 83:4650–4654; 1986.

Chapter
8

Selenium Status and Glutathione Metabolism

KRISTINA E. HILL

Selenium and Glutathione

Selenium, vitamin E, and sulfur amino acids have long been considered to serve as antioxidants that complement one another. Selenium is an essential component of intracellular and extracellular glutathione peroxidases. (See chapters 3 and 4.) Vitamin E is a membrane-associated molecule that scavenges free radicals, preventing damage to membrane lipids (Witting, 1980). Glutathione (GSH) reacts with free radicals nonenzymatically and is also a substrate for many enzyme systems. The central role of glutathione in oxidant defense has recently been strengthened by discoveries showing that it regenerates vitamin E and ascorbic acid from free radical metabolites of them (Meister, 1992). Deficiencies of selenium, vitamin E, and/or GSH often result in increased sensitivity to oxidant stress. The relationships of glutathione with the antioxidant nutrients are important. Figure 8.1 depicts the formation and fate of cellular GSH. Elements of the scheme that are affected by selenium deficiency are highlighted. The relationship between selenium and glutathione will be discussed in this chapter.

Alterations in GSH Status

GSH, γ-glutamylcysteinylglycine, is a ubiquitous nonprotein thiol. All animal cells synthesize GSH for intracellular use. It is the major cellular nonprotein thiol and is reponsible for detoxification of a large number of compounds. GSH is the source of reducing equivalents for reduction of hydroperoxides by glutathione peroxidase and is conjugated with electrophiles by glutathione S-transferase. In addition to GSH for intracellular use, the liver synthesizes GSH for transport into the plasma. Other organs, especially the kidney, degrade plasma GSH and take up its constituent amino acids. Whether plasma GSH serves a redox function in the extracellular space is not known. Selenium deficiency has been shown to affect GSH status in the liver, kidney, and plasma.

Liver

In the process of developing a model for investigation of hepatotoxicity in selenium deficiency, we examined GSH metabolism in the

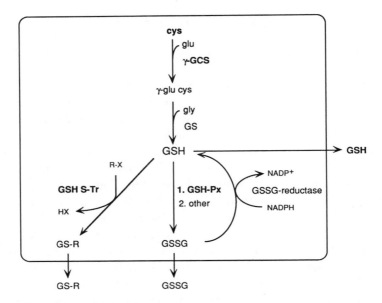

FIGURE 8.1. Relationship between selenium and glutathione (GSH). GSH is synthesized in the cell from its constituent amino acids (glu, cys, and gly) in two steps by the action of γ-glutamylcysteine synthetase (γ-GCS) and glutathione synthetase (GS). GSH formed in the hepatocyte has three potential fates: Transport out of the cell as GSH (reduced glutathione); enzymatic conjugation with electrophiles (R-X) by the glutathione S-transferases (GSH S-Tr) and transport of the conjugate out of the cell; and enzymatic or other reactions that produce GSSG (oxidized glutathione) which is transported out of the cell or reduced by the action of glutathione reductase (GSSG reductase). Enzymes whose activities are affected by selenium deficiency are shown in bold letters. Hepatocyte cysteine concentration and the release of GSH by the hepatocyte are also affected by selenium deficiency.

selenium-deficient rat liver (Hill and Burk, 1982). When isolated, selenium-adequate and selenium-deficient hepatocytes had the same GSH content (47 nmol GSH equivalents/10^6 cells). With time in incubation, intracellular GSH increased slightly in selenium-deficient hepatocytes compared to that in selenium-adequate hepatocytes (Fig. 8.2). Also, selenium-deficient hepatocytes released twice as much

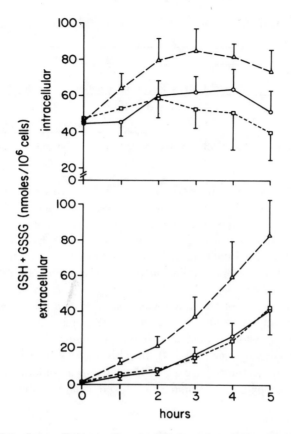

FIGURE 8.2. Intracellular and extracellular glutathione concentration of isolated hepatocytes measured by the glutathione reductase—5,5′-dithiobis(2-nitrobenzoic acid) (DTNB) recirculating assay. Control hepatocytes, ○; selenium-deficient hepatocytes, △; and vitamin E−deficient hepatocytes, □. Each symbol represents the mean of at least four experiments and one standard deviation is indicated by the bracket. Figure from Hill and Burk (1982).

GSH to the medium as did selenium-adequate hepatocytes (Fig. 8.2). Similar results were obtained with the isolated perfused rat liver model. The selenium-deficient liver released over four times as much GSH into the caval perfusate as did the selenium-adequate liver

TABLE 8.1. Glutathione released by isolated perfused liver and glutathione content of plasma[1].

| | GSH + GSSG | |
| | Perfusate | Plasma |
Diet group	(nmol GSH equiv/g liver · minute)	(nmol GSH equiv/ml)
Selenium-adequate	5.6 ± 0.9 (4)	11.2 ± 2.2 (7)
Selenium-deficient	23.8 ± 6.5 (3)	30.9 ± 7.1 (7)

[1] Data from Hill and Burk (1982). Values are Means ± SD for (n) animals.

(Table 8.1). However, there was no significant change in the level of biliary GSH in selenium deficiency. The increased GSH release in selenium deficiency was localized primarily to the basolateral membrane rather than to the canalicular membrane. Extension of this observation to the intact animal was confirmed by measurement of increased GSH content in plasma of selenium-deficient rats (Table 8.1). Thus, increased GSH synthesis and release from the selenium-deficient liver is an *in vivo* phenomena as well as an *in vitro* one.

Measurement of γ-glutamylcysteine synthetase activity showed that its activity was doubled in selenium-deficient liver compared to selenium-adequate liver (Table 8.2). This increased enzyme activity is responsible for the increased GSH synthesis in selenium-deficient isolated hepatocytes; in isolated, perfused selenium-deficient liver;

TABLE 8.2. γ-Glutamylcysteine synthetase activity in selenium-deficient and -adequate rats[1].

| | Selenium-deficient | Selenium-adequate |
Tissue	(nmol γ-glutamylcysteine formed/[mg protein · minute])	
Liver	8.4 ± 1.8*	4.5 ± 0.8*
Kidney	45.7 ± 7.2	48.6 ± 10.2
Heart	ND[2]	ND[2]
Lung	ND[2]	ND[2]
Brain	ND[2]	ND[2]

[1] Values are Means ± SD for at least four rats. Data for liver are from Hill and Burk (1982); other data are unpublished.
[2] Not detectable; activity was less than 1 and not linear with time or protein concentration.
* Means are significantly different ($P < 0.01$).

and in the selenium-deficient liver *in vivo* (Hill and Burk, 1982). γ-Glutamylcysteine synthetase activity was not increased in selenium-deficient kidney (Table 8.2). Thus, increased GSH synthesis is not a general finding in selenium-deficient tissues.

The increased hepatic γ-glutamylcysteine synthetase activity did not result in increased intracellular GSH concentration in selenium-deficient liver. This suggested that all of the GSH resulting from increased GSH synthesis in the selenium-deficient liver was transported into the extracellular space. The increased GSH release could be due to an increased demand for plasma GSH in selenium deficiency. It could be a compensatory mechanism for the loss of a selenium-containing component in the plasma.

PLASMA

After finding that selenium deficiency doubled plasma GSH concentration, we examined the affect of selenium deficiency on plasma GSH clearance (Hill and Burk, 1985). Selenium deficiency did not affect the systemic clearance or plasma half-life of GSH ($t_{1/2}$ = 3.4 ± 0.7 minutes in selenium-deficient and selenium-adequate plasma). Since GSH concentrations were doubled in selenium-deficient plasma compared to selenium-adequate plasma and systemic clearance was not changed by selenium deficiency, these results indicated that selenium deficiency doubled the rate of production of plasma GSH. This is consistent with the results obtained in isolated hepatocytes and isolated perfused livers.

Reversal of selenium-deficient plasma GSH levels to selenium-adequate levels was accomplished by dietary repletion of selenium (Hill et al., 1987a) and by injection of selenium (Hill and Burk, 1989). The return of plasma GSH to selenium-adequate levels was compared with the changes in selenoproteins that are also affected in selenium deficiency. Glutathione peroxidase, both intracellular and extracellular forms, and selenoprotein P are decreased in selenium deficiency (Yang et al., 1989). Selenium-deficient diet supplemented with 0.03 ppm selenium fed to selenium-deficient rats for 2 weeks corrected plasma GSH levels to the selenium-adequate value (Fig. 8.3). At this level of selenium supplementation, plasma glutathione peroxidase was corrected to 18% of selenium-adequate and liver

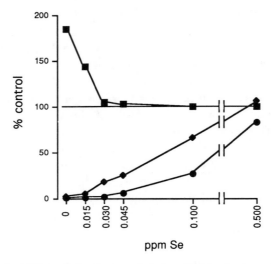

FIGURE 8.3. Effect of feeding graded levels of selenium for 2 weeks on plasma GSH (■), plasma glutathione peroxidase (◆), and liver glutathione peroxidase (●). The values shown are the percentage change caused by selenium supplementation of selenium-deficient rats (n = 4). Control rats were fed 0.5 ppm Se. Data from Hill et al. (1987a).

glutathione peroxidase was only increased to 2% of selenium-adequate. In a separate experiment, selenium (50 μg/kg) was injected ip and the time course of changes in plasma GSH, glutathione peroxidase, and selenoprotein P and liver glutathione peroxidase were measured. Selenium-deficient plasma GSH levels began to return to selenium-adequate levels within hours after the injection of selenium and were corrected completely by 24 hours (Fig. 8.4). Within this same time frame, selenoprotein P returned to selenium-adequate levels while plasma glutathione peroxidase reached 11% of selenium-adequate value. Liver glutathione peroxidase returned to 6% of selenium-adequate levels (data not shown). Thus, the metabolic change in GSH metabolism caused by selenium deficiency is reversible. It is corrected by lower dietary selenium levels than are required for production of selenium-adequate levels of glutathione peroxidase. Selenium injection corrected selenoprotein P and GSH to control

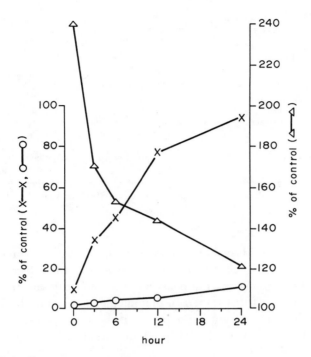

FIGURE 8.4. Time course of changes in plasma selenoprotein P concentration (X), glutathione peroxidase activity (O), and glutathione (△) following a single selenium dose (50 µg/rat). Three rats were used at each time point. Control values for selenoprotein P = 57.6 ± 0.5 µg/ml plasma; glutathione peroxidase activity = 757 ± 119 nmol NADPH oxidized/(ml plasma · minute); glutathione = 12.9 ± 1.9 nmol GSH equivalents/ml plasma. Reproduced from Hill and Burk (1989) with permission from Springer-Verlag.

values on the same time scale and before repletion of glutathione peroxidase took place.

KIDNEY

The interorgan metabolism of GSH involves GSH synthesis in the liver, release to the systemic circulation, and delivery in the blood to other tissues, where it is degraded (McIntyre and Curthoys, 1980). γ-

TABLE 8.3. Renal measurements in selenium-deficient and -adequate rats[1].

	Selenium-adequate	Selenium-deficient
a. Plasma GSH levels	(nmol GSH equivalents/ml plasma)	
Aorta	17.0 ± 5.4 (5)	40.0 ± 3.4 (5)
Renal vein	5.2 ± 0.9 (6)	9.5 ± 1.6 (6)
Renal extraction ratio	0.69	0.76
b. γ-Glutamyltranspeptidase activity	(μmol p-nitroanaline formed/[mg protein · minute])	
	1.91 ± 0.12 (4)	1.94 ± 0.20 (4)
c. Renal blood flow	(ml blood/[minute. 100 g body weight])	
	2.5 ± 0.5 (6)	4.4 ± 1.0 (6)

[1] Data from Hill and Burk (1985). Values are Means ± SD for (n) animals.

Glutamyltranspeptidase and cysteinylglycine dipeptidase are extracellular membrane-associated enzymes responsible for the degradation of GSH. After degradation, the constituent amino acids are transported into the cell. GSH distributed in this manner is hypothesized to be a transport form of cysteine and thus this is a mechanism by which cysteine from the liver is delivered to various organs of the body (Tateishi et al., 1977).

The kidney is an important site of plasma GSH removal and degradation. Therefore, we examined the effect of selenium deficiency on renal degradation and removal of GSH from the plasma (Hill and Burk, 1985). Consideration of renal GSH arteriovenous difference and renal blood flow led to the conclusion that selenium-deficient kidney removed 2.6-fold more GSH than selenium-adequate kidney (Table 8.3). γ-Glutamyltranspeptidase activity in the kidney is very high compared to that of other organs, but was unchanged from control in the selenium-deficient rat kidney (Table 8.3). This indicated that the increased turnover of plasma GSH in selenium deficiency was not due to increased degradative enzyme activity in the selenium-deficient kidney. Measurement of renal blood flow showed an increase of 70% over the flow measured in selenium-adequate rats (Table 8.3). Thus, increased delivery of GSH to the selenium-deficient kidney accounts for increased renal removal of GSH.

Degradation of increased amounts of plasma GSH by the selenium-deficient kidney results in an increased amount of cysteine being

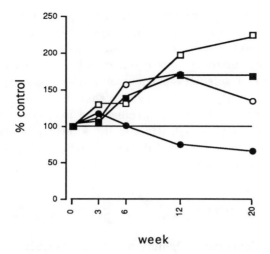

FIGURE 8.5. Changes in plasma glutathione (□), kidney glutathione (■), kidney taurine (●), and urinary taurine excretion (○) with the development of selenium deficiency. Values for selenium-deficient rats are expressed as a percentage of the value measured in control rats at the same time point. Five or six animals from each dietary group were used for each time point measurement. Data from Piao et al. (1990).

presented to the kidney. Cellular cysteine is incorporated into GSH, used for protein synthesis, or degraded to taurine and sulfate. The fate of sulfur amino acids in the selenium-deficient kidney was examined by measuring cellular GSH, cysteine, and taurine content and by determining urinary taurine and sulfate excretion (Piao et al., 1990). Male weanling Sprague-Dawley rats were maintained on selenium-deficient or selenium-adequate diets for 20 weeks. Figure 8.5 shows the changes in plasma GSH, kidney GSH, kidney taurine, and urinary taurine excretion with the development of selenium deficiency. As selenium deficiency developed, increased plasma GSH was measured at the earliest time point. This was followed by increased renal GSH content. Finally renal taurine decreased and urinary taurine excretion increased. The amount of sulfur excreted as taurine was approximately 10% of the amount of sulfur excreted as sulfate. Urinary sulfate excretion was not statistically different in

selenium-deficient and selenium-adequate rats. Therefore, these results suggest an increased flux from plasma GSH through the kidney
to urinary taurine but not to urinary sulfate.

No significant difference was found in cellular GSH, cysteine, or
taurine content of selenium-deficient and selenium-adequate heart,
brain, and testis (Piao et al., 1990). Therefore, changes in GSH
metabolism appear to be organ specific: The liver is responsible for
increased levels of plasma GSH, and the kidney is responsible for
removal of increased amounts of the plasma GSH and for excretion of
increased amounts of taurine.

Effects of GSH Changes in Selenium Deficiency

Aside from the effects of selenium deficiency on GSH synthesis and
degradation, selenium deficiency results in changes to enzymes that
utilize GSH (Fig. 8.1). In selenium deficiency, glutathione peroxidase
activity is decreased and glutathione S-transferase activity is increased. GSH is a cosubstrate required by both of these enzymes. As
a result of changes in substrate availability and enzyme activity, the
toxicity of xenobiotics is modified in selenium deficiency.

Glutathione Peroxidase

Glutathione peroxidase reduces hydrogen peroxide and organic hydroperoxides to water and organic alcohols, respectively. In 1973, it was
reported that glutathione peroxidase was a selenoenzyme (Rotruck et
al., 1973). Subsequently, it was determined that selenium was at the
active site of the enzyme (Wendel et al., 1975). As a result of
decreased selenium availability in selenium deficiency, glutathione
peroxidase protein levels and activity are decreased. The extent to
which the selenium-deficient organism is at increased oxidant risk
because of decreased glutathione peroxidase activity is uncertain.
Hydrogen peroxide can be metabolized to water by catalase and
organic hydroperoxides can be metabolized to alcohols by the non
selenium-dependent glutathione peroxidase activity of the glutathione
S-transferases. Thus, the reduction of hydroperoxides by glutathione
peroxidase may not be essential to the cell.

Studies in isolated hepatocytes and perfused organs have not always shown increased toxicity in selenium deficiency to hydroperoxides (Burk et al., 1978; Hill and Burk, 1984; Xia et al., 1985; Hill et al., 1987b). Addition of cumene hydroperoxide to selenium-deficient isolated hepatocytes did not show increased toxicity compared to similarly treated selenium-adequate isolated hepatocytes (Hill and Burk, 1984). Infusion of hydroperoxide into selenium-deficient isolated perfused rat liver (Burk et al., 1978) and into selenium-deficient isolated perfused rat heart (Xia et al., 1985) did not cause an increase in glutathione disulfide (GSSG) release as it did in selenium-adequate organs. Toxicity of hydroperoxide infusion was judged by release of lactate dehydrogenase in the effluent of the perfused organ and was unaffected by selenium deficiency.

Additional studies in the isolated perfused rat heart demonstrated that hydrogen peroxide infusion resulted in diastolic dysfunction (Konz et al., 1989). No effect on systolic function was observed. The threshold hydrogen peroxide concentration at which diastolic dysfunction occurs was lower in the selenium-deficient rat heart than in selenium-adequate rat heart. It is not known whether the diastolic dysfunction is related to the loss of glutathione peroxidase activity, another selenoprotein, or some other function of selenium.

In vivo experiments have shown that diquat, a redox cycling compound thought to produce hydrogen peroxide, causes massive lipid peroxidation in selenium-deficient rats at doses that do not injure selenium-adequate rats (Burk et al., 1980). However, the protection afforded by selenium against diquat has been shown to be unrelated to glutathione peroxidase activity. Thus, selenium deficiency makes the cell more susceptible to oxidative damage, but this is not necessarily due to the loss of glutathione peroxidase activity.

Glutathione S-Transferase

The glutathione S-transferases are a family of enzymes that conjugate electrophiles with GSH. The electrophile occupies a hydrophobic binding site on the transferase that is separate from the binding site for GSH. Among substrates conjugated with GSH by the transferases are organic hydroperoxides—e.g., *t*-butyl hydroperoxide and cumene hydroperoxide. This activity is referred to as non selenium-dependent glutathione peroxidase activity. Measurement of non selenium-dependent glutathione peroxidase activity associated with different glutathione S-transferase isoforms showed that glutathione S-transferase B (current nomenclature: 1-1) exhibited the greatest glutathione peroxidase activity with cumene hydroperoxide (Lawrence et al., 1978). It was suggested that increased glutathione S-transferase activity, i.e., non selenium-dependent glutathione peroxidase activity, in selenium deficiency was a compensation for the loss of selenium-dependent glutathione peroxidase activity.

A subsequent study examined the induction of protein concentrations of glutathione S-transferase isoforms $Y_{b1}Y_{b1}$, Y_cY_c, and Y_aY_a (current nomenclature 3-3, 2-2, and 1-1, respectively) in selenium-deficient rat liver (Arthur et al., 1987). Increased protein levels and increased transferase activity were measured for all isoforms examined. These results suggested that the increased transferase activity measured in selenium deficiency was another example of increased drug-metabolizing enzyme activity in selenium deficiency (Reiter and Wendel, 1984) rather than compensation for the loss of selenium-dependent glutathione peroxidase activity.

TABLE 8.4. Effect of acetaminophen on isolated hepatocyte viability[1].

Acetaminophen (mM)	Incubation time (hours)	Selenium-adequate	Selenium-deficient
a. Viability		(% viable)	
0	0	94 ± 3	92 ± 2
	4	73 ± 6	69 ± 11
25	0	94 ± 3	92 ± 2
	4	78 ± 7	74 ± 9
50	0	94 ± 3	92 ± 2
	4	31 ± 37	57 ± 22
b. GSH content		(nmol GSH equivalents/10^6 cells)	
0	0	42 ± 6	68 ± 5
	4	52 ± 16	68 ± 10
25	0	42 ± 6	68 ± 5
	4	15 ± 1	27 ± 9
50	0	42 ± 6	68 ± 5
	4	5 ± 4	21 ± 7

[1] Data from Hill and Burk (1984). Values are Means ± SD for at least three experiments.

Metabolism of xenobiotics by the glutathione S-transferases is a major route of detoxification for many compounds. The toxicity of chemicals detoxified by conjugation with GSH is less in selenium-deficient liver due to increased GSH synthesis. For example, the toxic metabolite of acetaminophen, N-acetyl-p-benzoquinoneimine, is detoxified by conjugation with GSH by glutathione S-transferase. Acetaminophen treatment is less toxic to isolated selenium-deficient rat hepatocytes than to selenium-adequate hepatocytes (Table 8.4a). Selenium-deficient hepatocyte intracellular GSH levels are not depleted by acetaminophen to the same extent as they are in selenium-adequate hepatocytes (Table 8.4b). *In vivo*, acetaminophen is less toxic to the selenium-deficient rat as evidenced by decreased hepatic damage (Burk and Lane, 1983). This suggests that the increased synthesis of GSH and increased glutathione S-transferase activity in selenium deficiency result in the ability to detoxify increased amounts of the acetaminophen toxic metabolite. Other compounds that are less hepatotoxic in selenium deficiency because of increased metabolism by glutathione S-transferase isoforms are iodipamide and aflatoxin B_1.

Summary and Conclusions

Selenium deficiency has multiple affects on GSH metabolism in the rat. These changes appear to occur primarily in the liver, kidney, and plasma. There is a twofold increase in hepatic GSH synthesis. This results in a twofold increase in plasma GSH concentration. Increased plasma GSH levels and increased renal blood flow result in increased delivery to and removal of GSH by the selenium-deficient kidney. The increased GSH removal by the kidney results in increased renal GSH concentrations and increased renal excretion of taurine.

The reason for the increased production of GSH in the selenium-deficient rat liver has not been elucidated. One possibility is that GSH can scavenge reactive oxygen species in a nonenzymatic manner and, thus, increased levels of GSH could protect against oxidants that normally would be removed by the selenoenzyme glutathione peroxidase.

In addition to increased GSH production, selenium deficiency results in increased hepatic glutathione S-transferase activity. Compounds metabolized by the glutathione S-transferases (e.g., acetaminophen) are detoxified more efficiently by the selenium-deficient liver and are less toxic to the animal. Organic hydroperoxides are metabolized to the corresponding organic alcohols by the non selenium-dependent glutathione peroxidase activity of the glutathione S-transferases. While it has been shown that the increased transferase activity in selenium deficiency is not a compensatory mechanism for the loss of the selenium-dependent glutathione peroxidase activity, this would be expected to result in modification of the toxicity of organic hydroperoxides in the selenium-deficient animal.

In conclusion, selenium deficiency results in changes in GSH metabolism and in the activity of enzymes that utilize glutathione as a substrate. The effect of these changes is to modify the toxicity of xenobiotics in the selenium-deficient animal.

REFERENCES

Arthur, JR, Morrice, PC, Nicol, F, Beddows, SE, Boyd, R, Hayes, JD, Beckett, GJ. The effects of selenium and copper deficiencies on glutathione S-transferase and glutathione peroxidase in rat liver. Biochem J 248: 539–544; 1987.

Burk, RF, Lane, JM. Modification of chemical toxicity by selenium deficiency. Fund Applied Toxicol 3:218–221; 1983.

Burk, RF, Lawrence, RA, Lane, JM. Liver necrosis and lipid peroxidation in the rat as the result of paraquat and diquat administration: Effect of selenium deficiency. J Clin Invest 65:1024–1031; 1980.

Burk, RF, Nishiki, K, Lawrence, RA, Chance, B. Peroxide removal by selenium-dependent and selenium-independent glutathione peroxidases in hemoglobin-free perfused rat liver. J Biol Chem 253:43–46; 1978.

Hill, KE, Burk, RF. Effect of selenium deficiency and vitamin E deficiency on glutathione metabolism in isolated rat hepatocytes. J Biol Chem 257: 10668–10672; 1982.

Hill, KE, Burk, RF. Toxicity studies in isolated hepatocytes from selenium-deficient rats and vitamin E-deficient rats. Toxicol Appl Pharmacol 72: 32–39; 1984.

Hill, KE, Burk, RF. Effect of selenium deficiency on the disposition of plasma glutathione. Arch Biochem Biophys 240:166–171; 1985.

Hill, KE, Burk, RF. Glutathione metabolism as affected by selenium deficiency. In: Wendel, A, ed. Selenium in Biology and Medicine. Berlin: Springer-Verlag; 1989, pp. 96–100.

Hill, KE, Burk, RF, Lane, JM. Effect of selenium depletion and repletion on plasma glutathione and glutathione-dependent enzymes in the rat. J Nutr 117:99–104; 1987a.

Hill, KE, Taylor, MA, Burk, RF. Influence of selenium deficiency on glutathione disulfide metabolism in isolated perfused rat heart. Biochim Biophys Acta 923:431–435; 1987b.

Konz, KH, Haap, M, Hill, KE, Burk, RF, Walsh, RA. Diastolic dysfunction of perfused rat hearts induced by hydrogen peroxide. Protective effect of selenium. J Mol Cell Cardiol 21:789–795; 1989.

Lawrence, RA, Parkhill, LK, Burk, RF. Hepatic cytosolic non selenium-dependent glutathione peroxidase activity: its nature and the effect of selenium deficiency. J Nutr 108:981–987; 1978.

McIntyre, TM, Curthoys, NP. The interorgan metabolism of glutathione. Int J Biochem 12:545–551; 1980.

Meister, A. On the antioxidant effects of ascorbic acid and glutathione. Biochem Pharmacol 44:1905–1915; 1992.

Piao, JH, Hill, KE, Hunt, RW, Burk, RF. Effect of selenium deficiency on tissue taurine concentration and urinary taurine excretion in the rat. J Nutr Biochem 1:427–432; 1990.

Reiter, R, Wendel, A. Selenium and drug metabolism—II. Independence of glutathione peroxidase and reversibility of hepatic enzyme modulations in deficient mice. Biochem Pharmacol 33:1923–1928; 1984.

Rotruck, JT, Pope, AL, Ganther, HE, Swanson, AB, Hafeman, D, Hoekstra, WG. Selenium: biochemical role as a component of glutathione peroxidase. Science 179:588–590; 1973.

Tateishi, N, Higashi, T, Naruse, A, Nakashima, K, Shiozaki, H, Sakamoto, Y. Rat liver glutathione: possible role as a reservoir of cysteine. J Nutr 107:51–60; 1977.

Wendel, A, Pilz, W, Ladenstein, R, Sawatzki, G, Weser, U. Substrate-induced redox change of selenium in glutathione peroxidase studied by X-ray photoelectron spectroscopy. Biochim Biophys Acta 377:211–215; 1975.

Witting, LA. Vitamin E and lipid antioxidants in free-radical-initiated reactions. In: Pryor, WA, ed. Free Radicals in Biology. New York: Academic Press; 1980, pp. 295–319.

Xia, Y, Hill, KE, Burk, RF. Effect of selenium deficiency on hydroperoxide-induced glutathione release from the isolated perfused rat heart. J Nutr 115:733–742; 1985.

Yang, JG, Hill, KE, Burk, RF. Dietary selenium intake controls rat plasma selenoprotein P concentration. J Nutr 119:1010–1012; 1989.

Chapter 9

Novel Strategies in Selenium Cancer Chemoprevention Research

Clement Ip and Howard E. Ganther

INTRODUCTION

Experimental studies with rodents indicate that selenium supplementation at levels above the dietary requirement is capable of protecting against tumorigenesis induced by chemical carcinogens or viruses (1–4). With few exceptions, the selenium compounds that have been examined are those readily available from commercial sources. Over 90% of such studies reported in the literature have used either selenite or selenomethionine as the test reagent. We have compiled the results of a large number of experiments involving supplementation with either selenite or selenomethionine and compared their chemopreventive efficacies using the dimethylbenz [a] anthracene (DMBA)-induced mammary tumor model in rats. On a selenium weight basis and over a graded dose range (from 1 to 5 ppm Se in the diet), our data showed that selenomethionine was not as active as selenite in mammary cancer inhibition (5). Tissue selenium concentrations in blood, liver, kidney, and skeletal muscle, on the other hand, were always higher in rats given selenomethionine compared with those given selenite. Thus the greater total body burden of selenium in selenomethionine-treated rats did not appear to confer a better protection against tumorigenesis. Based on this observation, the question that came to mind was whether selenium metabolism is necessary for its anticarcinogenic activity.

Two lines of indirect evidence have come forth from our work to suggest that this might be the case. The first set of supportive data concerns the influence of methionine availability on the chemopreventive efficacy of selenomethionine. We found that a low-methionine diet significantly reduced the protective effect of selenomethionine, even though tissue selenium was actually higher in these animals compared with those given a supplemental amount of methionine (6). When methionine is limiting, a greater percentage of selenomethionine is incorporated into body proteins in place of methionine. In other words, the anticarcinogenic activity of selenomethionine is severely compromised under a situation in which it is preferentially compartmentalized into tissue proteins instead of entering the metabolic pathway of selenium utilization and detoxification. The second set of supportive data came from the observation that the chemopreventive action of selenite was almost completely abolished by coadministration of arsenite (7), which is known to modify selenite metabolism (8). These two pieces of information, together with our earlier finding that a continuous intake of selenium is necessary to achieve maximal protection against cancer (9), strongly suggest that some active species of selenium with antitumorigenic potential is formed by the metabolism of selenium and is generated only when the supply of selenium is maintained at a certain level.

Experimental Approach and Conclusions Regarding the Relationship Between Chemical Form of Selenium and Anticarcinogenic Activity

With high intakes of selenium, the levels of intermediate metabolites are expected to rise, particularly the methylated derivatives. Figure 9.1 depicts the metabolism of selenite or selenomethionine to hydrogen selenide (refer to figure legend for details) and its sequential methylation to methylselenol, dimethylselenide, and trimethylselenonium ion (10). The objective of our research was focused on testing the anticarcinogenic activities of several synthetic selenium compounds that can enter the selenium metabolic pathway at different points. We aimed to address the following questions in our studies: (a) Does selenium have to flow through the intermediary inorganic hydrogen selenide pool for the cancer-protective effect to be manifested? (b) Does methylation of selenium enhance or diminish its chemopreventive efficacy? and (c) Is the degree of methylation important? By controlling the entry of selenium into various points of the metabolic pathway through selection of the appropriate precursor compounds to be tested, our goal was to correlate the chemopreventive efficacy of these novel selenium compounds with their metabolism to the various methylated forms (11). This approach would enable us to pinpoint more closely the active intermediate(s) that is involved in cancer protection. The precursor compounds that have been tested are those encased in boxes in Figure 9.1; the major sites where these compounds enter the metabolic pathway, as reported in previous publications (12,13), are also shown in this schematic diagram. All the chemoprevention experiments described below were done using the DMBA-induced mammary tumor model in female Sprague-Dawley rats.

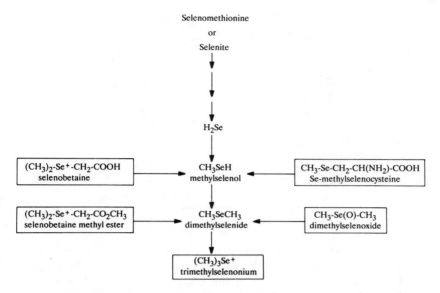

FIGURE 9.1. This schematic flow chart shows the main sites where seleno-betaine, Se-methylselenocysteine, selenobetaine methyl ester, and dimethyl-selenoxide enter the selenium metabolic pathway. The center portion of the diagram illustrates the metabolism of selenite or selenomethionine into the methylated products. The conversion of selenite to H₂Se involves the re-ductive steps through glutathione selenotrisulfide (GS-Se-SG) and glutathione selenopersulfide (GS-SeH), while selenomethionine is metabolized via the transsulfuration mechanism to selenocysteine first, and then through the enzymatic lyase reaction to H₂Se. Hydrogen selenide is regarded as a possible precursor for incorporation of selenium into selenoproteins.

The relative anticarcinogenic efficacy of the different selenium compounds is summarized in Table 9.1. For comparative purposes, the information is documented as the dose of each compound (ex-pressed as ppm Se) required to produce 50% inhibition of tumori-genesis in DMBA−mammary cancer model. The original data can be found in several of our publications (14−16). By correlating the chemical form and metabolism of the different selenium compounds (11) with their chemopreventive efficacy, we have arrived at the following five conclusions.

TABLE 9.1. Anticarcinogenic efficacy of different selenium compounds.

Compound	Dose of Se for 50% inhibition (ppm)
Se-methylselenocysteine	2
Selenobetaine	2
Selenobetaine methyl ester	2–3
Selenite	3
Selenomethionine	4–5
Selenocystine	4–5
Dimethylselenoxide	>10
Trimethylselenonium	(No effect at 80 ppm)

a. Good anticarcinogenic activity of selenium is obtained when selenium is introduced into the pathway beyond the hydrogen selenide pool. Between this entry point for selenium and its eventual conversion to excretory metabolites, the active forms presumably would be generated.

b. Certain selenium compounds, such as selenobetaine and Se-methylselenocysteine, which are able to produce a steady stream of methylated metabolites, particularly the monomethylated species, are more efficacious than selenite and are likely to have good anticarcinogenic potential.

c. Anticarcinogenic activity is lower for selenoamino acids that can be incorporated into proteins. Both selenomethionine and selenocystine show inferior activity compared to selenite. For selenomethionine, nonspecific incorporation into proteins in place of methionine may prevent the release of the monomethylated selenium moiety and thus attentuate its anticarcinogenic potential. The same is true for selenocystine, which is reduced to selenocysteine.

d. Dimethylselenoxide, which is reduced rapidly and quantitatively to dimethylselenide (about 90% of the dose is excreted in the breath as dimethylselenide), has very poor activity in chemoprevention.

e. The degree of methylation is also an important factor. Our results showed that the completely methylated form, trimethylselenonium, is relatively inactive, probably because it is rapidly excreted in urine and therefore has a modest spectrum of chemical or biochemical reactivity.

DEVELOPMENT OF NEW ANTICANCER SELENIUM COMPOUND WITH LOW TOXICITY

The development of new selenium compounds with high anticarcinogenic efficacy but low toxicity continues to be a priority in chemoprevention research involving selenium. Recently, El-Bayoumy and colleagues reported the synthesis of 1,4-phenylenebis(methylene) selenocyanate, which has an acute LD_{50} considerable higher than that of all other selenium compounds that have been tested positive for cancer-chemopreventive activity (17). Since this compound is derived from xylene, it is abbreviated to xyleneselenocyanate, or p-XSC, for simplicity. It should be noted that the design of p-XSC evolved from benzyl selenocyanate, abbreviated as BSC. Over the past decade, studies by El-Bayoumy and colleagues have demonstrated that BSC was effective in inhibiting tumor development induced by chemical carcinogens in the forestomach, mammary gland, and colon of experimental animals (18–20). Improvement of BSC was necessitated by the desirability to reduce its volatility as well as to widen the window that separates cancer chemopreventive activity and toxicity. On the basis of toxicological, metabolic, and pharmacokinetic studies, the structure of BSC was modified to generate the new compound p-XSC.

El-Bayoumy and co-workers reported that p-XSC was very effective in inhibiting DMBA-induced mammary carcinogenesis and adduct formation during the initiation phase (21). We have extended these earlier observations by investigating the dose response of p-XSC given either before or after DMBA administration (22). p-XSC was kindly provided by Dr. Karam El-Bayoumy at the American Health Foundation at Valhalla, NY. At a level of 15 ppm Se, p-XSC suppressed mammary tumorigenesis by 80% and 52% in the initiation phase and postinitiation phase, respectively. A dose-response effect was evident in the range between 5 to 15 ppm Se. When p-XSC was given at a level of 5 ppm Se continuously during the entire course of the experimental period, total tumor yield was reduced by half. This dose appeared to be about 4× less than the maximum tolerable dose (MTD). Thus successful cancer chemoprevention was achieved with this compound in the absence of any adverse effect and with a safety margin sufficiently distant from the toxicity range.

In order to compare the efficacy and tolerance of p-XSC with that of selenite and other selenocyanate analogs, the concept of chemopreventive index is introduced using the data from sodium selenite (reference compound), potassium selenocyanate, methyl selenocyanate, BSC (from Karam El-Bayoumy), and p-XSC. Chemopreventive index is calculated as the ratio of the maximum tolerable dose (MTD) to the effective dose that produces approximately 50% inhibition in tumor yield (ED_{50}). Compared to p-XSC, which has a chemopreventive index of 4.0, the other four compounds have a lower index, ranging from 1.3 for sodium selenite and potassium selenocyanate to 2.0 for methyl selenocyanate and 2.5 for BSC. A high chemopreventive index (MTD/Ed_{50}) signifies that a compound is well tolerated at doses required for cancer suppression. Using this set of criteria, p-XSC is decidedly superior to the other compounds as evidenced by a two- to threefold improvement in the index.

The bioavailability of selenium from these alkyl and aryl seleno-cyanates was also examined in attempt to gain some information regarding the rate of selenium release and its subsequent metabolism, since previous studies by us have indicated that the passage of selenium through its detoxification pathway is an important process in attaining chemoprevention by selenium. The restoration of liver glutathione peroxidase activity in selenium-deficient rats was used as a biomarker to estimate the metabolizability of the above selenium compounds. Our results showed that p-XSC was much less efficient in repleting glutathione peroxidase compared to selenite or the other selenocyanate analogs. This observation suggests that the selenium from p-XSC may be released more slowly into the metabolizable pool, thus accounting for the lower efficacy in maintaining glutathione peroxidase and the higher tolerance of the compound. p-XSC is a promising agent that can offer new insight on ways to minimize toxicity without sacrificing the anticancer potency of selenium.

DELIVERY OF SELENIUM IN A SELENIUM-ENRICHED FOOD PRODUCT

One of our goals in selenium chemoprevention research is to find ways to deliver sufficient quantities of selenium safely in a food system. Plants are known to convert inorganic selenium in soil to organoselenium analogs of naturally occurring sulfur compounds.

Vegetables with a rich source of sulfur might be expected to concentrate selenium if cultivated in medium so fertilized. This idea was tested with garlic, which is abundant in a variety of sulfur compounds. A major reason for choosing garlic as the experimental crop is that the allyl sulfides present in garlic are known to have anticarcinogenic activity (23). By substituting sulfur with selenium, we had hoped to produce more powerful anticancer agents. The hypothesis is supported by our previous research with structurally related selenium and sulfur analogs that concluded that, molecule for molecule, selenium is much more active than sulfur in cancer prevention (24). Garlic crops high in selenium were cultivated by Dr. Donald Lisk at Cornell University in Ithaca, NY, and provided to us for our experiments; and we recently reported that this selenium-enriched garlic is indeed superior to regular garlic in the suppression of mammary tumors in an animal model (25). Furthermore, the selenium in this garlic is capable of maintaining maximal activity of functional selenoenzymes at nutritional levels of intake (26). Our study therefore shows that selenium-enriched garlic represents a feasible way of delivering selenium both as an essential nutrient and as an anticarcinogen.

One could reasonably argue that the selenium-enriched garlic most likely contains many different selenium compounds that might account for these desirable attributes. But this is exactly why the approach of delivering selenium through a food system is an attractive one. Garlic contains an abundance of sulfur amino acids and their derivatives, as well as a variety of alkyl and alkenyl cysteine sulfoxides. The latter class of compounds are the precursors responsible for the pungent odor of garlic when it is crushed or sliced. Through a cascade of enzymatic and chemical reactions, allyl sulfides and disulfides are produced from the sulfoxides. Not only do these volatile sulfides contribute to the flavor of garlic, they are also active anticancer agents. When garlic is grown in a selenium-fertilized medium, selenium analogs of many of these sulfur-containing compounds are expected to be formed. At the present time, there is no information yet on which of these selenium-substituted compounds are responsible for the nutritional or anticarcinogenic activities in selenium-enriched garlic. A priority of this research is to identify the chemical forms of selenium in the garlic. It is interesting to note that tissue selenium levels are actually lower in animals ingesting the selenium-enriched garlic than in those fed a similar amount of selenium from selenite (25). This suggests that the selenium from garlic is probably excreted at a faster rate, but the lower tissue-retention characteristic does not diminish the anticancer efficacy of the selenium from garlic. Future research in this direction could potentially open a new avenue in the development of "designer food" that is suitable for implementing the strategy of general population chemoprevention.

REFERENCES

1. Milner, JA. Effect of selenium on virally induced and transplantable tumor models. Fed Proc 44:2568–2572; 1985.

2. Ip, C. The chemopreventive role of selenium in carcinogenesis. J Am Coll Toxicol 5:7–20; 1986.

3. Ip, C, Medina, D. Current concept of selenium and mammary tumorigenesis. In: Medina, D, Kidwell, W, Heppner, G, Anderson, EP, eds. Cellular and Molecular Biology of Breast Cancer. New York: Plenum Press; 1987, pp 479–494.

4. El-Bayoumy, K. The role of selenium in cancer prevention. In: DeVita, VT, Hellman, S, Rosenberg, SS, eds. Cancer Principles and Practice of Oncology, 4th ed. Philadelphia: J B Lippincott; 1991, pp 1–15.

5. Ip, C, Hayes, C. Tissue selenium levels in selenium-supplemented rats and their relevance in mammary cancer protection. Carcinogenesis 10:921–925; 1989.

6. Ip, C. Differential effect of dietary methionine on the biopotency of selenomethionine and selenite in cancer chemoprevention. J Natl Cancer Inst 80:258–262; 1988.

7. Ip, C, Ganther, H. Efficacy of trimethylselenonium versus selenite in cancer chemoprevention and its modulation by arsenite. Carcinogenesis 9:1481–1484; 1988.

8. Hsieh, HS, Ganther, HE. Biosynthesis of dimethyl selenide from sodium selenite in rat liver and kidney cell-free systems. Biochim Biophys Acta 497:205–217; 1977.

9. Ip, C. Prophylaxis of mammary neoplasia by selenium supplementation in the initiation and promotion phases of chemical carcinogenesis. Cancer Res 41:4386–4390; 1981.

10. Ganther, HE. Pathways of selenium metabolism including respiratory excretory products. J Am Coll Toxicol 5:1–5; 1986.

11. Vadhanavikit, S, Ip, C, Ganther, HE. Metabolites of sodium selenite and methylated selenium compounds administered at cancer chemoprevention levels in the rat. Xenobiotica, in press, 1993.

12. Foster, SJ, Kraus, RJ, Ganther, HE. Formation of dimethylselenide and trimethylselenonium from selenobetaine in the rat. Arch Biochem Biophys 247:12–19; 1986.

13. Foster, SJ, Kraus, RJ, Ganther, HE. The metabolism of seleno-methionine, Se-methylselenocysteine, their selenonium derivatives, and trimethylselenonium in the rat. Arch Biochem Biophys 251:77–86; 1986.

14. Ip, C, Ganther, HE. Activity of methylated forms of selenium in cancer prevention. Cancer Res 50:1206–1211; 1990.

15. Ip, C, Hayes, C, Budnick, RM, Ganther, HE. Chemical form of selenium, critical metabolites, and cancer prevention. Cancer Res 51:595–600; 1991.

16. Ip, C, Ganther, HE. Biological activities of trimethylselenonium as influenced by arsenite. J Inorg Biochem 46:215–222; 1992.

17. Conaway, CC, Upadhyaya, P, Meschter, CL, Kurtzke, C, Marcus, LA, El-Bayoumy, K. Subchronic toxicity of benzyl selenocyanate and 1,4-phenylenebis(methylene)selenocyanate in F344 rats. Fund Appl Toxicol 19:563–574; 1992.

18. El-Bayoumy, K. The effects of organoselenium compounds on induction of mouse forestomach tumors by benzo(a)pyrene. Cancer Res 45:3631–3635; 1985.

19. Reddy, BS, Sugie, S, Maruyama, H, El-Bayoumy, K, Marra, P. Chemoprevention of colon carcinogenesis by dietary organoselenium, benzylselenocyanate, in F344 rats. Cancer Res 47:5901–5904; 1987.

20. Nayini, J, El-Bayoumy, K, Sugie, S, Cohen, LA, Reddy, BS. Chemoprevention of experimental mammary carcinogenesis by the synthetic organoselenium compound, benzylselenocyanate, in rats. Carcinogenesis 10:509–512; 1989.

21. El-Bayoumy, K, Chae, Y-H, Upadhyaya, P, Meschter, C, Cohen, LA, Reddy, BS. Inhibition of 7,12–dimethylbenz(a)anthracene-induced tumors and DNA adduct formation in the mammary glands of female Sprague-Dawley rats by the synthetic organoselenium compound, 1,4-phenylenebis(methylene)-selenocyanate. Cancer Res 52:2402–2407; 1992.

22. Ip, C, El-Bayoumy, K, Upadhyaya, P, Vadhanavikit, S, Ganther, H. Formulation of a method to index the efficacy of inorganic and organic selenocyanate derivatives in mammary cancer prevention. Proc Amer Assoc Cancer Res 34:557; 1993.

23. Wargovich, MJ. Inhibition of gastrointestinal cancer by organosulfur compounds in garlic. In: Wattenberg, L, Lipkin, M, Kelloff, G, Boone, C, eds. Cancer Chemoprevention. Boca Raton, FL: CRC Press; 1992, pp 195–203.

24. Ip, C, Ganther, HE. Comparison of selenium and sulfur analogs in cancer prevention. Carcinogenesis 13:1167–1170; 1992.

25. Ip, C, Lisk, DJ, Stoewsand, GS. Mammary cancer prevention by regular garlic and selenium-enriched garlic. Nutr Cancer 17:279–286; 1992.

26. Ip, C, Lisk, DJ. Bioavailability of selenium from selenium-enriched garlic. Nutr Cancer, in press.

Chapter 10

Keshan Disease and Selenium Status of Populations in China

Yiming Xia, Jianhua Piao, Kristina E. Hill, and Raymond F. Burk

Keshan disease is a cardiomyopathy that occurs in certain regions of China. Named for Keshan County in Heilongjiang Province, where it was rampant in 1935 (Apei, 1937), the disease has also been recognized in many other locations. An inscription on a stone pillar in Huanglong County of Shaanxi Province suggests that Keshan disease occurred there in 1812 and thus is not a new condition (Shan and Xue, 1987).

Keshan disease has been a serious public health problem in China. Because of this, a number of research institutes and task groups were set up in the 1960s to study the disease and to work toward its prevention. These groups established that selenium deficiency is an underlying cause of Keshan disease and that selenium supplementation can prevent it. Selenium supplementation and an increasing content of selenium in the diet have reduced the incidence of the disease to low levels, and it is no longer a major public health problem. However, the pathogenesis of Keshan disease has never been elucidated.

A leading hypothesis is that selenium deficiency allows injury of the heart by impairing oxidant defenses. Oxidant injury is postulated to occur in other diseases as well, so an understanding of the pathogenesis of Keshan disease might advance understanding of other diseases. Biochemical characterization of populations in China has been pursued in recent years to characterize the selenium deficiency underlying Keshan disease and to determine its impact on oxidant defenses. Animal studies have also examined the effect of selenium deficiency on the heart.

LINKAGE OF SELENIUM DEFICIENCY WITH KESHAN DISEASE

There are three major epidemiological characteristics of Keshan disease (Ge et al., 1983; Yang et al., 1984). The first is its regional distribution. Keshan disease-endemic areas are focally distributed in a belt across China that extends from the northeast to the southwest. Within endemic areas are found "safety islands" in which the disease does not occur. These safe zones typically consist of a village and its environs. Inhabitants of severely affected areas have often sought refuge in these "safety islands" and some have sent susceptible children to live with relatives in them.

The second characteristic is that the disease primarily strikes children. Affected ones are typically younger than 5. Young women have been reported to develop the disease in the northeast. Keshan disease occurs only in rural areas and almost exclusively in members of farm families. The final characteristic is seasonal occurrence. In northeast China the peak incidence occurs in winter. In southwest China it occurs in summer. The annual incidence of Keshan disease in 11 northern provinces is shown in Figure 10.1. In the 1960s and early 1970s there was considerable fluctuation in the annual incidence with a peak every 3–4 years.

In the early 1960s selenium deficiency was determined to be the cause of white muscle disease in ruminants. This condition is characterized by muscular degeneration in young animals and sometimes involves the heart. It occurs only in selenium-deficient areas.

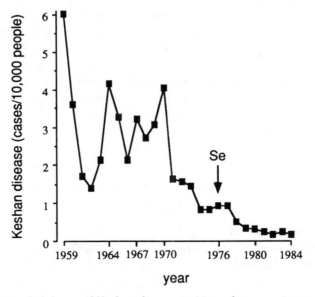

FIGURE 10.1. Incidence of Keshan disease in 11 northern provinces of China (Sun et al., 1982; Shan and Xue, 1987). Selenium addition to salt in affected areas began in 1976.

Chinese veterinarians recognized that white muscle disease was common in Keshan disease-endemic areas and suggested that selenium deficiency might contribute to the human condition. Keshan disease research groups showed that the endemic areas were selenium deficient. Crops grown in them had very low selenium content and the hair and blood of their inhabitants contained less selenium than hair and blood from people in unaffected areas (Yang et al., 1984). The selenium levels in "safety islands" were found to be slightly higher than those in affected areas.

Conclusive evidence that selenium supplementation could prevent Keshan disease was obtained by a large placebo-controlled study in Mianning County of Sichuan Province (Keshan Disease Research Group, 1979). It was carried out in 1974–1976 by the Keshan Disease Research Group of the Chinese Academy of Medical Sciences. Following that study, selenite supplementation of salt was instituted in high-incidence areas. Figure 10.1 shows that the incidence of Keshan disease in 11 northern provinces has been very low since then. There has been a decline in the incidence of the disease in other provinces as well because of selenium supplementation and increased shipment of food between selenium-deficient and selenium-adequate areas. In 1989 only 58 cases were reported in all of China and in 1990 only 45.

BIOCHEMICAL CHARACTERIZATION OF POPULATIONS AT RISK FOR KESHAN DISEASE

A series of three studies was carried out between 1987 and 1991 to determine some of the biochemical characteristics of populations at risk for Keshan disease. These studies were conducted by us in Liangshan Prefecture of Sichuan Province. The prefecture is a selenium-deficient area and a nutrition survey carried out by its antiepidemic station in 1985 estimated the per capita selenium intake from food to be 11 μg per day.

Two of its counties, 150 km apart, were chosen for study. Mianning County had been the site of the intervention study carried out in 1974–1976 (Keshan Disease Research Group, 1979). Because of the high incidence of Keshan disease there, supplementation of its salt

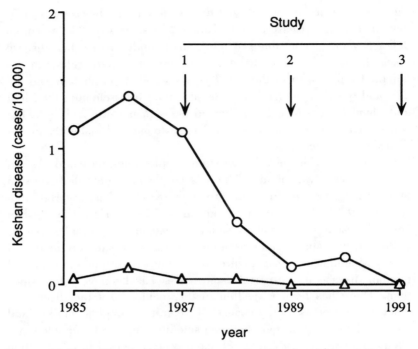

FIGURE 10.2. Incidence of Keshan disease in Mianning ($\triangle$) and Dechang ($\bigcirc$) counties. Both counties are located in a selenium-deficient area but selenium has been added to the salt in Mianning County since 1983. The three studies described in the text are indicated.

TABLE 10.1. Selenium status in Dechang and Mianning Counties in 1987[1].

	Selenium content (µg/dl)		Glutathione peroxidase	
	Blood	Plasma	Plasma (U/L)	Red cells (U/g Hb)
Dechang				
Boys[2]	1.8 ± 1.0	1.3 ± 0.5	29 ± 15	2.8 ± 1.7
Men[3]	2.2 ± 0.7	1.6 ± 0.4	51 ± 16	4.6 ± 2.9
Mianning				
Boys[2]	4.7 ± 0.9	4.0 ± 1.1	87 ± 15	8.4 ± 3.3
Men[3]	5.3 ± 0.9	4.2 ± 1.1	118 ± 21	11 ± 3.6

[1] Values are means ± SD, n = 15–22. Data from Xia et al., 1989.
[2] Age range 8–12 years.
[3] Age range 17 years and older.

supply with selenite had been instituted in mid-1983, increasing the per capita daily selenium intake to 80 μg. Mianning County served as the control with normal selenium intake. Dechang County had never been supplemented with selenium and served as the selenium-deficient area in the studies. Figure 10.2 shows the reported incidence of Keshan disease in the two counties from 1985 through 1991. Selenium supplementation had virtually eliminated the condition from Mianning County by 1985. The incidence in Dechang County was appreciable in 1985 but it declined after 1987. No new cases of the disease were reported in either county in 1991.

SELENIUM STATUS IN DECHANG AND MIANNING COUNTIES

The study carried out in 1987 included measurement of selenium and glutathione peroxidase activity in blood and plasma of boys 8−12 and men 17 and over (Xia et al., 1989). Table 10.1 shows that all measures of selenium status indicated that Dechang had a lower status than Mianning. The values from Dechang placed it in the range of Keshan disease-endemic areas, which typically have blood selenium levels of 2 μg/dl or less (Yang et al., 1984). The values from Mianning were safely above the Keshan disease range.

The 1989 study investigated age and sex effects on selenium status. Figure 10.3 shows that the population varied in selenium status according to age. The youngest (2−5 years old) and the oldest (>60 years old) subjects had lower selenium status than subjects of intermediate ages. No significant sex effect was noted. These data are consistent with Keshan disease occurring in young children because that age group had the lowest selenium status of the groups studied. They do not explain the reported occurrence in young women.

By 1989 the selenium status of boys in Dechang County had improved from the Keshan disease range to a safe range (Fig. 10.4), and the incidence of the disease had fallen further (Fig. 10.2). Figure 10.4 also shows that blood selenium concentration in men rose from 2.2 to 5.1 μg per dl by 1991. Thus, selenium status improved in the inhabitants of Dechang County between 1987 and 1991 and this accounts for the disappearance of new cases of Keshan disease there. The improvement in selenium status between 1987 and 1989 was probably caused by increased consumption of foods obtained from

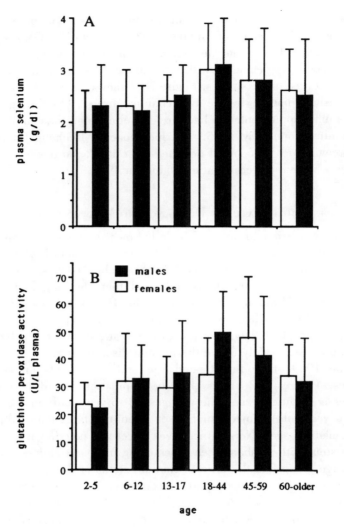

FIGURE 10.3. Effect of age on plasma selenium content and glutathione peroxidase activity in selenium-deficient subjects. The study was performed in Dechang county in 1989. It is study 2 in Figure 10.2. Values are means ± SD, n = 12–28.

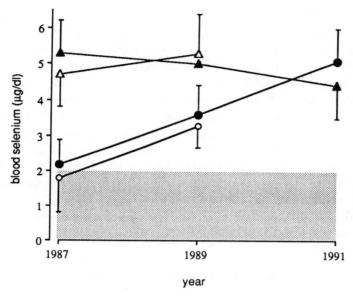

FIGURE 10.4. Blood selenium level in men 17 years of age and older (closed symbols) and boys 8 to 12 years old (open symbols). Subjects are from the selenium-deficient Dechang County (circles) and Control Mianning county (triangles) in the three studies indicated in Figure 10.2. Values are means ± SD, n = 13–50.

selenium-adequate areas because no increases were found in the selenium content of rice grown in Dechang County (data not shown). The further improvement by 1991 could have been partly due to inadvertent distribution of selenized salt in Dechang, which began occurring in 1990.

EFFECTS OF SELENIUM STATUS ON OTHER OXIDANT DEFENSES

Selenium protects against some oxidant stresses. The protection is thought to be mediated by selenoproteins such as the glutathione peroxidases and selenoprotein P. However, selenium deficiency also affects glutathione metabolism (Hill and Burk, 1982) and brings about changes in a number of enzymes that do not contain the element (Reiter et al., 1989). For that reason, glutathione and several antioxidant enzymes were measured in the blood of selenium-deficient and control subjects in the 1987 study (Xia et al., 1989).

Plasma and red-blood-cell glutathione concentrations in all groups of subjects were in the range considered to be normal. Red-blood-cell catalase and superoxide dismutase activities were not affected by selenium status. Finally, plasma vitamin E concentration was not affected by selenium status, but it was slightly below the normal range in both groups. It ranged from 3.8 to 4.3 mg/dl. Thus, the subjects from Dechang, who were susceptible to Keshan disease, were selenium deficient and mildly vitamin E deficient. The subjects from Mianning were only mildly vitamin E deficient and had normal selenium status. This is potentially important because an animal model of cardiac damage in selenium deficiency (see below) requires that vitamin E deficiency be present simultaneously.

Studies of Keshan Disease

Manifestations of Keshan Disease

Four different clinical presentations of Keshan disease have been described (Yang et al., 1984). The acute form is associated with acute heart failure and a high incidence of cardiogenic shock. Chest pain often occurs. Cardiomegaly is usually not present and pathological examination of fatal cases reveals a patchy necrosis throughout the myocardium. Coronary arteries are normal. Patients with this form of Keshan disease frequently die, but treatment with intravenous vitamin C is considered to be efficacious and may salvage some (Yang et al., 1984). Administration of selenium to these acutely ill patients is not effective treatment.

Subacute Keshan disease runs a course of weeks to months. Patients have signs and symptoms of heart failure and cardiomegaly is present. Treatment with selenium can interrupt progression of the disease and prevent death. Cardiomegaly and cardiac function impairment are often sequelae.

The insidious onset of heart failure occurs in chronic Keshan disease. It is manifested by dyspnea on exertion and edema. The heart is dilated and pathological examination demonstrates diffuse myocardial fibrosis with loss of muscle fibers. The condition is not reversible. Latent Keshan disease is similar to the chronic form except that there are no symptoms.

The process underlying Keshan disease is necrosis of myocardial cells. The rapidity and extent of this necrosis determine the clinical presentation.

STUDIES OF PATIENTS WITH KESHAN DISEASE

A large-scale study of Keshan disease was carried out during 1984–1986 in Chuxiong Prefecture, Yunnan Province. It was conducted by 293 scientific workers (including author Y.X.) representing 16 laboratories from seven provinces. Epidemiology, ecological environmental aspects, clinical manifestations, pathology, and biochemistry of Keshan disease were studied. Study subjects included 3,648 healthy children in 56 villages. Some were in areas affected by Keshan disease and some were in areas not affected. One hundred sixty-seven children with Keshan disease were studied and 27 autopsies were carried out on children who died from subacute Keshan disease. Autopsy controls were studied, as well as some controls from Jilin Province, where Keshan disease does not occur. The latter were healthy subjects who died suddenly and from whom tissue was

TABLE 10.2. Selenium content and glutathione peroxidase activity of heart and liver in children dying from Keshan disease and from other causes[1].

	Selenium (µg/100 g)	Glutathione peroxidase (U/mg protein)[2]
Heart		
Keshan disease	2.5 ± 1	10 ± 5*
Controls	5.5 ± 3	26 ± 21*
Liver		
Keshan disease	5.2 ± 3	7 ± 4**
Controls	8.9 ± 5	38 ± 11**

[1] Children dying from causes other than Keshan disease are controls. Values are means ± SD, n = 3–11.
[2] The substrate used was H_2O_2.
*, ** Values with the same superscript are significantly different ($P < 0.05$) by the t-test.

obtained. The results of this study were published in book form (Yu et al., 1988). A few of the findings will be presented here.

Table 10.2 compares selenium and glutathione peroxidase activity in heart and liver of children dying from Keshan disease with results from children dying of other causes. Both groups of subjects lived in the same areas. There was a tendency for the subjects with Keshan disease to have lower heart and liver selenium levels than controls. Their glutathione peroxidase activities were statistically significantly lower than those of controls. Subjects from Jilin Province had heart selenium levels of $13 \pm 3 \mu g/100 g$ and heart glutathione peroxidase activity of $73 \pm 12 U/mg$ protein. Those values were considerably higher than the values of the subjects living in the areas affected by Keshan disease (Table 10.2). These results are consistent with reports that subjects living in areas where Keshan disease occurs have a poor selenium status. Moreover, they suggest that the patients dying of Keshan disease might be a subset with an even poorer selenium status.

Other studies were carried out on the cardiac tissue. Ulrastructural studies showed that mitochondrial alterations were associated with low selenium content. Biochemical results were different between Keshan disease-affected hearts and controls. Notable among these was an increase in calcium content in selenium deficiency, which could be an indicator of cell injury. Low selenium status correlated with changes in spectrin–actin binding in erythrocytes. The Chinese investigators interpreted the results of this comprehensive study as suggesting that weak oxidant defenses are important in the etiology of Keshan disease.

Effects of Selenium Deficiency on Rat and Pig Hearts

Animal studies have been carried out to assess the effect of selenium deficiency on cardiac metabolism and function. We used the isolated perfused rat heart for a series of experiments because it is a well-characterized experimental system and selenium-deficient rats are readily available.

The first two investigations assessed the effect of selenium deficiency on metabolism of hydroperoxides by glutathione peroxidase (Xia et al., 1985; Hill et al., 1987). Selenium deficiency decreased cardiac glutathione peroxidase activity to 5% of control. Infused hydroperoxide was metabolized via glutathione peroxidase in control hearts as indicated by it causing an increase in intracellular GSSG and release of GSSG into the effluent. Infusion of hydroperoxide into selenium-deficient hearts did not raise intracellular GSSG concentration or cause release of GSSG. This was interpreted as evidence that selenium-deficient hearts had impaired hydroperoxide metabolism and that they might be susceptible to injury by those oxidant compounds.

To assess the susceptibility of selenium-deficient heart to injury by hydroperoxides, a working perfused heart model was used (Konz et al., 1989). This model employed a latex balloon in the left ventricle so that pressure in that chamber could be monitored. Systolic and diastolic pressures were stable for 70 minutes during baseline perfusion in selenium-deficient and control hearts. Infusion of hydrogen peroxide (375 nmol/minute) into selenium-deficient hearts led to a rise in end-diastolic pressure at 45 minutes. There was no effect on systolic pressure. Control hearts functioned normally for the entire 70 minutes at this level of hydrogen peroxide infusion. These results indicate that the impaired glutathione-dependent hydroperoxide metabolism, which is characteristic of the selenium-deficient heart, is linked to impaired diastolic function under conditions of hydroperoxide challenge. They suggest that cardiac dysfunction and injury might occur in selenium deficiency if an oxidant stress occurs that leads to increased hydroperoxide concentrations.

Pigs develop a cardiac injury resembling acute Keshan disease when they are fed a diet deficient in selenium and vitamin E (Van Vleet et al., 1977). The injury does not occur in pigs deficient in only one nutrient. This condition was studied as a potential model for Keshan disease (Konz et al., 1991). Pigs were fed control, selenium-deficient, vitamin E–deficient, or doubly-deficient diets from weaning. Thirteen of 20 doubly-deficient pigs died spontaneously. Many of them had apparently been healthy but died suddenly. None of the singly-deficient or control pigs died spontaneously. Cardiac catheterizations were performed in 9 control and in 11 doubly-deficient pigs to assess physiological function. There were no significant differences in diastolic or in systolic function between these groups. However, end-diastolic pressure was higher in the four doubly deficient pigs that later died spontaneously than in the control pigs. This suggests that the injury in this condition is associated with diastolic dysfunction.

Two different animal models have been studied. Selenium deficiency predisposes the heart to injury in each, but in neither one does selenium deficiency alone cause injury. The stresses leading to the injury in the selenium-deficient hearts were different in the two models but both were oxidative in nature. Thus, it appears that selenium deficiency predisposes the heart to oxidant injury. Glutathione peroxidase appears to be the selenium function that protects the perfused rat heart. Selenoprotein P has been postulated to scavenge free radicals and might play a role *in vivo*.

ROLE OF SELENIUM IN THE PATHOGENESIS OF KESHAN DISEASE

Selenium deficiency is a necessary condition for the development of Keshan disease. Numerous studies have shown that populations in which the disease is endemic have a low selenium status (Yang et al., 1984). No other potential pathogenetic factor has been demonstrated in these populations with the consistency of selenium deficiency, although marginal plasma vitamin E levels are often present.

Animal models indicate that selenium deficiency is not sufficient to cause cardiac injury. Perfused hearts from severely selenium-deficient rats had normal systolic and diastolic function under baseline conditions (Konz et al., 1989). Selenium-deficient pigs did not develop cardiac injury (Konz et al., 1991). Observations in humans are in agreement with the animal studies. Severely selenium-deficient populations are known in which Keshan disease has not occurred (Lombeck et al., 1977). Also, only a few individuals in the susceptible Chinese populations develop the disease.

Study of animal models indicates that selenium deficiency predisposes them to cardiac injury. In the perfused rat-heart model, the injury was brought about by hydrogen peroxide infusion. In the *in vivo* pig model, it was caused by vitamin E deficiency. Both these challenges can be considered to be oxidant stress. Studies in China have suggested that infections, which produce oxidant stress, might precipitate Keshan disease.

Thus, a hypothesis for the pathogenesis of Keshan disease that is compatible with the available human and animal data can be stated: Selenium deficiency is a necessary condition for the development of Keshan disease, but an additional factor, probably an oxidant stress, is required. Factors that can potentially cause oxidant stress include deficiencies of nutrients such as vitamin E, copper, and vitamin C; chemicals such as sulfonamides and nitrofurans; and inflammatory processes associated with white cell and macrophage activation.

ACKNOWLEDGMENTS

Research by the authors is supported by NIH grants HL 36371, ES 02497, and ES 00267.

REFERENCES

Apei, H. Report of etiological survey on Keshan disease. Research Reports of Continental Academy (in Japanese); 1:1–10; 1937.

Ge, K, Xue, A, Bai, J, Wang, S. Keshan disease-an endemic cardiomyopathy in China. Virchows Arch Pathol Anat 401:1–15; 1983.

Hill, KE, Burk, RF. Effect of selenium deficiency and vitamin E deficiency on glutathione metabolism in isolated rat hepatocytes. J Biol Chem 257: 10668–10672; 1982.

Hill, KE, Taylor, MA, Burk, RF. Influence of selenium deficiency on glutathione disulfide metabolism in isolated perfused rat heart. Biochim Biophys Acta 923:431–435; 1987.

Keshan Disease Research Group. Observations on effect of sodium selenite in prevention of Keshan disease. Chinese Med J 92: 471–476; 1979.

Konz, KH, Haap, M, Hill, KE, Burk, RF, Walsh, RA. Diastolic dysfunction of perfused rat hearts induced by hydrogen peroxide. Protective effect of selenium. J Mol Cell Cardiol 21:789–795; 1989.

Konz, KH, Walsh, RA, Hill, KE, Xia, Y, Lane, JM, Haap, M, Burk, R. Cardiac injury caused by selenium and vitamin E deficiency in the minipig: biochemical and hemodynamic studies. J Trace Elem Exp Med 4:61–67; 1991.

Lombeck, I, Kasperek K, Harbisch, HD, Feinendegen, LE, Brewer, HJ. The selenium state of children. I. Serum selenium concentrations at different ages; activity of glutathione peroxidase of erythrocytes at different ages; selenium content of food of infants. Eur J Pediatr 125:81–88; 1977.

Reiter, R, Otter, R, Haney, HM, Wendel, A. Selenium-dependent metabolic modulations in mouse liver, In: Wendel, A, ed. Selenium in Biology and Medicine. pp 85–89. Springer Verlag, Berlin.

Shan, S, Xue, A. The morbidity fluctuation, prevention and treatment of Keshan disease in Shaanxi province. In: Yu, W, ed. The Study on Prevention and Treatment of Keshan Disease in China. Publishing House of Chinese Environmental Science; 1987, pp 61–68 (in Chinese).

Sun, J, Lu, Y, Wu, G, Teng, R. A survey of the epidemic of Keshan disease in the north of China. Chinese J Endemiology 1:2–5; 1982 (in Chinese).

Van Vleet, JF, Ferrans, VJ, Ruth, GR. Ultrastructural alterations in nutritional cardiomyopathy of selenium-vitamin E deficient swine. I. Fiber lesions. Lab Invest 37:188–196; 1977.

Xia, Y, Hill, KE, Burk, RF. Effect of selenium deficiency on hydroperoxide-induced glutathione release from the isolated perfused rat heart. J Nutr 115:733–742; 1985.

Xia, Y, Hill, KE, Burk, RF. Biochemical studies of a selenium-deficient population in China: Measurement of selenium, glutathione peroxidase and other oxidant defense indices in blood. J Nutr 119:1318–1326; 1989.

Yang, G, Chen, J, Wen, Z, Ge, K, Zhu, L, Chen,X, Chen, X. The role of selenium in Keshan disease. Adv Nutr Res 6:203–231; 1984.

Yu, W, et al. Collected Works of a Comprehensive Scientific Survey on Keshan Disease in Chuxiong Prefecture. People's Medical Publishing House; 1988 (in Chinese) Beijing.

Chapter 11

Nationwide Selenium Supplementation in Finland— Effects on Diet, Blood and Tissue Levels, and Health

Pertti Varo, Georg Alfthan, Jussi K. Huttunen, and Antti Aro

Finnish rocks and soils are low in selenium: The concentration range is only 0.03−0.10 mg/kg. As a result, the selenium content of Finnish agricultural soils is low (0.2−0.3 mg/kg). Low temperatures and high humidity characteristic of the climate in Finland together with relatively low pH and high iron content of the soil favor deposition of selenium in reduced forms (1) known to be poorly available to plants. Thus, the geochemical and climatic conditions explain the fact that Finland is a low-selenium area both with regard to the soil and the biosphere.

After the introduction of more efficient animal husbandry methods in the 1950s and 1960s, muscular dystrophy and other diseases associated with insufficient selenium intakes became a problem in Finland. Despite the general practice of supplementing all commercial animal feeds with sodium selenite (0.1 mg selenium/kg dry feed) since 1969, deficiency symptoms have regularly been encountered in domestic animals; and selenium medication has been necessary. In the late 1970s, it was shown that all Finnish agricultural products contained exceptionally low amounts of selenium (2). The dietary intake of selenium varied in the 1970s depending on the ratio of imported to domestic grain in the diet, but most of the time it was as low as 25 µg/10 MJ (2,400 kcal).

DECISION TO SUPPLEMENT FERTILIZERS WITH SELENIUM

Reports on selenium intervention studies in China (3) combined with epidemiological studies in Finland suggesting that a low serum selenium concentration is a risk factor both for coronary disease and for cancer (4,5) raised concerns about the sufficiency of selenium nutrition in Finland. Domestic grain was regarded as being of poor quality because of its low selenium content, and self-medication with commercial selenium preparations became popular. These factors formed the basis for discussion of the possibility of supplementing the Finnish diet with selenium. Fertilization was thought to be a safe and efficient way to increase the selenium intake of the population, because plants act as a buffer between fertilizer and man, and inorganic selenium compounds are transformed to organic forms by the plants.

Early studies on the use of selenium in fertilizers had mainly focused on selenite. A series of studies in Denmark and Finland (6–9) demonstrated that most of the selenium that was added to agricultural soil as selenite was rapidly altered into a form that was poorly available to plants. In contrast, selenium added as selenate stayed in an available form for several months. The selenium content of spring wheat, barley, and timothy grass could be effectively increased by using fertilizers containing selenate. The amount of selenium needed to increase the selenium content of grass was smaller compared to the amount needed to increase the concentration of cereal plants.

The Ministry of Agriculture and Forestry of Finland decided in 1983 to supplement the multimineral fertilizers with selenium in the form of sodium selenate starting in the fall of 1984. An expert group appointed by the government proposed that the fertilizers for grain production would be supplemented with 16 mg/kg and those for fodder and hay production with 6 mg/kg as sodium selenate (10). The primary goal was to produce a tenfold increase in the selenium concentration of cereal grains. It was foreseen, however, that all agricultural products would be affected as well. The expert group has also monitored the effects of selenium fertilization and reported annually on the effects on soils, waters, animal feeds, grain crops, foods, and human sera (11). The amount of selenium added to the fertilizers was kept constant until 1990, when it was reduced to 6 mg/kg for all fertilizers (12).

This overview describes the effects of the selenium fertilizers on diet, blood and tissue levels, and health in Finland in 1984–1992.

EFFECT OF SELENIUM SUPPLEMENTATION OF FERTILIZERS ON FOOD SELENIUM

The effect of selenium fertilization on the selenium content of different types of foodstuffs is seen in Table 11.1.

GRAIN

The original selenium concentration of all cereals grown in Finland was 10 µg/kg or below (2). In comparison, the selenium concentration of

TABLE 11.1. Selenium content (mg/kg dry matter, Mean ± SE) of Finnish retail-store foodstuffs in 1984–1992.

	n[1]	1984[2]	n[1]	1990[3]	n[1]	1992[4] (March)
Wheat bread, French loaf	24	0.05 ± 0.04	16	0.23 ± 0.02	4	0.14 ± 0.01
Rye bread, whole	24	0.07 ± 0.05	16	0.06 ± 0.02	4	0.04 ± 0.01
Potato	2	<0.01	16	0.11 ± 0.03	4	0.07 ± 0.01
Beef, steak	24	0.17 ± 0.06	16	0.64 ± 0.08	4	0.54 ± 0.05
Pork, fillet	24	0.35 ± 0.07	16	1.09 ± 0.09	4	0.84 ± 0.11
Milk, whole	24	0.06 ± 0.01	16	0.23 ± 0.02	4	0.17 ± 0.01
Cheese, Edam type	24	0.09 ± 0.02	16	0.42 ± 0.04	4	0.29 ± 0.01
Egg	24	0.69 ± 0.15	16	1.27 ± 0.13	4	1.16 ± 0.26

[1] Number of samples.
[2] Before selenium fertilization.
[3] The amount of sodium selenate in fertilizers used for grain production (16 mg/kg) and in fertilizers used for fodder and hay (6 mg/kg).
[4] The amount of sodium selenate in all fertilizers (6 mg/kg) since 1991.

European cereals varies usually between 20 and 50 μg/kg and that of North American cereals between 200 and 500 μg/kg (13). The level of selenium to be added to fertilizers was chosen to raise the selenium concentration in cereals about tenfold. Figure 11.1 shows the changes in the selenium content of bread cereals grown in Finland from 1984 to 1991. The average selenium content of spring wheat exceeded 200 μg/kg in 1985, the first year of supplementation. In 1989 it was nearly 300 μg/kg, and in 1991, after the selenium level in fertilizers was lowered, it decreased to the average of 125 μg/kg. The increase in winter cereals (rye and winter wheat) was considerably less, the concentrations varying between 20 and 70 μg/kg (14). There are at least two explanations for this difference. Winter cereals are usually given only light selenium-supplemented multimineral fertilization in the fall during sowing, while nitrogen fertilizers without selenium are applied in the spring. Selenate may be reduced to selenite and thus bound to the soil during the winter season. Further, some of the selenate may be leached.

Oats and barley are grown in large quantities in Finland for animal feeding. They are sown in the spring, and consequently their response to selenium fertilization was nearly identical to that of spring wheat.

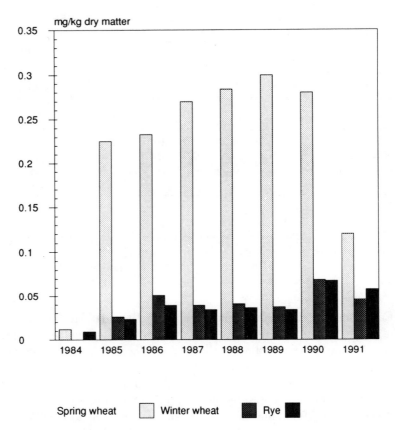

FIGURE 11.1. Selenium content of wheat and rye grown in Finland in 1984–1991. Selenium fertilization became effective in 1985.

The average selenium concentrations have varied from 220 to 260 μg/kg. Figure 11.2 shows the farm-to-farm variation in the selenium content of barley produced in 1989. The majority of the samples lies between 100 and 300 μg/kg. However, some of the farms still produced grain of nearly original selenium content (about 10 μg/kg), while concentrations in others exceeded the average level severalfold. The variation may have importance in animal feeding, since farm animals eat fodder produced in one single farm throughout their lives. On the other hand, in human nutrition only the average level has

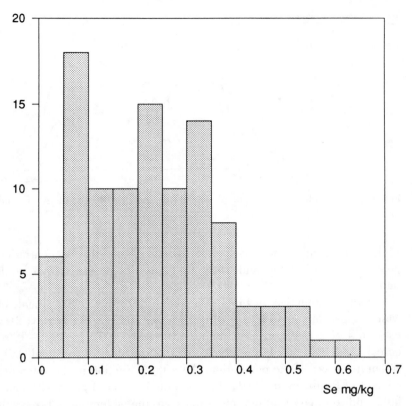

FIGURE 11.2. Farm-to-farm variation in the selenium content of barley grown in Finland in 1989.

significance, as the modern food-service system effectively mixes the grain and flour collected from individual farms. This practice cuts off both high and low levels.

Finland occasionally imports grain because of an inadequate or low-quality harvest, and domestic grain and imported grain are mixed for milling in ratios stipulated by the Ministry of Agriculture. A substantial part of the grain is imported from North America. The imported grain has raised the selenium content of flour and bread even during the years of selenium fertilization, as the selenium content of North American grain was higher than the grain produced in

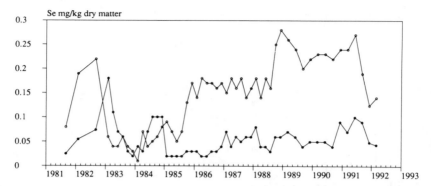

FIGURE 11.3. Selenium content of wheat (O) and rye (●) bread in Finland from 1981 to 1992.

Finland with selenium-enriched fertilizers. Thus, the concentration peaks in 1982, 1984, and 1988 in Figure 11.3 result from grain imports.

Cereal consumption in Finland is about 200 g/day (120 g wheat, of which approximately 15% is winter wheat; 50 g rye; 5 g barley; 10 g oats; and 15 g rice and other imported cereals) (15). In 1985–1990 cereal products contributed about 20% (25 µg/day) of the total daily selenium intake of the population. After the reduction in the selenium content of fertilizers in 1991, the selenium content of grain will again fall, and the contribution of cereals to the selenium intake will probably decrease to about 15 µg/day.

MEAT

The selenium content of beef produced in Finland in the mid-1970s was low—an average concentration of about 50 µg/kg dry matter. Pork contained more selenium (about 200 µg/kg dry matter), probably because of regular selenite supplementation of commercial feeds. Even this level was low compared to the reported values from other countries.

Selenite raises the selenium content of muscular tissues less effectively than does organic selenium (16). This explains the dramatic effect of the selenium fertilization on the selenium content of meat. The concentration in beef in 1990 was about 600 µg/kg dry matter (more than a 10-fold increase from the 1970s), and that of pork about 1,100 µg/kg dry matter. The selenium content of broiler chicken was about 800 µg/kg dry matter in 1991 (17).

Meat and meat products are currently the main dietary source of selenium in Finland. The contribution to the total selenium intake is about 40% (nearly 50 µg/day). After the reduction in the selenium content of fertilizers, the first signs of a decrease in meat selenium were observed in December 1991. (See also Table 11.1.) A new plateau will probably be reached during 1992. However, the relative significance of meat products as a source of selenium may increase because of the proportionately greater reduction in selenium intake from cereals.

DAIRY PRODUCTS AND EGGS

In the mid-1970s the selenium concentration of milk was very low (about 30 µg/kg dry matter; 3–4 µg/L). It slowly increased in the early 1980s, probably because of increasing use of selenite-containing commercial feeds and mineral concentrates and selenium medication of cattle. The effect of selenium-supplemented fertilizers on milk composition was rapid and substantial. Selenium-supplemented fertilizers were used for the first time in May 1985. The milk samples collected in June 1985 already contained about 130 µg selenium/kg dry matter instead of the earlier level of 50 µg/kg dry matter. The plateau, 175 µg/kg dry matter in the summer and 225 µg/kg dry matter in the winter, was reached in a few months (18). After the decrease in the amount of selenium in fertilizers in 1991, a change into the opposite direction was observed already in the same summer.

The selenium content of eggs was relatively high (about 450 µg/kg dry matter) already in the mid-1970s because of the use of selenium-enriched feeds. After 1985 the concentration gradually rose to the level of 1,200 µg/kg dry matter. The contribution of dairy products and eggs to the total selenium intake was about 30 µg/day (over 25%) in 1990.

FISH

Before selenium fertilization the relative importance of fish as a source of selenium was much higher than today, and the contribution varied from 10 to 25% of the total intake depending on the amount of imported grain. The present contribution is approximately 6%. The selenium content of fish has remained unchanged—i.e., between 500 and 1,500 µg/kg dry matter—depending on the species and the fat content of fish (19). The average amount of selenium obtained from fish is presently about 5 µg/day/person.

POTATOES

Selenium fertilization has increased the selenium content of potatoes at least 10-fold as compared to the level of the mid-1970s. The level in 1990 was about 100 µg/kg dry matter, and in 1991 it was about 60 µg selenium/kg. The average selenium intake from potatoes was about 3 µg/day in 1985–1990 and 2 µg/day in 1991.

VEGETABLES

The response to the supplementation has varied by the type of vegetable (20). Tomato is a low responder (present concentration about 30 µg selenium/kg dry matter), while high concentrations have been encountered in different crucifers such as white cabbage (600 µg selenium/kg dry matter) and cauliflower (700 µg/kg dry matter).

DIETARY INTAKE

The average daily selenium intake in the mid-1970s, when grain was not imported, was 25 µg/person. In the early 1980s, when grain was imported, the intake was 40–50 µg/day (21). However, most of the time the selenium intake was below the lower limit of the safe and adequate intake for selenium as defined by the U.S. National Academy of Sciences (50 µg/day) (22).

The selenium supplementation of fertilizers affected the average intake substantially (Fig. 11.4). A plateau of 110–120 µg/day was reached in 1987, and it remained constant until 1990. The reduction of the amount of selenium in fertilizers from 1991 was reflected in food selenium content during the last 2–3 months of 1991. Based on selenium determinations in March 1992, the estimated intake was ca. 95 µg/day. A new plateau will probably be reached in 1992 and is likely to be between 80 and 90 µg/day.

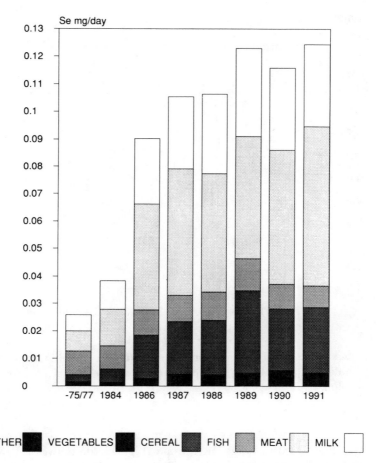

FIGURE 11.4. Average dietary selenium intake (energy level of 10 MJ) in Finland before and during selenium fertilization.

HUMAN STUDIES

SERUM AND WHOLE BLOOD

Serum selenium concentration in European populations ranges from 0.80 to 1.65 μmol/L (23,24). The serum selenium concentration in Finland varied in the 1970s between 0.63−0.76 μmol/L (25,26), a

μmol/l

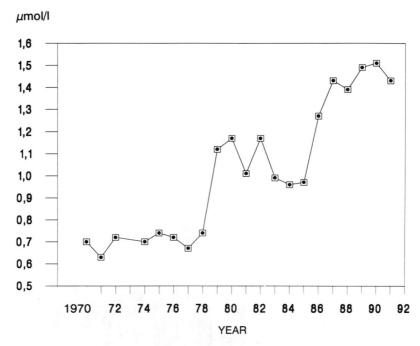

FIGURE 11.5. Mean serum selenium concentration of healthy adults in Finland during 1971–1991. Each point represents the annual mean of several samplings.

level that was the lowest in Europe (Fig. 11.5). Between 1979 and 1985 the concentration fluctuated between 0.89 and 1.23 μmol/L depending on the amount of imported high-selenium wheat.

Since 1985 the serum selenium level has been monitored both in urban and rural populations. Before selenium fertilization the mean serum selenium concentration was slightly higher in the urban follow-up group than in the rural group (Table 11.2). By 1988 the mean serum selenium level in both groups had increased to 1.40 μmol/L. The maximum level, 1.52 μmol/L, observed in 1989, was due to increased use of imported high-selenium North American wheat in 1988–1990. In 1991 serum selenium levels returned to the 1988 level (Fig. 11.5).

TABLE 11.2. Serum selenium concentrations in Finnish populations before and during selenium fertilization[1].

	n	Age	Before (1983–1985)	n	During (1988–1991)
Healthy adults			(μmol/L)		(μmol/L)
Helsinki urban	24	37	0.95 ± 0.08	24	1.52 ± 0.15
Leppävirta rural	45	45	0.84 ± 0.12	45	1.51 ± 0.17
Elderly men					
Eastern Finland	169	73	0.94 ± 0.22	169	1.57 ± 0.29
Southwestern Finland	205	73	0.89 ± 0.12	205	1.64 ± 0.26
Elderly women: Helsinki					
Institutionalized	30	83	0.67 ± 0.12	30[2]	1.36 ± 0.20
Free-living	29	79	0.87 ± 0.16		—
Pregnant: 1st trimester					
Helsinki	20		0.89 ± 0.11	20	1.35 ± 0.18
Turku	20		0.84 ± 0.08	20	1.35 ± 0.21
Joensuu	20		0.82 ± 0.07	20	1.43 ± 0.12
Jyväskylä	20		0.86 ± 0.11	20	1.38 ± 0.11
Mothers and children					
at delivery: Helsinki					
Mothers	15		0.76 ± 0.07	21	1.40 ± 0.14
Children	15		0.59 ± 0.06	21	0.86 ± 0.12
Neonates					
Helsinki	20		0.60 ± 0.08	20	0.81 ± 0.11
Turku	20		0.53 ± 0.07	20	0.90 ± 0.10
Joensuu	20		0.51 ± 0.07	20	0.82 ± 0.10
Jyväskylä	20		0.53 ± 0.11	20	0.81 ± 0.12

[1] Mean ± SD.
[2] Fourteen new subjects included replacing those who had died.

Serum selenium levels have also been monitored in several groups thought to be at risk for selenium deficiency. Cord blood samples were studied in 10 different geographical areas before selenium fertilization. The levels were similar throughout the country, and therefore samples from four large towns in southern Finland were chosen for the follow-up. The mean increase in serum selenium concentration observed after selenium fertilization was 52% (Table 11.2). Pregnant women during the first trimester and mothers at delivery both had slightly lower serum selenium levels compared to nonpregnant healthy women before the fertilization (25). After fertilization the serum selenium level of the two groups increased by 63% and 85%, respectively, but were still lower than those of nonpregnant women.

Two cohorts of elderly men were sampled for serum selenium concentration before (1984) and during (1989) selenium fertilization. The increase in serum selenium concentrations in both cohorts was essentially similar to that observed in middle-aged healthy subjects in urban areas (Table 11.2). In 1989 the range was 0.88–2.53 μmol/L (70–200 μg/L). Elderly institutionalized female patients constituted another risk group due to their low energy consumption. Before fertilization three subjects among the 30 women studied on three occasions consistently had a serum selenium value below 0.57 μmol/L (45 μg/L), a level that has been suggested to increase the risk of cardiovascular diseases and cancer (4,5,26). Selenium fertilization raised the mean serum selenium concentration in this group by 104%. No subjects with a serum selenium value less than 0.57 μmol/L were found in the follow-up.

Whole-blood selenium concentration in the urban follow-up group was also determined annually in 1985–1991. The level was 1.15 ± 0.12 μmol/L (Mean ± SD) before the onset of the fertilization, and it reached a steady-state of approximately 2.50 μmol/L by 1989.

Toenails

The determination of toenail selenium concentration has gained increasing attention as a long-term biomarker of selenium intake (27). We have studied this biomarker in two populations: Before the selenium fertilization in 1984–1985 in men aged 59 years (n = 136) from Helsinki (28) and during fertilization in 1988 in men aged 55 years (n = 43) from central Finland (29). None of these subjects had used selenium supplements. The mean ± SD selenium concentration of toenail clippings increased from 0.45 ± 0.06 mg/kg to 0.69 ± 0.10 mg/kg, respectively. Preliminary results from a study among farmers sampled in 1991 indicate that a steady state had not yet been reached in 1988, as the level in these subjects was 0.96 mg/kg (30). Like the serum selenium level, the toenail selenium level was low before fertilization and comparable only to values reported from New Zealand (27). European data are available only from the Netherlands, where the concentration has been reported to vary from 0.60 to 0.78 mg/kg (31,32).

Table 11.3. Human tissue selenium concentration before (1983–1985) and during (1988–1989) selenium fertilization[1].

	n	Before	n	During
		(mg/kg[2])		
Males[3]				
Liver	53	0.95 ± 0.27	12	1.58 ± 0.29
Fetal tissues[4]				
Liver	10	1.87 ± 0.18	12	2.25 ± 0.28
Heart	10	0.91 ± 0.27	12	1.30 ± 0.21

[1] Mean ± SD.
[2] Dry weight.
[3] Death from accidental causes, mainly traffic accidents, Helsinki area.
[4] Abortions performed in the Helsinki area.

TISSUES

Liver contains a major fraction of the body stores of selenium. Liver selenium is in a relatively mobile form reflecting dietary selenium intake over a time period of weeks rather than months (33). The liver selenium concentration of middle-aged men obtained at autopsy from southern Finland before the selenium fertilization started was among the lowest reported from Europe (34) (Table 11.3). Selenium fertilization increased the liver selenium concentration by over 60%, to a level that is still below those reported from the Netherlands (1.75 mg/kg) (35) and Scotland (1.80 mg/kg) (36).

The selenium concentration of fetal liver and heart tissue increased by 20% and 40%, respectively. A regional comparison is not feasible due to the lack of data from other countries.

EFFECTS ON SERUM, ERYTHROCYTE, AND PLATELET GLUTATHIONE PEROXIDASE

Two supplementation studies were conducted in the same healthy, middle-aged men in central Finland: One before (1981) and the other during (1988) selenium fertilization, using 200 µg selenium/day as selenate, selenite, selenium-rich yeast, or selenium-rich wheat for 11–16 weeks (37,38). Selenite and selenate raised the activity of platelet glutathione peroxidase by 50–70% before fertilization but only by 30% after 3 years of fertilization. In subjects supplemented with selenium-rich yeast a significant increase in the enzyme activity was observed only before fertilization. None of the different selenium supplement types had any effect on either plasma or red-blood-cell glutathione peroxidase activity.

ENVIRONMENTAL STUDIES

SELENIUM IN WATERS

In 1990 lake water samples were collected from 13 lakes that were surrounded by cultivated fields and from 18 lakes that were not affected by fertilization. The Mean ± SD selenium concentration of lake water was 62 ± 18 ng/L, with a range of $25-114$ ng/L. There was no difference in the mean selenium concentration between the two types of lakes (64 ng/L vs. 60 ng/L, respectively) (39).

SELENIUM IN WATER PLANTS

Annual leaf samples of yellow water lily (*Nuphar Luteum*) were collected in 1986 to 1991 from 19 forest ponds, lakes, and rivers in southern Finland. The selenium levels remained constant throughout the whole period. There were differences between the samples from different types of waters (water lily from forest ponds 16 ± 4, lakes 26 ± 8, and rivers 46 ± 15 µg/kg dry matter). These differences probably reflect general nutrient content of the waters rather than the effects of selenium fertilization.

ANTHROPOGENIC EMISSIONS OF SELENIUM IN FINLAND

The total annual anthropogenic emission of selenium to the atmosphere in Finland has been estimated to be 28 tons in 1989. The two main sources were nonferrous metal production (72%) and primary energy production (28%). The total fallout of selenium from precipitation was estimated to be 18 tons, 65% from rain and 35% from snow. This is approximately equal to the amount of selenium used in fertilizers (20 tons in 1989) (40). It must be emphasized, however, that the chemical forms of selenium in precipitation are most likely much less available for plants than sodium selenate from the fertilizers.

EFFECTS ON HUMAN HEALTH

Except for the cardiomyopathy described in low-selenium areas of China the role of selenium in human disease is still uncertain. However, clinical and epidemiological evidence has been presented in support of the hypothesis that a low dietary intake of selenium is related to the development of atherosclerotic disease and cancer in man. Selenium deficiency has also been incriminated in the etiology and prognosis of a multitude of other human diseases, but the evidence is mostly based on case studies and on poorly controlled clinical trials.

Decreased dietary intake of selenium might influence the risk of cardiovascular diseases either by promoting the progression of atherosclerosis or by affecting the processes that trigger acute myocardial infarction and cardiac death in subjects with atherosclerotic coronary arteries. The former mechanism would affect the rate of cardiovascular diseases in the population during the course of many years, whereas the latter mechanism would change the rates immediately.

Mortality from ischemic heart disease has been declining continuously in Finland since the late 1960s. As shown in Figure 11.6, the rate of decline was almost linear in the 1980s and did not change after the onset of selenium fertilization nor in 1987–1991 when the selenium intake of the population had been higher for some years.

The mechanisms by which selenium might influence the development of cancer are hypothetical but, if existent, are not likely to influence the morbidity or mortality immediately after the change in the intake. Data on cancer mortality is available in Finland until 1991 and on site-specific cancer incidence until 1988. No changes that could be attributed to increased dietary selenium intake have been observed.

Because the changes in disease rates result from a multitude of other factors, it will be difficult, if not impossible, to determine whether an increased selenium intake influences the health of the

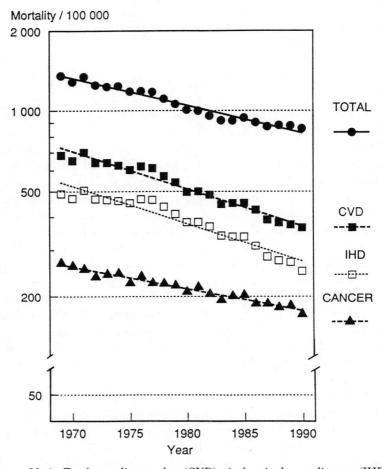

FIGURE 11.6. Total, cardiovascular (CVD), ischemic heart disease (IHD) and cancer mortality (per 100,000) in Finnish men before and during selenium fertilization.

nation. Thus, conclusions on the health effects of selenium must be based on experimental and clinical studies, on epidemiological studies within the populations, and on controlled clinical trials.

SUMMARY AND CONCLUSIONS

For geochemical reasons Finland is a low-selenium area. Based on studies of the selenium content of human foods, epidemiological investigations, and clinical trials of selenium supplementation, it was decided in 1984 to raise the selenium intake of the population by adding selenium to multimineral fertilizers. As a result, the mean dietary intake of the population has increased from 30–40 µg/day to over 100 µg/day in the early 1990s. The selenium intake of the population is now within the limits considered to be safe and adequate. No dramatic changes in the incidence or mortality from cardiovascular diseases or cancer have been observed since the onset of supplementation.

REFERENCES

1. Koljonen, T. The behavior of selenium in Finnish soils. Ann Agric Fenn 14:240–247; 1975.
2. Koivistoinen, P. Mineral element composition of Finnish foods. Acta Agric Scand Suppl 22:171; 1980.
3. Keshan Disease Research Group. Epidemiologic studies on the etiologic relationship of selenium and Keshan disease. Chin Med J (Engl) 92: 477–82; 1979.
4. Salonen, JT, Alfthan, G, Huttunen, JK, Pikkarainen, J, Puska, P. Association between cardiovascular death and myocardial infarction and serum selenium in a matched-pair longitudinal study. Lancet 2:175–179; 1982.
5. Salonen, JT, Alfthan, G, Huttunen, JK, Puska, P. Association between serum selenium and the risk of cancer. Am J Epidemiol 120:342–349; 1984.
6. Gissel-Nielsen, G, Bisbjerg, B. The uptake of applied selenium by agricultural plants. 2. The utilization of various selenium compounds. Plant and Soil 32:382–396; 1970.
7. Yläranta, T. Sorption of selenite and selenate in the soil. Ann Agric Fenn 21:103–113; 1983.
8. Yläranta, T. Raising the selenium content of spring wheat and barley using selenite and selenate. Ann Agric Fenn 23:75–84; 1984.

9. Yläranta, T. Effect of selenite and selenate fertilization and foliar spraying on selenium content of timothy grass. Ann Agric Fenn 23:96–108; 1984.

10. Ministry of Agriculture and Forestry. Proposal for the addition of selenium to fertilizers. Working Group Report No. 7; Helsinki 1984 (in Finnish).

11. Ministry of Agriculture and Forestry of Finland. Annual reports of the Selenium Working Group 1986–1990.

12. Ministry of Agriculture and Forestry. Annual report of the Selenium Working Group. (in Finnish). Working Group Report No. 28; Helsinki; 1990.

13. Varo, P, Koivistoinen, P. Annual variations in the average selenium intake in Finland: cereal products and milk as sources of selenium in 1979/1980. Int J Vitam Nutr Res 51:62–65; 1981.

14. Eurola, M, Ekholm, P, Ylinen, M, Koivistoinen, P, Varo, P. Effects of selenium fertilization on the selenium content of cereal grains, flour, and bread produced in Finland. Cereal Chem 67:334–337; 1990.

15. National Board of Agriculture. Food balance sheet. Helsinki; 1991.

16. Ekholm, P, Varo, P, Aspila, P, Koivistoinen, P, Syrjälä-Qvist, L. Transport of feed selenium to different tissues of bulls. Br J Nutr 66:49–55; 1991.

17. Ekholm, P, Ylinen, M, Koivistoinen, P, Varo, P. Effects of general soil fertilization with sodium selenate in Finland on the selenium content of meat and fish. J Agric Food Chem 38:695–698; 1990.

18. Ekholm, P, Ylinen, M, Eurola, M, Koivistoinen, P, Varo, P. Effects of general soil fertilization with sodium selenate in Finland on the selenium content of milk, cheese and eggs. Milchwissenschaft 46:547–550; 1991.

19. Eurola, M, Ekholm, P, Ylinen, M, Koivistoinen, P, Varo, P. Selenium in Finnish foods after beginning the use of selenate-supplemented fertilizers. J Sci Food Agric 56:57–70; 1991.

20. Eurola, M, Ekholm, P, Ylinen, M, Koivistoinen, P, Varo, P. Effects of selenium fertilization on the selenium content of selected Finnish fruits and vegetables. Acta Agric Scand 39:345–350; 1989.

21. Varo, P, Alfthan, G, Ekholm, P, Aro, A, Koivistoinen, P. Selenium intake and serum selenium in Finland: effects of soil fertilization with selenium. Am J Clin Nutr 48:342–349; 1988.

22. United States National Academy of Sciences. Recommended Dietary Allowances, 10th ed. Washington DC: National Academy of Sciences, 1980.

23. Thorling, EB, Overvad, K, Geboers, J. Selenium status in Europe—human data. A multicenter study. Ann Clin Res 18:3–7; 1986.
24. Lockitch, G. Selenium: clinical and analytical concepts. CRC Crit Rev Clin Lab Sci 27:483–541; 1989.
25. Alfthan, G. Longitudinal study on the selenium status of healthy adults in Finland during 1975–1984. Nutr Res 8:467–476; 1988.
26. Knekt, P, Aromaa, A, Maatela, J, et al. Serum selenium and subsequent risk of cancer among Finnish men and women. J Natl Cancer Inst 82:864–868; 1990.
27. Morris, JS, Stampfer, MJ, Willett, W. Dietary selenium in humans. Toenails as an indicator. Biol Trace Elem Res 5:529–537; 1983.
28. Ovaskainen, ML, Virtamo, J, Alfthan, G, Pietinen, P, Haukka, J, Taylor, P, Huttunen, J K. Toenail selenium as an indicator of selenium intake among middle-aged men in a low-soil selenium area. Am J Clin Nutr 57:662–665; 1993.
29. Alfthan, G, Aro, A, Arvilommi, H, Huttunen, JK. Deposition of selenium in toenails is dependent on the form of dietary selenium. In: Biomarkers of Dietary Exposure, 3rd Meeting Nutritional Epidemiology. Proceedings. Rotterdam 23–25th. January 1991, pp 110 (abstr).
30. Alfthan, G, Kumpulainen, J, Aro, A, Miettinen, A. Selenium status of rural subjects consuming their own produce six years after onset of addition of selenate to fertilizers in Finland. In: Selenium in Biology and Medicine, 5th International Symposium on Selenium. Proceedings. Nashville, TN, 20–23rd. July 1992 (abstr).
31. van Faassen, A, Cardinaals, JM, van't Veer, P, Ockhuizen, T. Selenium status parameters: response to a six-week dietary modification and intra- and inter-individual variability. In: Brätter, P, Schramel, P, eds. Trace Element Analytical Chemistry in Medicine and Biology, vol 4. Berlin: Walter de Gruyter; 1987, pp 289–300.
32. van Noord, PAH, Collette, HJA, Maas, MJ, de Waard, F. Selenium levels in nails of premenopausal breast cancer patients assessed prediagnostically in a cohort-nested case-referent study among women screened in the DOM Project. Int J Epidemiol 16:318–322; 1987.
33. Levander, OA, DeLoach, DP, Morris, VC, Moser, PB. Platelet glutathione peroxidase activity as an index of selenium status in rats. J Nutr 113:55–63; 1983.
34. Iyengar, GV. Reference values for the concentrations of As, Cd, Co, Cr, Cu, Fe, I, Hg, Mn, Mo, Ni, Pb, Se, and Zn in selected human tissues and body fluids. Biol Trace Elem Res 12:263–295; 1987.
35. Aalbers, TG, Houtman, JPW, Makkink, B. Trace-element concentrations in human autopsy tissue. Clin Chem 33:2057–2064; 1987.

36. Lyon, TDB, Fell, GS, Halls, DJ, Clark, J, McKenna, F. Determination of nine inorganic elements in human autopsy tissue. J Trace Elem Electrolytes Health Dis 3:109–118; 1989.
37. Levander, OA, Alfthan, G, Arvilommi, H, et al. Bioavailability of selenium to Finnish men as assessed by platelet glutathione peroxidase activity and other blood parameters. Am J Clin Nutr 37:887–897; 1983.
38. Alfthan, G, Aro, A, Arvilommi, H, Huttunen, JK. Selenium metabolism and platelet glutathione peroxidase activity in healthy Finnish men: effects of selenium yeast, selenite, and selenate. Am J Clin Nutr 53:120–125; 1991.
39. Wang, D, Alfthan, G, Aro, A, Kauppi, L, Soveri, J. Selenium in tap water and natural water ecosystems in Finland. In: Aitio, A, Aro, A, Järvisalo, J, Vainio, H, eds. Trace Elements in Health and Disease. Cambridge: Royal Society of Chemistry; 1991, pp 49–56.
40. Wang, D, Alfthan, G, Aro, A, Soveri, J. Anthropogenic emissions of selenium in Finland. Appl Geochem Suppl 2:87–93; 1993.

Index

DATE DUE

JUL 1 5 1997	
APR 1 6 1994	
DEC 0 9 1994	
JUN 2 3 1996	
FEB 1 2 1997	
APR 2 3 1997	
JAN 0 4 1999	
MAY 0 9 2001	